# MINDSCREAM

# MIND

# SCREAM

by
## R.D. ZIMMERMAN

**DONALD I. FINE, INC.**
*New York*

MANY THANKS TO N. FOR THE INSPIRATION, TO PAMELA HOLT, LIBRARIAN EXTRAORDINAIRE AND TO MY AGENTS JONATHON AND WENDY LAZEAR. ALSO, I'M DEEPLY INDEBTED TO DR. SAM ABELSON FOR HIS INTEREST, INPUT AND TECHNICAL ADVICE—THANKS!

Library of Congress Cataloging in Publication Data
Zimmerman, R. D. (Robert Dingwall)
    Mindscream.

    I. Title.
PS3576.I5118M56   1989        813'.54        88-45874
ISBN 1-55611-137-1

Designed by Irving Perkins Associates

Manufactured in the United States of America
10  9  8  7  6  5  4  3  2  1

**FOR MY SUSPENSE SUPPORT GROUP,
THE SUSPENDERS**

# PROLOGUE

It was the silence that woke her, the absolute stillness of the late night that pulled her from a dreary sleep. There had been steps, soft and furtive. But now there was nothing. That's what she heard. Quiet. A lock of gray hair hanging in her face, she blinked, her aged eyes sucking in the faint glow of the nightlight. It was the middle of the night and she understood. Someone was in her bedroom.

But where was she? This wasn't her home. This bed. It had metal railings, a metal footboard. What was it? A hospital bed? Wait, that dresser. Pretty. Dark wood, nice brass handles. And the chair, big and squishy, covered in a worn floral print. Yes. She'd chosen that fabric herself. That was her chair. So what was it doing here in this cold little room with the harsh linoleum? How had—

Clothes rustling, an arm moving. Then silence. And deep, husky breathing. Who was that? Yes, yes, she could sense it clearly now. Another person. Someone had crept into her room and was lurking in here, shifting in the shadows.

Oh God, she thought, frozen with fear. She was all alone. And she was so tired, her old body so lazy with sleep. She had to get up, to run, to flee. But she couldn't. Her body just wouldn't move. What was wrong? Why couldn't she even flex a muscle? She dug her elbow into the crisp white sheets, pushed. There. Good. Then again

. . . and all at once she flopped on her back and saw him. A tall dark figure towering over her.

She gasped, "Who . . . who . . ."

He was atop her at once, slamming a hand over her mouth, capping the fear about to rise from her throat. She twisted and screamed, but his palm deadened her plea. She wiggled her head, then an instant later he slapped something over her lips. Something taut and sticky. Tape. He had sealed her mouth shut!

He leaned next to her and whispered, "Everything's all right. I'm a friend."

Lord! Help! Her terror growled in her throat, searched for an escape. She sucked air in through her nose, tried to stretch her mouth wide. The tape was thick, though. Coarse. She tried to raise her head, but he reached down and pressed it firmly back on the pillow.

"Just relax. You're in a special home," said the man, holding a small vial in one hand. "And I'm a friend."

What? No. No, she didn't know him. Get out! Get out of here! It was the middle of the night and she was alone and this stranger was going to kill her.

"Don't worry," came his low voice. "This won't hurt."

He reached in and took her left wrist, his strong, soft fingers wrapping around her thin bones. Her entire body went rigid, she attempted to pull away but could barely flinch. Then the stranger began rolling up her sleeve, pushing her nightgown higher and higher up her arm. Oh, God. He was going to—

She saw it. A rubber cord dangling in the dark from one of his hands. As he lowered it toward her, her heart shrunk with fear. No. No. Please don't hurt me. Please!

Beneath the tape, she screamed a stiffled, "N-no . . . !"

Not paying any attention, he wrapped the cord around her upper arm, then tied it snugly. Oh, God, she thought, looking over. Who was this person? What was he going to do to her? Why couldn't she move?

He began stroking her, pushing gently on her inner arm. Feeling. Feeling for something. This is disgusting! Stop touching me! Stop!

Suddenly and oddly, he ripped open a little wrapper. Inside was a tiny pad, and he rubbed her arm, wiped it nice and clean. Clean? She didn't understand. It didn't make any sense, not until she saw him hold up a syringe. A shot? What? Where was she? She . . . she had to get away. Away, she thought. I have to escape! Concentrating, she lifted her left arm, levitated it slightly off the bed. Oh, Lord. She could barely move. But she had to. She had to flee!

"Be still!" he shouted, pinning her arm back down on the bed.

Quickly and expertly he stabbed the needle into her arm, the tip of it piercing her old skin. He then flipped loose the rubber cord and pressed the solution into her. Oh Lord! She tried again to move. But his weight on her . . . so heavy . . .

Her veins suddenly began to warm, simmer. Something afire slid through her body. Her blood. It was molten, burning!

"Ach!" she gasped.

At once he jerked the syringe from her, then reached for her neck. He pressed into her, felt for something. She stared at him, eyes bulging, some great pressure, some inhuman force building within her. Her right side. She looked down. Saw her right fingers curling, pulling inward, upward. Her entire arm. It was bending, trembling, and she couldn't stop it. No. Now it was her leg, too. Her entire right side. Humming. Burning. Numb. It was numb! She couldn't feel anything!

She looked up to the stranger. He was pulling away. Backing off. What—

Suddenly he reached down to her and grabbed at a corner of the tape. With huge fingers, he crudely yanked the adhesive band from her mouth, tearing skin and lip away with it.

"Ah!" she cried.

Something exploded in her head. She opened her eyes. The light, part of it was gone. Half of it extinguished. She gasped. Couldn't get air. She blinked again. Please! Light! Let me see! Please! Gasping, she strained, batted her eyes. Yes. There. Full vision. Maybe the man could get help, maybe he could . . .

He was leaving, slipping out the door. Abandoning her. No! No, come back! I need help. You must—

All of a sudden her body shook, her mind screeched with pain. Everything went black. Pain blasted through her skull. A liquidy something dripping and then . . . then . . .

# 1

Nina and Alex hadn't had sex for the almost two months. It probably would have been all right, but they were afraid of an infection, afraid of an orgasm. There were enough problems and they just wanted to be careful, and that included avoiding uterine stimulation. Almost ten years ago Nina had had two miscarriages, one right after the other, and this was her first pregnancy since. At age forty-two, she figured this was her last chance—the one she'd thought she'd never have—and so Alex and she had gladly agreed to abstain.

"There, feel?" she said, grinning.

As she lay on the couch, Nina Trenton, blonde and handsome, with an angular face, took her husband's hand and placed it on her abdomen. She moved his hand around, then settled it on one spot. There, she thought, right there, and she closed her blue eyes and marveled yet again. Yes, this little person growing inside her was a miracle. And now things were going just fine. There had been a few problems; seven weeks ago Nina had started having regular contractions, about five an hour, and her cervix had begun to dilate. Since then, however, she had been taking Terbutaline to calm her womb. She was lying down for all but four hours a day, and she and Alex hadn't made love, just as the doctor had ordered. And it had worked. Now entering the last part of the third trimester and with only five weeks left, Nina realized she might go full term. She and the baby were in the homestretch. Next week Nina could even start being up for longer periods.

"Feel? That's her bottom."

Alex Hale laughed, his boyish grin nearly as innocent as when Nina had met him sixteen years ago. Really, she thought, studying him in his navy blue sweats, he hasn't changed that much. More mature, but just as easy going, too. Only the flecks of gray in his dark hair and the circles beneath his rich brown eyes gave evidence of his age and busy life as a lawyer. Well, she thought, he was older, but he loved to run and that had kept him in pretty good shape. Soon she'd be jogging again, too.

"Are you serious?" He rubbed her gently, but couldn't sense what she did. "You can't tell."

"Yes, I can. The midwife showed me the difference between her head and her bottom."

He laughed again, and Nina brought his hand up to her mouth and kissed it. They were going to have a little girl, whose black and white ultrasound picture was stuck to the refrigerator.

Nina was so glad to be out of the Chicago advertising world. Yes, they'd done the right thing moving from the big city and up here to Mendota, Wisconsin. Not only was her father in an Alzheimer facility where he was given terrific twenty-four hour supervision, but he was under the supervision of the best specialist in the country. Plus they were close to him. He was less than fifteen minutes away and even now Nina was still able to visit him almost every day. Indeed, Mendota had been the right choice. Good for her father and good for them. There was just something so normal and basic about this place, a little town gathered along a river and surrounded by dairy farms. Even this house, a big old red Victorian, seemed to reflect values and a life Nina had thought no longer existed.

As she lay on the tan living room couch, where she had been since noon, Nina pulled Alex closer. Walking on his knees between the couch and the coffee table, he came up beside her and bent over. She wrapped her arms around him and kissed him, at first lightly, then deeply, and she felt his gentle hand on one of her swollen breasts.

"Oh, God, I want you," murmured Alex.

She hugged him and whispered, "You're talking about someone who can't see her toes."

He pulled away a bit, so that his face was only inches from hers.

Grinning, he said, "I love you." He kissed her on the nose. "I love you, I love you, I love you."

He'd always been like this, always carried his support and affection right out there in front. God, she was happy to be pregnant, elated to be so far along. It hadn't been easy. The greatest stress came from the memory of the two miscarriages. But like now, Alex had been there, coaching, soothing, urging Nina to believe that, yes, they could have a child, a healthy one, too. Once Nina had entered the second trimester and had had an ultrasound and amniocentesis with good results, she, too, began to believe.

Nina felt his eyes, dark and steady, upon her. sensed his intensity, his total concentration. N thought. Can't have this. She kissed him on run." and nudged him upward.

"You, my friend, need a cold shower breath and

His eyes still fixed on her, he took sighed. "Alas, I think I need both. ger. Are you going

"I'm sorry, but it's only fo a to make it?" d, "Barely."

He crossed his eyes, a

With that he rose, leaving Nina propped up and cushioned by an assortment of pillows. Her eyes on him, she watched as Alex, dressed in his dark blue sweats, crossed from the living room and into the foyer, a large space broken only by the staircase. Seating himself on the bottom step, Alex pulled on his running shoes.

Nina rolled as far as she could and saw the dark sky out the bay window. It had to be going on eight, and the warmth of the March day had certainly retreated by now.

"Do you think you should go?" she asked. "It's going to be awfully slippery."

"Don't worry. You know I already sprained my ankle once on spring ice, and I don't intend to do that again." He stood, braced himself on the doorframe to the living room, and stretched his calves. "I won't be long—I'm just going down to the park and back. Will you be all right? Need anything?"

"No," she said, reaching for a pile of photographs on the coffee table. "I'll be working on the album." She saw him studying her, and added, "I'm fine."

"You're sure you're sure?"

She rolled her eyes. "Positive. Now go on and get some exercise."

"I'll be back in less than a half hour." He stood, and cl "Everything's going to be great."

He she said, daring to believe, too. They were so door ope "I love you!"

porch, then From where she lay, Nina heard the front chilly March n ose, heard his steps across the gray front She adjusted a p the last of him as he ran off into the

a stack of photos in ehind her head and settled back, pictures for a couple of ye nd. She hadn't sorted any get the recent ones into her r and she was anxious to through the photos, she came a ther album. Flipping

s ones of her father

just before he'd gotten bad and they'd had to sell the old house; she'd show them to him tomorrow. Next came ones of Alex in the marathon last fall. Grinning, she looked at several of herself in which she proudly posed showing off her belly. She'd been so happy when she couldn't fit into her jeans anymore, when the scale started to inch upward and when her breasts began to swell. She laughed when she looked at herself in one of the photos. She was so tiny then, so . . .

Suddenly Nina gasped and bit her lip as the first of the contractions began, gripping her in the back and then traveling and growing in intensity as it moved toward her abdomen. She dropped the photos and clutched herself. Her uterus seemed to be shrinking, crushing her insides in a painful cramp. She cried out, afraid and not understanding. None of the ones before had ever been so strong, so consuming. What did it mean? How long would it last? And how soon, she thought, glancing out the window, would Alex return?

# 2

"Ah!" cried John Morton as his eyes burst open.

Gasping, he lurched forward and glanced about the room. Beige carpet. Plaid couch. Television. Mikey, his son, sitting Indian style in front of his favorite television show, a cartoon featuring herculean robots. Several framed prints. The kitchen door.

The older man dabbed the sweat from his wrinkled brow and leaned back. His heart was racing as if to kill; the muscles across his chest were tight like shrunken leather straps. Relax, he told himself. That was only a dream. Just a dream. He'd simply fallen asleep in the chair and had had a terrible vision. A nightmare where he'd seen himself buried alive. But none of it was true. He was here in the living room of his apartment above the Ridgewood Mortuary, it was a late March night, and he was alive. One of two funeral directors in this small Wisconsin town.

That, however, wasn't enough reassurance. He had to check on the new case, the body downstairs. Wiping his lips, he stood. He looked at the back of Mikey, who sat less than two feet from the screen of the color TV, images and colors and sounds crackling right before him. The young man, his hair brown and straight, wouldn't miss him at all. Morton would just hurry down to the workroom, the place where all the cleansing and preparation and embalming was done, and be right back.

From the three-bedroom apartment carved into a corner of the mansion's second floor, the old man passed into a wide hall. His trembling fingers felt for a switch, flicked it, and a string of fluorescent lights fluttered on. He hung on to the banister of the curving stairway and passed by the tall windows draped with heavy gold brocade. From the two-story entry, which had a desk and plant strategically placed in the center, he came to a door painted a bland green, opened it and headed down the back stairs. In the basement, he entered the showroom, a long well-lit gallery running the entire length of the east side of the building and containing row after row of coffins. Off to one side stood an electric shoe polisher with red and black buffers.

Pulling a key from his pocket, the mortician unlocked a heavy door and passed into the preparation room. There, slabbed out and covered by a sheet on the tilted white ceramic table, was the fat insurance man. At just the sight of the deathly still body with its head cradled in a ceramic block, a lungful of air rushed out of Morton. Thank God. He, John Morton, was alive, and this fat man lay as if life had long ago run out on him, as if his body had already been pumped with formaldehyde, causing the protein in the cells to coagulate and thereby prevent decomposition. The body just had to stay that way until after the viewing tomorrow, following which Morton and his son would make the delivery and receive another five thousand. Morton only hoped there was enough of the coffee-colored drug to last until tomorrow night. Oh, please, he thought. No problems. Don't let there be any problems with this one. He trembled, not knowing why he feared the worst.

The tall, elderly Mr. Morton stood next to the sink and

kitchen-like cabinets in the basement of his funeral home, where he had lived and worked for more than forty years. No wonder he was tired, he thought as he gazed around at the yellow walls, the slop sinks and the instrument cases filled with scalpels and hemostats, petroleum jelly and needle injectors. No wonder his dreams had grown wild and his hands shook so and his back burned with such pain. So many cases, so many of them in and out, buried and forgotten. A lot of heavy work, disinfecting the body with the green hexophene soap, probing the insides with the trocar to remove the contents of the hollow organs, then finally dressing the lifeless form. It was far too much for him these days. His figure bent with each year, and his face had sunk until he could pass for Ichabod Crane. He'd never have lasted so long without Mikey's eager help. Put on the plastic apron, Mikey, and lift here. That's right, always wear gloves. Now put the old lady here on the table. The young man there on the church truck. Like a tractor that boy was, thick and determined and obedient every second, letting Morton run the controls of his mind.

Good Mikey, thought his father. The boy had problems but they weren't his fault, and his heart was purer than that of any other human he'd ever met. Morton loved him so, his only child, born when both his wife and he were in their early forties and had long since given up hope of having a child. That was some thirty-one years ago, Morton realized, and Mikey had been practically within calling distance ever since. The poor kid, tricked by nature. Even today, Morton still felt so guilty about his child. But wasn't he doing everything he could for him? Wasn't concern for Mikey's health why he'd agreed to this business in the first place? Of course. Anything to help Mikey, to protect him, to add a few years to that twisted life. Yes, there was the money, but that was enough just to keep the place open now, then help them later. And it would all be over soon, within a year if they were lucky. Soon after Mikey and he would be off, a couple of snowbirds fleeing Wisconsin's wet winters for the dry heat of Mexico. Just think, he mused. Mikey's health assured and he retired at last. Already they'd had an offer from a group to buy the funeral home. It wouldn't, he knew, be long now.

Morton and Mikey had picked up this insurance man at the hospital early this afternoon, less than a day after he'd been brought to the morgue. The cases that were sent to Morton—the ones that he received a flat five thousand to process—were all dead of supposed heart failure. That common cause of death sometimes worried Morton, but not this time. Who would doubt that this man with the round face, the bulging double chin, and enormous stomach had died any other way? In fact, some had probably been predicting it for years.

With his son's help, Morton had carted the body in, washed and prepped it, then laid it out. Tomorrow morning Mikey would lift the man and Morton would tug on a fine blue suit. Next, Morton would do the hair, then apply the makeup, which had a rich opaque tint to mask the pallor. All would be well by the time they came—the widow, the daughter, the son-in-law who'd taken over the insurance agency, the son who'd moved to Milwaukee. They'd gawk and they'd cry, mumble a few words, take a few horrified glances at the puffy body, and know that within a few short hours this man and his suit and his shoes would all be burned to ashes at the crematorium. A mere collection of burned tissue and pulverized bone.

With the March sun having set some time ago, Morton checked his watch. Seven thirty. Time, he thought, for another shot. Then another in exactly twelve hours. There was just enough of this Haitian solution for that, for two more doses.

From a chipped white instrument case on the sidewall, its shelves lined with white towels, Morton selected a stethoscope and slipped it on. He then pushed back the sheet draped over the fat man and placed the cool round disk on the hairless chest. Morton stopped breathing and listened. There was no pounding, no pulse of life. He moved the silvery disk up and down and across the fatty chest, distinguishing nothing. Then he put the disk on the man's neck. This was just another case, he told himself. Don't worry. This man is simply another—

Oh, Christ, what was that?

He pressed the stethoscope into the man's flab. What was that, that sound like the slow squeezing of water from a sponge? Flushing with fear, Morton bent over and tilted his head. There! Wait, no . . . He moved the disk again and again. Then sighed. There was nothing, just as, of course, there shouldn't be.

Thank God, he thought, pulling off the stethoscope and laying it on a table near the embalming machine. He'd worried about what dosage to administer to such a large person, how to do it without going too far. This was, after all, a quirky drug, manufactured in a crude laboratory, but so far Morton's calculations had proved correct.

Quickly, he went to the kitchen cabinets lining one wall, reached for a fresh syringe and ripped off its sterile wrapper. Morton next stretched to the top shelf and took the small vial. As if he were an expert tailor threading a needle, he slipped the tip through the rubber cap and began to pull the plunger. The darkish solution was sucked from the bottle and began filling the syringe. Just then, however, his entire arm began to burn as if a hot poker had been been laid upon it.

"Ah!"

The muscles and tiny nerves in Morton's left hand, the one holding the vial, twisted and stiffened beyond his control. Under the duress of the arthritic spasm, his fingers jerked grotesquely as if controlled by a demonic puppeteer. Horrified, he watched his fingers take on a life of their own, bending and tightening, clutching the little glass vial one moment, then releasing it the next. Oh, no, he begged, as he saw the tube slip from his fingers and tumble through the air. Please! He had to stop it, to catch it, and he lunged forward. His old body, though, was too crooked, too slow.

"No!"

As fast as death, the glass vial toppled through the air, smacked and shattered on the tiled floor. Terrified, Morton stood helplessly and watched as the liquid began to dribble toward the drain. Dear Lord, he thought, what am I going to do about the insurance man and his bereaved ones, who are due in the morning?

# Chapter

# 3

Alex hadn't jogged more than thirty feet when he stopped. Standing in the late-March snow, the cold moisture seeping through his running shoes, he stared at the large yellow-brick funeral home across the street. Once a lumber baron's mansion, now a stopping point for the dead, Alex had thought he'd grown accustomed to living across from such a place. But he hadn't. Months after moving onto the block, he still feared that being so neighborly with death would bring him bad luck.

A series of lights shot on as he studied the Ridgewood Mortuary. Then the large, always well-dressed figure of old Mr. Morton cut past several windows. Alex took a deep breath and started for the yellow-brick building. Alex the lawyer, Alex the guy who could never say no, had been asked by his neighbors to stop by and talk to Morton. There was a rumor circulating that the funeral home might be sold and turned into a sorority. But no one wanted that. Everyone on Leaf Street preferred a quiet funeral home to a wild sorority and a parking lot full of kids and cars.

His hand in his dark hair, Alex glanced back once at their big red Victorian house. He didn't need to tell Nina that she was right, that tonight wasn't such a great night to go running. Too many icy patches. No, he'd just stop over at the funeral home, have a quick chat with Mr. Morton and return home. Alex had to do it, had to get it over with. He was supposed to have done it a week ago.

Stepping over a small pile of disintegrating snow, Alex made his way across the narrow street and into the parking lot that was slick with a sheen of ice. Lights burned in the top windows of the funeral home. Their apartment. Where Mr. Morton and his reclusive son lived. Then in the basement still more lights fluttered and burst with life. Fluorescent lights in a work room? Perhaps. That was probably where the bodies were prepped. Probably where the sorority girls planned to set up their stereos and Ping-Pong tables. Christ, wondered Alex, who in their right mind would want to live there, laugh there, study there, screw there?

Within seconds he was passing the garage at the rear of the building. He really didn't want to do this tonight. But he should. Should? Alex shook his head. In his forties and still unable to say no, a legacy from his soft-hearted Italian father. One day all the obligations he took on were going to kill him, of that he was sure. But he was getting better about that, about not taking on the weight of the world. Yes, it was good they'd moved up here. It had been an incredible strain trying to cope with Nina's father Bill; now it was such a relief knowing he was receiving the best care available. Most importantly, their fourteen-year marriage, free at last of Bill's primary care needs, was fresh again. They'd solved that problem and escaped the city. And miraculously, Nina's womb now held a hope they had thought could never be theirs. Amazing, he thought, I'm going to be a father after all.

He stepped around the building and to the side door. Searching in vain for a doorbell, he finally tapped on the aluminum storm. When there was no immediate response to his rattling, Alex started to turn away. This must have been so much nicer as a private residence, when all this back here was a garden instead of an asphalt parking lot . . .

He caught himself, knocked again and called, "Hello?"

Maybe Morton's busy, thought Alex. Maybe he's pumping the blood out of a body and filling it full of formaldehyde or cleaning solution or whatever it is they preserve bodies with. Or maybe he's sewing up a face, putting makeup on it, making the thing presentable. Yeah, he wondered, isn't there some sort of gelatin they squirt into depressed faces to make them look full and alive again? Or . . .

Stop it, Alex, he told himself. You're being ridiculous. Just go on, don't worry about it. And with that he swung open the storm door, twisted the handle and pushed the wooden door.

"Mr. Morton?" he called.

Alex stood with one foot inside on the brown carpeting, one foot out on the slippery step. Swirls of cold charged past him into the little back hall with the narrow steps that led up and down.

"Hello? Mr. Morton?"

Reflexively he stepped in to block the rush of cold air. He stood motionless, but then chided himself. This is a place of business. Nothing else. So why are you standing so still, so quiet? Because . . .

Rising from below came a deep voice that was worn like an old record. Mr. Morton. It had to be, and from the muffled rising and falling of his words, from the periodic bursts of quiet, Alex could tell he was on the phone. Business, undoubtedly. There was that brusque clip to it. Did that mean the topic was bodies?

Alex started to make his way down. It's all right to proceed, he told himself. This isn't Morton's residence. No, and this isn't someplace terrible down here, either. Just look at how nice it is, all that fresh brown carpeting and the walls nicely papered in gold and green. Everything's fine, Alex, he said over and over in his mind. He exhaled deeply and tried to loosen up. After all, it was quite apparent he wasn't descending right into the middle of a morgue with a row of bodies laid out like steaks. If anything, downstairs would be a few neat desks and a line of caskets. A showroom, just like a car dealership. Alex smiled. The Chevy of the undertakers, that's what Morton was. Basic.

"Hello?" called Alex again, pausing just before the staircase doubled back on itself.

Motionless, he stood staring at a Chinese vase perched atop a rosewood stand on the landing. When no response came and when Morton continued on the phone, his voice louder than ever, Alex moved on. The old guy must be deaf not to have heard him by now, thought Alex. He turned the corner and continued down the last flight.

He hesitated one last time, then shook himself. Why was he so nervous? What could possibly lie ahead?

Morton shouted into the phone, "You have to bring it at once!"

Alex flinched. What was he talking about? A body? He recoiled at the thought, knew he should turn around, slip out. No. He'd come this far. The showroom or whatever was coming into view, an expansive, well-lit place, and Morton himself was right down there, just three steps more.

"I told you, I dropped the last vial," rose the voice from below. "All I have is half a syringe full. That won't last until tomorrow morning. This is a large one, I tell you."

His mouth suddenly dry, Alex couldn't utter a word. He should make his presence known, let Morton know he was here. But he couldn't, and he didn't want to be hearing this. Shit, what had he stumbled into?

"It'll be the end of us, I tell you, if his family comes in for a viewing tomorrow and just one—" Morton stopped, paused, then added, "Good, the last thing we want to do is attract the attention of the police. I'll meet you in twenty minutes down by the park."

For a moment it seemed to Alex that his feet were made of mucky clay and that he'd never be able to move them from these stairs. Only with great effort was he able to raise one foot up and back, then the other. As quiet as possible now, he forced himself to retreat. That's it, he told himself. Nice and slow. You're okay. But what was going on here? Something? Nothing? And what was all that talk about vials and trouble and the police? Surely Morton couldn't be talking about a dead person? But, Christ, maybe he was. Maybe he was referring to a large person whose family would be coming tomorrow or . . . or . . .

Alex's feet began to work quickly, too quickly. Backing out he forgot about the landing and his foot reached for a step that wasn't there. He clawed at the gold and green wallpaper, couldn't stop himself, felt himself whoosh through thin air, then hit the landing. His right arm flailed back, hit the base of the rosewood stand. As he tumbled back, he glanced up over his brow and saw the Chinese vase rock from side to side. The sway of the vase grew greater and greater until it tipped from the stand and dove into nothingness.

"Shit!" he muttered.

He had to try to catch it, attempt to prevent the ceramic container from crashing on the floor in hundreds of little, noisy pieces. He'd be caught by Morton if it did and he'd have to explain what he was doing here. He'd have to buy the mortician another vase, too. Half lying, half sitting on the landing, Alex spun around, jabbed out a hand and caught . . . a leg. A person's leg.

"What . . . ?"

His eyes shot up. Holding the vase in two hands and standing above Alex was a man of no great height. As if he'd never been outside, his skin was sheet white, while his face was faintly etched with fine dry lines. Perhaps in his early thirties, he had a tall, wide forehead, a flat face, small ears and eyes that were stretched at tight angles.

"I caught," said the young man with a big, broad smile. "Papa, I caught!"

Alex cowered against the wall. Morton's son. Alex had seen him a number of times, following his father to the hearse, helping his father unload a coffin, shoveling very slowly the walk. This was him, Morton's son who suffered from Down's syndrome.

"Papa, I caught!" he shouted.

As Alex clambered to his feet, a voice below hollered, "Mikey?"

Almost instantly, Alex saw the tall, gray-haired Morton appear at the bottom of the staircase. A syringe cocked in one hand, the old man stared up at Alex and was suddenly flush with horror.

"What's . . . what's going on here?"

Mikey held up the vase. "I caught!"

Morton's eyes squinted as they aimed at Alex. "You're from across the street, aren't you?"

"Yes," said Alex. He didn't know where to begin or how to get out of here. He fell back on his best attorney voice, the one that was deep and direct. "Several of the people in the neighborhood asked me to—"

"How long have you been here?"

His confidence waned. "Not long. Not long, really. I was just about to go for a jog when I saw your lights."

"Is your wife with you . . . or any of the neighbors?"

"No," he said, and immediately regretted his response.

Morton looked past Alex to his son. "Mikey, were you and this man on the stairs when I was on the phone?"

Slowly, as if afraid he'd done something wrong, Mikey nodded, then lifted up the vase. "I . . . I caught."

"Good boy, good boy." Morton raised the needle.

"Now we're going to play another kind of game, Mikey. Put down the vase and catch this man. Go on, grab him and hold him."

Before Alex realized it, Mikey had done exactly as his father had asked and there were two thick arms wrapped around his chest. This was ridiculous, thought Alex. He'd simply wanted to inquire about the sale of the funeral home. This couldn't be happening. He twisted to the side, looked down and saw Mikey's white fists locked over his chest.

"What in the hell . . . ?"

Morton pulled himself up the steps, the syringe, a natural extension of his body, held carefully in his right hand.

"Hey, I just came over to have a neighborly chat," said Alex. "What in the hell's this all about?"

The older man raised the syringe and said, "You've left me no other choice."

"What? What do you mean?"

The lawyer part of Alex wanted to talk this out, wanted to come to some sort of agreement. But then, trapped in Mikey's arms, the scared part of Alex took over. He dipped slightly and lunged back. But Mikey barely faltered and his lock on Alex didn't break. Next, he started to twist, but the more he struggled, the tighter became Mikey's lock on him.

"Football!" shouted Mikey, laughing with crazed power.

"That's right, Mikey," said Morton, climbing closer.

Alex stared at the syringe in the old man's hand. Christ, he thought, what was going on? What was this about? He started thrashing, pushing against the wall with one running-shoe-clad foot. This couldn't be happening. He was here simply because he was the only lawyer on the block. He didn't want any trouble. Shit. He kicked out, toppled over the vase, sent it rolling down the stairs and to its shattered end.

"What are you doing?" demanded Alex. "What do you want?"

Alex pulled his head back as Morton, tall and frail, came right up on the landing, his face only inches away. Alex stared into the wrinkles, the large pores of the old man's drooping face. Pulling as hard as he could, he tried to free his right hand, but couldn't. Shit, who was to think Mikey was so strong?

Then suddenly Morton's hard old fingers were ripping at Alex's sweatshirt. The rough hands pushed and prodded until the cloth was torn from the neck down to the chest.

"Jesus Christ!" screamed Alex, jerking his head from side to side. "Stop it!"

The fear charged through Alex. His veins flooded with blood. He tried to resist, but couldn't, as Morton leaned on him, pinning him against Mikey's shoulder. Alex felt the air come in tiny gulps. He tried once again to lunge out of Mikey's grasp and once again he failed. And then—aimed at his exposed chest—he saw the needle. Glinting light, rising high. No!

"No!" he screamed.

Morton plunged it into him, the tip of the needle breaking Alex's skin with a bee-like bite, then sliding deep between rib and muscle. Alex looked down. The needle had pierced his chest wall and plunged—Oh, God, no, he thought—into his heart. Syringe dangling out of him, he looked up, begging for mercy, but Morton's face was tight and bitter and angry.

"You heard too much!" said Morton through clenched teeth as he plunged the dark liquid directly into Alex's pulsing heart.

And then the drug hit and Alex screamed. Morton

jerked the needle free, and Alex yelled and tried to reach out. His body gyrated as if he'd just grabbed a live wire. That passed and then it struck again and Alex felt his eyes bulge from his head and his tongue disappear down his throat. God, no! he was screaming inside himself, unable to open his mouth.

Somewhere outside his body, he heard a voice say, "Okay, Mikey, let . . . go . . ."

Alex knew he was stumbling but he didn't know how. Then he felt himself prodded along as if he were a kid being cajoled into jumping into a black whirlpool. All the muscles on his right side tightened and bent back on one another. Many hands came up from behind, pushed and shoved. He cried out in pain but no sound came out. When he opened his eyes, he saw blackness and felt cold. He was outside. They were throwing him out. Clutching at his own throat, his chest, he trudged on: Just get home! His body went rigid, he looked up and saw stars above. Stumbling against the side of the yellow-brick building, he pulled himself along. One foot, the next. Yes, run. Hurry to Nina! Rush to the baby! He came around the corner and saw lights in the red Victorian. Run, he screamed somewhere inside. Run!

The contraction passed within minutes, leaving Nina on the couch wide-eyed and frightened. She rolled onto her side, nudged two pillows beneath her stomach and lay there, not knowing what to expect.

Abruptly, the phone in the big house began to ring way over there, across the living room and on the desk in the den. Not again, Alex, she thought. He'd forgotten to stretch the cord to its limit, leave the phone by her, by the couch and the half-assembled photo album.

As the phone rang once, twice, she tried to ignore it. She wanted outside contact, though. She wanted especially not to be alone now, and by the third ring Nina was up and had swung her feet to the floor. With the fourth ring, she was just on her feet. Her blue eyes looking down, she couldn't help but wonder if that contraction had been the real thing.

Nina's half-English, half-Scandinavian face couldn't hide her alarm. Gently rubbing her stomach, she crooned, "Hold on, sweetheart. Just hold on." To the ringing phone, she said, "You hold on, too."

She knew already that it was a friend because only friends knew to let it ring a long, long time. And it kept ringing. Eight. Nine. Nina shook her head. She shouldn't be doing this, but she wanted to talk to someone, to tell someone about what she'd just experienced.

Finally she made her way into the small den that was in a corner between the living room and dining room. There she stopped at a desk parked in a corner and carefully lowered herself into a chair. She took a deep sigh, brushed aside her thick blond hair, and lifted the phone.

"Hello?"

"You're getting slow," said a man's deep voice. "I was only going to let it ring another fifty times."

Nina held her stomach and relaxed at once. It was Dr. Dundeen, her father's physician and head of the Extended Care Research Institute. Adjoining Mendota General Hospital, the facility had been home to Nina's father for almost a year.

"What can I say? I keep getting more pregnant."

Pregnant indeed, she thought. She'd called Dundeen this afternoon because she was going to have to miss two or three visits to her father in the upcoming week. There was only so much time she could be on her feet and she had her own doctors' appointments to keep.

"How are you feeling?" asked Dundeen, who, in light of her family history, had counseled her on the dangers of her pregnancy.

"Really well, I think." She hesitated only a moment before saying, "But I just had this enormous contraction."

"Is your husband there?"

"He went out for a run. He'll be right back."

"Good. Just take it nice and easy—and let him do everything around the house," said Dundeen. "Now what can I do for you? I got your message—sorry I couldn't get back to you earlier."

"That's all right." Dundeen, she knew, worked twelve to fourteen hours a day and tended to return calls in the evening. "I'm not going to be able to see my father every day next week, and I was worried that—"

A muscle tightened in Nina's lower back, twisting and

cutting her breath short. Another contraction. She gasped, bit her lower lip. She should be timing these. She should be lying down.

"Ah . . ."

The pain pulled deeper now, burned up her spine, then cut deep into her womb. Her body tightened and she caught her breath. This one was bad, the strongest, she thought, clutching the phone in one hand, her belly with the other. So deep. Oh, God, Alex, come back. Come back . . .

The concerned voice on the other end called through Nina's pain. "Nina, are you all right? Are you there?"

Before she could respond a fist pounded hard at the front door. The handle twisted, somebody pushed to get in. Alex. God. So wonderful but so forgetful. First the telephone and now the keys. When were they going to learn that they didn't need to go locking everything up as in Chicago?

Nina bit her lip, gasped. "Dr. Dundeen . . . Alex is at the front door." My God, she thought, this could really be it. "And I'm having another contraction."

"Start timing them," he calmly advised. "If they continue, telephone your obstetrician. If there's anything I can do, just call. I haven't delivered a baby in years, but I do know a few things. I'm leaving the office now, but my answering service can page me. Regarding your father, let's talk tomorrow. Call me—early morning would be best."

Weak but reassured, Nina replied, "Thank you."

Nina set down the receiver, held her stomach and closed her eyes. Was it indigestion? Was it just the baby kicking? No, this was more. Much more.

The pounding at the door continued.

"Coming, Alex!" she called.

Just as quickly as it had come, the contraction passed. She caught her breath, then pushed herself up and made her way across the oak floor. She passed from the den through to the living room and into the large front hall. Resting for just a moment, she leaned against the staircase and looked over at the opaque glass that filled the top half of the door. The porch light cast a deep shadow on the milky glass, and at once Nina realized it wasn't Alex out there. No, it was someone taller, leaner perhaps and slightly stooped.

She called out, "Who is it?"

Would she ever, she wondered, lose her big city suspicions? Up here in Mendota, some three hours north of Chicago, people opened their doors all the time to strangers without even the slightest thought of gangs.

"It's me. Mr. Morton from across the street. Please open up."

Nina started for the door but then stopped. She didn't know Mr. Morton. Sure, she'd waved at him and his son a few times. But what could he want? Why had he come, especially at this hour? Should she open the door to him? And why had he tried the door himself?

This is Wisconsin, she chided herself. Don't worry. He's just a neighbor. Of course you should let him in, and she stepped to the door, twisted the brass deadbolt with one hand and turned the doorknob with the other. If only Alex and she would just relax about the locks she wouldn't have to go shuffling around like this.

She opened the door to the night and the old man, and said, "Hello, how are . . . ?"

At once she knew something was very wrong. She could see it in his dark eyes. This wasn't a cup-of-sugar visit, this wasn't a lost-cat call either. Not at least by the way Morton was kneading his knuckles one against the other, not by the way his body was flinching and moving and his eyes shifting with horror. Suddenly frightened, she tensed, and took a step back.

"Mrs. Hale, I . . . I . . ." He reached out with one hand

and grabbed her wrist. Then his eyes shrank as he said, "Something terrible has happened."

She'd kept her own name, Trenton, but she let his error slide. "What is it? What's the matter?" As she broke his grasp on her arm and pulled back, she could see the fear in his face. "Is there something I can do for you?"

He opened his craggy mouth but could not speak. Helplessly, he stepped aside and motioned toward the street with one shaking hand. Squinting, Nina could barely make out a dark blue pile in the snow.

"Your . . . your husband . . ."

"What?" she said, not understanding.

She looked again, and there, crumpled across the street, was a shape she recognized, knew better than her own. But she couldn't believe it, didn't want to, even as the adrenaline began to surge into her system.

"Alex?" She hesitated in shock and was only able to repeat herself. "Alex?"

Mr. Morton's head bounced up and down. "I . . . I saw him come jogging back toward your house. He started . . . started to trip. He was clutching his chest and then . . ."

Nina threw herself forward. "No!"

"I . . . I think it might be his heart," said Morton, trying to catch her. "That's rather what it looked like from the way he fell, you know. I've already called an ambulance and I . . ."

She shoved aside the old man and threw herself out the door. Clutching her belly, she ran across the slippery gray planks of the porch.

"Alex!" she screamed, her breath steaming into the cold night.

She left the old man rattling on about what he'd tried to do to save Alex, about how he'd tried to revive him there in the snow. But what was he talking about? Of course Alex was all right. He'd never leave her. Especially not now. Not before the baby. Yes, they were going to have a baby. Yes, after all these years she'd finally become pregnant.

"Alex!"

Her scream turned lights on in every house, brought people running to the street. Almost at once a siren could be heard slicing through the night, but it was dimmer, not as terrified as Nina's plea.

"Mrs. Hale!" a voice cried out from behind her. "Watch out for the steps!"

But she paid Mr. Morton no attention as she grabbed the handrailing and charged down the steep porch stairs. There, in the dirty late-March snow was a pile, and that pile was her husband. Motionless, yes, even lifeless, he lay in the night like a discarded pile of clothes. No. God, no. Alex was dropped there like a rejected pile of flesh and bones, an abandoned body.

"Alex!"

Terror seized Nina's entire body as she struggled, clutching her stomach, down the stairs. Her puffy face twisted grotesquely and was suddenly awash with tears. She flung one arm out, tried to reach across the distance to grab him. She had to reach him, pull him back, hold him and never let Alex go.

She was nearly at the bottom of the stairs when it happened. Her right foot landed on the third step and slid across a thin film of early-spring ice, the kind that's a puddle by day and death by night. As if she were on a roller coaster, her stomach sank in anticipation of all that was to come. First her foot shot out, then her leg stretched inhumanly to the side, pulling and twisting and ripping muscles. Then, with no hope of stopping herself, she plunged forward. Suddenly there was nothing beneath her and she was diving through the air, totally at gravity's whim.

"Ah!" she screamed.

In those split seconds before she landed, Nina folded

inward. The baby. She had to protect the baby. Wrapping her left arm around her belly, Nina jabbed out her right to try and break the fall. Less than a second later, her right hand smacked against the cold cement walk and her rigid arm snapped under the pressure. And as hard as she could, she threw herself back and twisted around so that she wouldn't land on her front side. It worked. Her right shoulder hit the ground, then her head, and finally she rolled onto her back. Still, the pain screamed from her soul and radiated through her like hundreds of volts of electricity. Everything went black, blacker than the sunless sky overhead.

Clutching her stomach, writhing on her back and unable to see her husband, Nina shrieked, "Alex!"

And minutes later all she was aware of lying there in the crusty snow was that the men from the screaming ambulance ran first not to Alex but to her, the one who still lived.

# Chapter

# 5

Seated on his blue bike with training wheels, Mikey waited and rocked from side to side, first the small left training wheel hitting, then the right. Left then right. Right then left. He liked to see how long he could make the bike stay up before the wheel hit the ground. Biting his lip, he looked down. Watch it, he told himself, but then he twitched and the bike tipped to the side. Oh, well. He tried again. And again.

In the park down the hill from Leaf Street, he waited all alone in the night. Periodically he turned, squinched up his eyes, looked but saw no one. He wasn't sure why he was here. What had his father told him? Wait? Yes, that was it. He was supposed to wait right here so he could help his father.

He smiled and rubbed the few whiskers on his chin. He liked to help. Mikey got to shovel snow and he got to carry things, too. But what he liked most was when his father let him help downstairs. The tests. Seated now on his bike, Mikey made a fist with a pointed knuckle sticking out, just as his father had taught him. You do this, thought Mikey, concentrating, and then you rub the chest with the pointy part. Or you reach in between the legs and you grab a bunch of skin and you squeeze as hard as you can. Mikey tried it on himself, pinching the inner part of his leg.

"Ow!"

That hurt, he thought, smiling. It hurt because his father had taught him how to do it, and his father let him help a lot. Mikey liked that.

He'd wanted to rush home when he'd heard the shrieking siren, especially when it grew louder and louder and whooshed right past. He always did as his father said, though, and so he stayed and waited for the man in the car. Yes, that's why he was here. The package. That's all Mikey needed. Then he could rush back, pedal his dented bike as fast as he could, go and see what was going on up there. It had to be something really, really, really exciting.

He heard more noise and his eyes searched the pulsing sky above Leaf Street. The chaos dulled, but now Mikey could hear in the distance many cars and muffled shouting and he wanted to be there, too. From the commotion he guessed there were many people out on his street. Was it something good or bad that had happened in that big red house? A game? If so, maybe he should go. Maybe they wouldn't push him away this time. After all, the nice people lived there, the man and blond lady who always waved. Mikey waved back, too.

Mikey stopped rocking. If the game was way up there, why was he here? Why was he sitting here in the dark so very far from home? Suddenly he couldn't remember. He remembered his father telling him something, but what was that? What did he say? He began to rock from side to side more quickly. He was never allowed to go this far alone, and yet . . . Was he waiting for his father? Didn't he have something to do? Mikey looked at the training wheels as first one touched, then the other. He looked at the sky as it surged with color and noise. It was night and he was out here without his father.

He gazed around. It was so dark and there weren't any people here in the park. Just a few benches, lots of trees and the little river. He stopped rocking his bike and looked over his shoulder. He liked the river. Water was fun. Sometimes he and his father would walk down here and he could play in the water, throw some twigs in and watch them float away. He liked boats. But now he had gone very far by himself and his father would be very mad if he knew Mikey had gone so far. Mikey laughed. His father would be very, very mad. Especially because it was so dark. Especially because Mikey was all by himself and so close to the water. But the flashing sky was so pretty.

Behind him, he heard a shoe slide across the cement sidewalk. He spun around and saw a dark something move. Tall and big. A second later a man emerged, wearing a long, dark coat and holding a bag. Mikey screwed up his eyes and bit his lip as he studied the emerging man.

"Good evening, Mikey."

"Hi," he said, his voice soft and warm.

His eyebrows pushed together and he stared at the man. Who was he?

"Don't you remember me?"

Mikey shook his head. He kind of remembered the man but he kind of didn't, either.

"Well, don't worry. I'll help you soon." The man looked beyond Mikey and his blue bicycle. "Is your father still up at the house?"

Mikey raised his shoulders then dropped them. Next he twisted around and pointed to the colorful, red-flashing sky up the hill.

"Yes, I know," said the man, his voice tense. "There's been a problem."

"Game!"

Another noise twisted into the night, its screaming pitch whirling through the chilled air. It was coming from town and growing louder and louder.

Quickly, the man spit out his next words. "Mikey, I have to go." He shoved out a brown bag. "Here, give this to your father. And be careful. There's a glass bottle inside. Can you do that?"

Mikey looked past the man toward town. It was a big noise now. And there were more lights, too. This was fun.

"Mikey!" the man shouted. "Give this to your father—and be very, very careful with it!"

All of a sudden he pushed the paper bag into Mikey's stomach. Mikey automatically clutched it, looked for the noise coming from town, turned and looked up toward his house. When he twisted around again, the man was gone, eaten up again by the shadows. Where the stranger in the long, dark coat had been was no one, nothing. Mikey looked from side to side, and farther away caught the faint glimpse of someone disappearing into the park.

"Bye!" called Mikey, raising one hand in a wave.

It was quite noisy now, and Mikey saw the red-flashing lights fly up the road from town, across the bridge over the little river and then right past him. Nearly forgetting about the brown paper bag clutched under his arm, Mikey stood, pushed down on a pedal with one of his heavy legs and started after the twirling lights and screechy noise.

# Chapter

# 6

It was August now, the late summer warm and rich. Six months. Nina could scarcely believe it. She had last seen Alex six months ago and her baby was already a half year old.

As Nina drove her maroon Mazda on to the Extended Care Research Institute, the past lapped at her. She recalled being whisked down this very road to Mendota General Hospital, the ambulance screaming the entire way. She could still vividly feel the pain in her womb, she still called out in her mind for her husband. Too, she still remembered being pulled from the ambulance and looking up at her father's window next door at the ECRI. How odd. Her father locked in his ward, she immobile on a cart, and Alex . . .

Then as she entered the emergency room it had all sped up to a blur. They'd immobilized her wrist in a plastic splint, used a fetal monitor to note the baby's heart tones, thus learning that the fetus was in life-threatening distress. Nina knew she'd screamed over and over for her husband, and she recalled all the empty faces looking down on her. Somehow, sometime, she'd been administered general anesthesia. Soon after she delivered by cesarian section a five-pound-four-ounce baby girl. Nina woke once, sobbed at the sight of this beautiful little thing that had emerged from within her, then started crying and begging for news of her husband. None came, however, and the drugs seized her, drowning her in a black pool of sleep.

When Nina had awakened the next day, there she was again. A baby girl. Long, elegant fingers. Face full and flush with life. A button nose. Eyes squinched shut. The nurse had handed her to Nina, and Nina had taken the baby in her arms, pressed her close to her swollen breasts. She smelled so sweet, so fresh. So wonderful. Nina had held her and fed her and rocked her. And cried. Jennifer. Little Jenny. That was Alex's choice. Alex, who, she had learned, had been in the ambulance behind her and pronounced dead on arrival.

Driving on to see her father today, with Jenny strapped in a car seat in the back, Nina still couldn't grasp it all. Pulling into the parking lot shared by the Institute and Mendota General, she didn't know how she had lived through it. Among other things, with a broken wrist there was so much she simply hadn't been able to do. Alex's parents had stayed on for nearly five weeks, primarily just to change Jenny's diapers.

With the car parked, Nina unfolded an umbrella stroller, then lifted Jenny from the back. Oh, baby, thought Nina, kissing her wispy hair. So beautiful. So wonderful. The worst thing about all that had happened was that whenever someone asked how old Jenny was, Nina knew automatically—to within the hour—how long Alex had been dead. If there were anything that could be changed, it would be this, for now this perfect baby was the marker of her father's death.

Squinting into the sun, Nina eyed the very new and modern Extended Care Research Institute, a wing of black glass and silvery metal that jutted off the side and to the rear of the hospital. The addition, built just two years ago, provided the most advanced and thorough care for memory-impaired people like Nina's father, as well as acted as a testing and living research center. Not only was her father under constant surveillance, but both Jenny and Nina were being studied as well. Just this morning, Dr. Dundeen had called and asked her to stop by the lab.

Nina proceeded through the lobby that was shared by both the hospital and Institute, then passed through a set of sliding doors and into the ECRI itself. Instead of going directly upstairs to her father's room, Nina wheeled Jenny past the main office and to one of the labs. There she found Dr. Dundeen bent over a microscope.

"Terrific, you're right on time," said Dundeen, switching off the instrument. "Come on in and have a seat."

It was a small room, sparse and white walled. A long counter lined one side, some cabinets above it. There was a collection of test tubes and dishes down by a sink, the microscope and a small refrigerator. Dundeen had once told her he did most of his research in a lab at his house, using the facilities here mostly for gathering data.

He said, "Look at this baby. She's going to be a blond like you."

"We'll see. Alex was dark."

"Of course . . ."

As Nina seated herself, she looked up at him. Not a particularly tall man, he was solid and square, with grayish-brown hair that had receded a good deal. His face, anchored by a wide jaw and eyes that were dark and striking, was pleasant. He had a severe, straight mouth that he could lighten with a quick smile.

"I was just going to be running some experiments in the next few days," began Dundeen, "and I wanted to obtain cell specimens from both you and your baby. I just need a blood sample. Is that all right?"

"Sure."

Nina seated herself on a stool and watched as Dundeen put on a face mask and latex gloves. An amazing person, thought Nina. He doesn't work because he has to, but because he wants to. Devoted, that's what he is. The ECRI, Nina had learned, wouldn't actually exist without him. He was not only one of the foremost Alzheimer specialists, but sole descendant of one of Wisconsin's wealthiest lumber families. To a large part, the Institute had been founded and endowed by Dundeen himself.

Lifting a syringe, Dundeen said, "This will only take a moment."

She sat still as the doctor scrubbed her arm, then effortlessly yet carefully inserted the needle and withdrew her rich dark blood. Satisfied, he labeled the sample, then reached for a new needle.

"In studying Alzheimer's," he said, "we have to look at it from every angle—diet, health history and family history. With three generations of Trentons right here in town, I have to take advantage of all of you."

"You can have a few of my daughter's cells and that's it," laughed Nina. "Otherwise she's all mine."

Nina lifted Jenny into her lap and steadied her as Dundeen repeated his task on the infant. Moments later, he had the specimen and labeled it, then pulled off his gloves and turned around.

"Nina, I could have had one of my assistants gather these samples, but, frankly, I wanted to take a moment to see how you were doing."

Always the doctor, she thought. Always the white coat, the white shirt and tie. Always the sincere concern. No wonder everyone trusted him.

"You've been so nice to me," began Nina. "Even before all this. Just knowing you're taking care of my father has been such a relief. You don't know."

He leaned against the black countertop. "Good. But, Nina, I want to say that in treating the Alzheimer patient we have two major goals. First, we strive to maintain the patient's social skills at the highest level of functioning for the longest period of time. Second, we feel that treatment should be directed at the patient and family as a single unit." He paused, and added, "Nina, I've seen this before. I've seen caregivers such as yourself forget to take care of themselves."

She took a deep breath and glanced at a collection of test tubes on a far counter. Then her eyes fell on the plain linoleum. Everyone had advice for her on how to handle her finances, how to raise a child on her own, how to deal with her father. While all of that she dismissed as she chose, Dundeen's words were, she knew, something she should heed.

Nina lifted her baby to her shoulder, began patting her back, then a bit defensively said, "This has been incredibly hard—Alex dying and Dad in here. I can't tell you how awful these past months have been. But I'm feeling better." She took another deep breath and looked directly into the kind face. "Really I am. Just in the past week or two I've felt like I was coming out of a thick fog."

"Good, I'm glad to hear that."

Nina kissed Jenny's head. How had this happened? How? First her mother four years ago, then Alex and next her father. His mind had been seized, captured, by Alzheimer's. Who knew how long his long end would last. And how, wondered Nina yet again, had a family melted away so quickly? Jenny and she were all that was left. Her memories of how wonderful they had all been— their health, their brightness—were all so recent, and yet . . .

"Nina?"

"What?"

"Are you attending the support group?"

"No." She hadn't in months, not since the first troubles with her pregnancy. "It's just so hard to get out. Jenny's not weaned, you see, and I can't leave her for more than a couple of hours. I suppose I could take her with me, but it might be such a disruption and—"

"Give it some serious thought." Dundeen collected the tools and set them in a sink. "I think you'd benefit a great deal from the group—they are, in fact, supportive. Having a loved one with Alzheimer's is, as you know all too well, devastating."

"Yes . . ."

Wasn't she skipping the group simply because she didn't want to deal with things? Absolutely. She just wanted to get through each day one at a time. She took a deep sigh. Six months. It was cold then, warm now. Soon a chilly fall would appear. Perhaps it was time.

"Are you getting out at all?" he asked.

"Well . . . well . . ." Her baby began to squirm, and Nina now cradled her. "I visit Dad every day."

He smiled. "I know, and that's wonderful. But don't forget to get out socially. It might even be good for you to go away for a while. To really relax and recuperate. Your father would be all right—we always keep a close eye on him. If nothing else, why don't you go down to Chicago for a long weekend? You're from there, aren't you?"

"Yes . . ."

It was true, she thought. She hadn't been out at all. She also knew she could go on living like this forever, never working again, going nowhere except the Institute. She had plenty of money. Alex's life insurance policy had been substantial, and then there was all of her father's money, too. Before he'd gotten too bad and aware of what awaited, he'd transferred most of his assets to her and signed a durable power of attorney designating Nina attorney-in-fact.

Her eyes drifted along the countertop, to the sink, back to the test tubes, then to the microscope and to his deep eyes.

"I really am just now beginning to get over the shock. But you're right. I need to start getting out."

"Good. And in particular I want you to attend the support group."

She smiled and bowed her head. "Yes, doctor." She paused, then seized the opportunity to switch the topic. "How's my father?"

"As well as can be expected. I think we have his outbursts under control. We're also treating him with some cholinergic agents—RS-86, if I'm not mistaken—and also ACTH, which is a neuropeptide."

A cure, that's all she wanted. Don't tell me what it is. Just get it for him. Make him remember again. Make him whole again.

"Anything new on the horizon?" she asked.

"There are many things being tested, some waiting for approval."

"Tell them to hurry." Jenny began to squirm even more and Nina placed her gently in the umbrella stroller. "My father hasn't much time." She added, "Then again, I suppose none of us does."

Dundeen, who had been glancing down at a chart, suddenly looked at her sharply, his eyes demanding to meet hers, which they held for a split second. Appearing reassured, he then sighed.

"That," said Dundeen, "is the problem with life." He came over and extended his hand. "Well, I have to start my rounds, but, please, I'm here to help. Let me know if there's anything I can do."

"Thank you. I appreciate knowing there's someone I can call."

If Nina found anything in the doctor's manner odd, she ignored it. She was so indebted to him—for attending to her father and making sure he not only received the most advanced treatment but that he was comfortable, too. And now, she supposed, as she wheeled the stroller out of the lab, Dundeen was right again. It was time at least to begin thinking about moving on.

Alex. As Nina made her way into the hall she thought of nothing, saw nothing but Alex. In her mind she envisioned the spot in the street where he had fallen. There had been snow then. Ice, too, in layers as thin as videotape. It had been dark and cold and damp. He had gone running, sensed something wrong in his chest, then clutched his heart, perhaps run even faster as he tried to reach the big red Victorian. Tried to reach her. He almost had, but his life had given way just short of his goal. If only she had heard him, if only she had talked him out of running that night . . . if only . . .

"Oh, God," she said, pushing Jenny toward the elevator.

Dundeen was right. It would all be so much easier if only she could accept Alex's death and move into the future. But she couldn't. She just couldn't. She knew him, knew his body, his mind, his everything. Two people couldn't have been closer. He was in good health—always jogging, exercising, eating lots of vegetables. Training for those stupid marathons. Him and his damn sprouts and granola. No steak for him. Yes, he was in perfect health.

That was it. The reason she couldn't let go of Alex and move on. There was something she believed deep within and was only now, as the fog of the past months was lifting, beginning to admit. Yes. She couldn't accept what had happened to him because she didn't believe it. His, she sensed in her soul, was not a simple death.

# Chapter

# 7

In a garage apartment on the north side of the Ridgewood Mortuary, Bruce Fitzgerald rubbed his thick brown moustache and studied the day's newspaper. His weary eyes focused on the short obituary column, and he found the notice almost at once.

**Sullivan**
Anthony R., age 46, of 4586 East River Road. Owner Blue Bright Cleaners, passed away after complications from an automobile accident. Survived by his loving wife, Ruth; son Peter J.; two daughters, Mrs. Todd (Pam) Lawrence, Elizabeth M. Visitation Tuesday 12–2 PM at Ridgewood Mortuary. Private interment Riverbluff Cemetery.

Fitzgerald took his pencil and circled the paragraph once, twice and yet another time. Then the tall, brown-haired man tore the newspaper around the words, lifting the small obituary from the paper. He tossed the day's paper on the floor, opened a three-ring notebook and, as neatly as if he were preparing someone's taxes, pasted the notice onto a page. Beneath, he wrote the date and place of death. He also recorded that at noon on the previous day John Morton had picked up and brought the body of the deceased to the Ridgewood Mortuary. He paused, then added that yesterday there had been one UPS delivery and two visits from the florists.

And, as the process of death and burial progressed, Bruce Fitzgerald would take further note of exactly who visited the mortuary and when they arrived and departed. All of this would include, of course, the details of Mr. Sullivan's burial and any other pertinent information. Would this man's body, wondered Fitzgerald, be cremated? Probably. If only, he thought, he could obtain some information from the hospital where Sullivan had died. Yes, that was an obvious course to follow. Didn't he know someone who worked in the records department? No. Not really. Just a friend of a friend. Still, that was a contact he could pursue, perhaps develop.

He heard a car engine outside and turned at once. From up here—one block over from Leaf Street—the view was unimpeded yet not conspicuous. Through the thick branches of an oak tree, he saw the black pavement spread behind the mortuary, next the narrow Leaf Street and then a row of large Victorian houses. An hour or so ago he'd observed the woman from the red house as she loaded up her child and drove off. The noise now, however, was not from there. Rather, it came from the hearse, which, Fitzgerald thought, was long in returning. Where could he have gone? What could he have been doing?

The man stroked his brown moustache, then reached across the table he'd positioned next to the window. His fingers wrapped around the black binoculars, raised them to his eyes. The lenses needed no adjustment. Both John Morton and his son Mikey were in clear focus. He scanned the vehicle. Mud. There was mud splattered on the wheels. That's odd, Fitzgerald thought. It hadn't rained in almost two weeks.

And then behind the short curtains in the rear of the hearse he spotted it: a long, dark, wooden box. When

Morton had left, the vehicle had been empty. Now it held a coffin. Could this be the very coffin—picked up at some warehouse?—for the deceased dry cleaner already inside the mortuary? Or might, wondered Bruce Fitzgerald, this casket presently contain a corpse, perhaps one that would never be listed in the obituary column?

# Chapter

As Nina rode the elevator to the top floor of the ECRI, Alex still wouldn't leave her mind. She could hear his voice so clearly, see him so vividly. Even though he was gone, some part of him haunted her senses. She knew that young men, even dedicated runners, sometimes died of heart attacks. There was that guy a few years ago, the famous marathon runner, who simply dropped dead. And there had to have been many others, too. But why Alex? What had happened that night? What had gone wrong? A clogged artery? A dysfunctional valve? An undetected congenital defect?

Someone had to know, she realized. There must be an answer, a recorded, bureaucratic one that was more informative than the simple phrase "heart attack." Perhaps she'd been told, but if so she'd blocked it out. It had been so chaotic those first few weeks that she'd ignored all the officialese, concentrating solely on her pain and on her newborn. Maybe, though, if she understood more about Alex's death she'd be able to leave him behind more easily. Hell, she thought, she didn't even know if there'd been an autopsy. But where to begin? Dundeen. Surely he'd be a good one to talk to. In the next day or so she'd ask him what the procedure would have been and if there might be a file on the death of her husband. Good idea. Learning and understanding would speed the old mourning process.

The glass security doors on the top floor were, as always, locked in an effort to prevent the patients from wandering. A prominent sign read: PLEASE ALLOW ONLY FAMILY AND STAFF TO EXIT THROUGH THESE DOORS. Without hesitation, Nina reached to a keypad and entered the number 1989. A split-second later there was a dull buzz, and Nina pulled the door open and pushed the stroller through. As she did every day, she again entered the world of her father and other high-functioning Alzheimer patients.

Over the hall speakers quietly played a Tommy Dorsey tune, and Nina made her way down the soft mauve carpeting. She passed the nurses' station and stopped at a window. In a fenced-in yard below she saw a dozen patients wandering aimlessly about. Oh, Dad, she thought. Dear, old Dad. What's going to happen to you? How long can you hang on?

As she continued on, it struck Nina again how much they'd thought of here at the ECRI. The mauve carpeting had a border of dark teal that ran continuously, except in front of the common rooms. Called "tracking," because most patients wouldn't cross a solid border, it tended to keep patients from strolling into other's rooms and from walking into offices. And adorning the hall windows were big flowery curtains reminiscent of the forties; there were, however, no vines, because patients sometimes saw those as terrifying snakes. Even the pictures on the walls harkened back in time—prints of rabbits, dogs, men sailing. Yes, thought Nina, you needed a good sense of history to work with this disease.

A plaque on the third door from the end held a picture of Nina's father, his name and a short biography. How odd. The picture was there so the staff could distinguish who belonged in which room; the short bio served to announce that this person had a history and had once been a real, productive human being. The photo wasn't there for her father because he couldn't recognize himself as a man of seventy. No, in his mind he was young and virile; as the disease progressed, the younger he saw himself. Alzheimer's was in a very real way a kind of ghastly fountain of youth.

Nina hesitated, drew her breath, then rapped gently and called, "Hello?"

"Come on in!" hollered William Trenton.

The deep, gravelly voice instantly brought a smile to Nina's face. Half of Chicago and everyone on La Salle Street knew the voice of Bill Trenton; her father had been a stockbroker, an outspoken one, and had been on the phone constantly. With its sharp yet warm tones, that voice, Nina's mother had always said, belonged to a radio sports announcer.

*"Nina, have you seen my keys?"*

*"They're on the front hall table, Dad, just like always."*

*"Oh."*

*She watched the tall, fit figure of her father as he headed into the den for his jacket. The death of her mother three months ago had been hard on him, that was clear. The blue eyes were a little less bright. The blondish-gray hair a little thinner and duller. His sharp wit had all but disappeared, replaced by self-doubt. But what else could be expected? What could be more draining or hard on a family than a long-drawn cancerous illness? Didn't Nina's father have a right to be a little slow, a little depressed, a little unsure of life?*

*Always the dapper dresser, he returned decked out in loafers, jeans, a bright blue cashmere cardigan and his winter parka.*

*"Dad, you look great, but you don't need the coat."*

*"I don't?" He glanced out the window at the spring day.*

*"No, the weather's perfect. It's already up to sixty."*

*He shook his head and unzipped the parka. "Good God, I don't even know what season it is. Your old man's getting a little daffy."*

*"Don't be silly, Dad. Now come on." Their Sunday walks had become a regular thing, a way to counter his recent reclusive habits. "Let's go."*

*"Yeah, yeah." Suddenly panic spread across his face like a deep rash and he started jabbing his hands into his pockets. "Nina, where are my keys? My God, someone didn't take them, did they? Nina, have you seen my keys?"*

Nina and Jenny entered a room that was less like a hospital and more like a combination bedroom-and-den decorated carefully with things from her father's Chicago home. Everything had been in the family for years, from the large oak headboard to the mahogany bedside table to the oriental rug and the curtains that had hung in the library. All had been chosen with great thought. The idea was to mask the linoleum and white walls and to surround her father with familiar things from his past.

"Hello!" he called. "Have a seat."

Her father, dressed in a red plaid shirt, yellow sweater and gray slacks, sat in a chair in front of the TV, the little color one he used to watch football on. He always looked good, well kept—those dazzling eyes, a handsome face now chiseled with classic lines—but today he looked even better.

"Good morning. It's good to see you. You look great." Dr. Dundeen had said to always reassure and compliment him, and today her enthusiasm was anything but forced. She hadn't seen him like this in weeks, if not months. Aiming the stroller at him, Nina bent down to Jenny and rubbed one finger under her chin. "Look who we've come to visit, Jenny. Come on, give us . . . There, that's a big smile!"

From the other side of the room, Bill laughed. "May I hold her?"

"Of course."

Nina crossed the room and handed Jenny to her father. With a relative degree of familiarity and ease, he took the baby and sat her on his knees. He bounced her several times, squinched up his nose and rubbed it against hers. A laugh like a series of little bubbles emerged from Jenny.

"Oh, you like this, don't you?" said Nina's father. "Yes, I know you do."

Nina sat on the bed and smiled, too, as her father played with Jenny. This was how it should be. Always. Perhaps there was hope, perhaps there was a way of stopping the slow progression of her father's disease. If only it could be halted now, today, just where it was, and allowed to do no further damage.

"I bet you're growing every day," said Bill.

As the two of them played, Nina's eyes were caught by the old silver-framed photo of her mother on the bedside table. How she missed her mother—now more than ever.

"This is a happy baby," said Nina's father, pulling more smiles out of Jenny.

"Do you think?"

"Absolutely. And look at those beautiful blue eyes. My God, they're huge. Such beautiful blue eyes. This is a gorgeous child." He gazed up at Nina. "Whose baby is this?"

Nina's finger sunk into the bed. "M-mine."

"Oh, that's nice."

She was stunned by the setback. Little by little, her father had begun to recognize his granddaughter, even calling her by name a few times. But now . . . It was the new memories, Dr. Dundeen had always said, that were the most difficult, the ones most quickly forgotten. The disease ate from the present and into the past until there was nothing left but flesh and bones and a mind that command them.

Nina once again glanced at her mother's photo. How lucky, she thought. How lucky her mother was not to have witnessed this.

Her father looked back up at her with that familiar hollow expression, and Nina tensed as if she were about to be physically struck. Even before he said it, she knew this was the question she had been fearing all along.

"Who are you? Do I know you?"

Nina's stomach caved in on itself. She tried to form the words, but couldn't.

"I'm . . . Nina, your . . . daughter."

"Oh. I thought you looked familiar." He smiled, and said, "I have a son, too. His name is Brian. You haven't seen him, have you?"

Nina bit her lip and shook her head. "No, Daddy," she said, at the same time thinking, begging her father not to put her through this. Not Brian. Not again.

Alzheimer's disease. The first signs of it had started four years ago, just after Nina's mother had died. Following her death, it had progressed rapidly for almost two years until he was no longer able to live by himself. Nina and Alex had brought him to live with them, turning the den of their condo into a bedroom. That had worked fine for the next year, with Bill not leaving the apartment during the day. Then, however, he forgot how to turn off lights, flush the toilet, turn off the range. And one day he placed a newspaper right up on the stove, and the kitchen caught fire. Half of the cabinets were ablaze by the time a neighbor smelled smoke, and it was only a miracle that no one, including Bill, was hurt and the entire building not destroyed. From that day on, Bill, the famous broker of La Salle Street, was never left alone. He had a babysitter. Soon thereafter, Alex and Nina decided to leave the city, choosing Mendota for its only claim beside tranquility: the Extended Care Research Institute.

Nina braced herself on the bed. Her eyes shut, she tried

to hold back the tears, but couldn't. They squeezed out of her eyes, dribbled down her cheeks.

"Are you all right?"

"Yes . . . Daddy." Ever since she was thirteen it had been *Dad* or *Father*. Recently, though, many things had regressed. "I'm fine."

"Do you want the maid?"

"I'm fine." Christ, how often had she said those words over the last few months? How often had she lied? "No, don't get the nurse."

Bill stopped bouncing Jenny, and abruptly the baby began to cry. Just as suddenly, the smile vanished from his face.

"What are you crying about?" he nearly shouted.

Jenny's eyes opened in alarm. She paused for a half a second, and then her face puckered in tears and shrieks.

"Stop it!" With two fingers he slapped Jenny on her cheek. "Stop it, do you hear?"

"Daddy, don't!"

Nina panicked, but didn't move. Dr. Dundeen had said his outbursts—fits of violence that had plagued the sweetest father in the world—were under control. Just be calm, Nina told herself. It won't happen again. Dr. Dundeen assured her that—

Suddenly Bill's face was filled with rage. "What do you mean, this baby's crying? You have to find her mother, give her back. She has to stop." He brought back his open hand. "I'll—"

"No!"

Seeing the danger, Nina leapt from the edge of the bed and lunged for Jenny. She jerked the child out of her father's hands and pulled her to her chest.

"That baby's crying and she has to stop!" shouted Bill, jumping to his feet.

"She's scared!"

Jenny wailed louder, her screams piercing everything.

"Stop her!" yelled Bill, swiping at Nina with one hand. "Daddy!"

Nina huddled over her baby, cradling her against her bosom, and sobbed. Her father didn't remember her. How could he have forgotten her? She looked up at him, tears in her eyes, and Bill screamed again, screamed louder than the baby, and then he turned away.

"Shut that thing up!" he cried, clutching his ears and thrashing his head from side to side. "Oh, won't someone find Brian for me?"

He charged toward the dresser, swung out with his hand. An antique china shaving mug, a bottle of cologne, photos of Nina and Alex and one of Jenny, all were wiped away, cascading onto the floor and shattering into bits.

"Daddy, no!" Running into the hall, Nina yelled, "Nurse! Nurse, help!"

Two nurses—a red-haired woman and a black man— bolted out of different rooms.

"My father!" she shouted, clutching Jenny and motioning into the room. "He's going to hurt himself!"

Bill cried a long low sound as if something were feasting away at him. "I . . . I can't remember!"

The former stockbroker grabbed the remote control from the TV and hurled it against the wall. The plastic device shattered and tumbled to the floor.

"Daddy, Daddy, please!" called Nina from the hall, not daring to go in. "Please, don't. It's all right. Everything will be all right!"

"Where's Brian?" he sobbed. "Won't someone get Brian for me?"

In Nina's tight arms, Jenny's little body became as stiff as a board. The child gulped down air and then shrieked as loud as an animal, the cry long and almost without end. Once her lungs were empty, she gasped and wailed again and again. Patients gathered in the hall in little groups, some held hands, and all stared.

The red-haired nurse burst past Nina and into the room, then the male nurse hurried in, pulling the door closed behind him. A moment later, the door burst open and the black man, his face broad and kind, wheeled out the umbrella stroller.

With a thick, rolling Caribbean accent, he said, "Don't worry, don't worry. This happens all the time. I ask the doctor what causes this but the doctor does not know. It just happens, so don't worry." A wide, sympathetic smile spread across his face. "He's scared, that's all. We'll take care of him."

"But . . ."

As the door closed, he said, "You go down the hall and rest yourself. We'll take care of him. Don't worry, don't worry."

Behind the door, Nina heard the man and woman's soothing voices as they tried to calm her father. Not trying to reason, only bring him under control, they spoke simply as if he were a child of three in the midst of a tantrum. But Bill wouldn't listen. He screamed again and hurled something across the room. The male nurse shouted to the other to duck, and an instant later glass shattered on the wall.

As Nina clutched her shrieking baby, she, herself, started to cry. This couldn't be happening. She had to find Dr. Dundeen—he had to have something stronger to give her father. A powerful shot or pill. He could give it to Bill and then he wouldn't charge out of control ever again.

Oh, God, thought Nina, rushing off. She'd beg Dundeen for something more, too. Yes, that's what she wanted, what Bill had to have. A potent medication that would clear the plaques and tangles from her father's rotting brain, a miracle drug that would make him remember his only daughter.

# Chapter

Before Dr. Dundeen could begin his rounds, a patient's wife cornered him and bombarded him with questions and tears. Minutes later, he started off, carrying his clipboard and the small leather case containing the syringes and synthetic solution. He'd been testing and observing one patient in particular, and he needed to ascertain her reaction to this formula. If only, he thought, there was a good animal model to use in research. It would speed things up so much, make it all so much easier. Humans, however, were the only creatures to suffer the progressive memory loss of Alzheimer's, and so he was forced into alternative research methods.

Lord. Every day people bombarded him. Every day he repeated his litany. No, we don't know what causes it. No, we don't know how to prevent or treat it. No, there isn't even a diagnostic test; it was simply a diagnosis of exclusion—electroencephalography, computerized tomography, and the like. He could give them more. He could tell them the blunt pathological facts: neurofibrillary tangles, senile plaques, granulovacular degeneration and a brain that was marked by decay in the frontotemporal and cortical areas. He could go on about a loss of dendrites and axons, a dramatic decline in choline acetyltransferase, the enzyme that made the chemical messengers, acetycholine, but . . . but . . .

People didn't want to hear that, just as they most

certainly wouldn't want to hear if they had inherited the disease. They would be horrified, Dundeen knew, if they learned they were genetically programmed to develop Alzheimer's yet could do nothing to prevent it. No, people only wanted to know why a husband no longer remembered where he had lived for the last twenty-five years or why a mother exposed herself in front of the grandchildren. They wanted to know why a bus driver could no longer drive or why an accountant had forgotten how to count. They just wanted to know why their loved one's mind was becoming a useless organ that was losing a lifetime's memories.

Well, Christ, thought Dundeen. He didn't know. He didn't have all the answers, not yet. If only there was more time. Already Alzheimer's was the fourth-leading cause of death in adults and in the not so distant future it would be affecting one out of every three families in America. So, would his research succeed in defusing the explosion of memory-impaired people? He just didn't know. He was so very close, and yet . . .

Sometimes, he thought, rubbing his head, the pressure was just too great. He couldn't bear it. Among other things, almost twenty-five years later he was still haunted by the memory of his father, who lost his mind to early-onset Alzheimer's—the instance when the disease struck not those in their sixties, seventies or eighties, but those in their forties and fifties. Whenever Gregory Dundeen thought of his father, the event that towered above all others was the rainy night he had gone out searching for the older man. Having escaped from the secluded estate, the older Dundeen was wandering around town in his pajamas, calling out for Muffins, his pet cocker spaniel that had died over fifty years earlier. The most horrendous thing about it was that back then there had been no name for the disease. All the townspeople had thought old Dundeen had simply gone crazy, that his tens of millions of dollars had poisoned his soul.

Wasn't that an end that terrified him above all others? Wasn't that, after all, the main reason Gregory Dundeen had gone into medicine?

As he proceeded down the hallway of the second floor, fingers of pain suddenly seized at the back of his head. They felt like claws, sharp ones, poking into his skull, and he stopped, closed his eyes. Catching his breath, Dundeen leaned against the wall, ran his hand over his balding head. This was too soon. He shouldn't be needing another dose of medication. Not yet. Not for another two hours. Just relax, he told himself. The pain began to melt. Yes, he could make it.

In room 212 of the moderate-functioning ward he found his patient, Ellen Cherney, a former fashion designer from Chicago. In her mid-sixties, she still bore high cheekbones and a thick head of silvery hair, but gone were the bright-colored, bold clothes she herself had designed. Now she sat on the edge of her bed wearing a man's T-shirt, baggy green pants and rubber boots. Next to her lay a red down parka streaked with stains.

"Hello, Ellen," said Dundeen. "How are you feeling today?"

Running her hand through her hair, Ellen Cherney said, "I'm fine." She smiled at him blankly. "Who are you?"

"A friend." Carefully pressing shut the door, Dundeen said, "I'm your doctor."

He'd visited her frequently, yet each time was as if his were a completely fresh face. He went along with it, too. If he told her that she knew him, that she had seen him repeatedly, if he made her try to guess his name and she was unable, her frustrations would only be compounded. And he didn't need anyone cantankerous. No, he needed her calm. Ellen Cherney was valuable to him for her blood pressure. It was high and he needed to learn if her body could tolerate the drug.

"Ellen, would you come over and sit in your chair?"

said Dundeen, motioning toward a seat by the window.

"Oh, all right, but when am I going to eat?" Still lithe, she scooted off her bed. "I'm hungry."

"In a half hour."

"Okay."

As she shuffled over in her rubber boots, Dundeen placed his clipboard and case on a dresser. With his back to her, he unzipped three sides of the leather kit and folded it open. Inside were four plastic-encased Singlject syringes, a tourniquet, alcohol wipes and a vial of the synthetic solution. He removed one of the syringes and tapped its plastic case, thereby breaking the seal. Leaving the Singlject on the dresser, he turned to her, tourniquet hidden in his hand.

"Ellen, would you roll up your right sleeve, please?"

"Yes, but when am I going to eat? I'm hungry."

"In fifteen minutes," replied Dundeen, knowing it made no difference what he replied. She would forget within the minute.

"Oh, good, because I'm very hungry."

Ellen sat there, picking at a spot on her pants and not suspecting a thing. Just nice and calm. That's what he wanted. No problems. Simple and quick. He just needed to learn her body's reaction. Perhaps at last he had succeeded . . .

Kneeling by her side, Dundeen kept the rubber cord low and out of sight. Then he gently extended her right arm and searched the inside of her elbow for an appropriate vein. With his fingers, he pushed until a bluish vein swelled to the surface of her chalky white skin. This arm would do, he thought, and raised the tourniquet.

"What are you doing?" she asked.

"Just checking your arm here."

"Why?"

"Because I'm going to give you a shot."

"Oh. Are you a doctor?"

"Yes, and my job is to make you better," he said,

wrapping the cord around her arm. "Now just sit still. I'm a friend and I want to help you."

No sooner had he tied the cord, however, than the woman jerked back her arm, clutching it against her waist.

"No!" she shouted. "I don't want a shot. I don't like shots!"

He felt his anger growing, but held himself in check. Just be calm, he told himself as he knelt by her. Don't frighten her. Just reassure. He'd been through hundreds of such situations.

"Ellen, please. I just want to help you."

"No!"

He hated bribery, but sweets for some unknown reason worked magic with Alzheimer patients. "If you're good I'll give you a big brownie."

She stared at him, eyes drawn small as she pondered the offer. But it was obvious she wasn't going to trust him. She jerked off the tourniquet and threw it on the floor.

"No! Get out of here!"

Suddenly her hand came hurling out, plunging into Dundeen's chest. He fell back slightly and watched as Ellen Cherney leapt from her chair and scrambled to the head of her bed. Drawing her legs up underneath her, she held a pillow out in front.

Dundeen's head began to throb again. "Damn it, Ellen, just sit still!" He didn't have time for this. It should be easy. He stormed toward her. "I—"

"Help!" she screamed as if she were fending off a rapist. "Help!"

Oh, shit. All he had to do was pin her down, jab the needle into her, monitor her reactions. To hell with what she wanted. To hell—

"Help! Help!" Ellen continued to cry.

He grabbed hold of her hospital bed and stopped himself. Don't. Don't be crazy, he told himself. You can't administer the shot now. It would be too dangerous. He squeezed the metal railing. Damn her. How was he going to make any progress when stupid people like Ellen Cherney got in his way? Infuriated, he turned back to the dresser and quickly zipped shut his leather case.

A moment later, just as Dundeen had expected, one of the nurses, Barb, came rushing in. A young woman with red hair, she took one look at Ellen Cherney, then Dr. Dundeen.

"Oh, doctor, I didn't know you were in here. Is everything all right?"

"I suppose." He took a deep breath, willing control. "But ... but I don't think this is going to be my day."

"You have to help me!" pleaded Cherney. "This man wants to give me a shot!"

"Now, now, Ellen. I just gave you your medication for the morning," said the nurse, approaching the older woman. "Calm down."

"But he was going to give me a shot! And ... and he closed the door so no one would see!"

"No, Ellen." Dundeen forced a tired smile. "I wasn't going to give you a shot." He raised his empty hands. "See, I don't have anything."

"But you wanted to stick me with a big needle!" she shouted.

Dundeen glanced briefly at the nurse, then back to his patient. "No, you're forgetting, Ellen. You asked me to come in and talk with you."

The older woman turned to the nurse. "He's lying! He was feeling for my veins and—"

"Now stop," said the young woman. "This is your doctor and he wouldn't lie to you. He wouldn't ever do anything to hurt you, either."

"But—"

In his coat pocket, Dundeen's beeper began to buzz. He turned it off, and said, "Perhaps she'll calm down if I leave. Would you stay for a while? Or perhaps you should take her down to the activity room."

"That's a good idea. She'd like that." The nurse said to Ellen, "You want to go draw? Some of your friends are down in the activity room. Let's go see what they're doing."

As Dundeen gathered his clipboard and case, he noticed it by the foot of the bed. The rubber tourniquet, lying just where Ellen had thrown it. He quickly eyed the nurse, then reached into his pocket. An instant later, he let his pen tumble to the floor.

"I'm going to answer my page," said Dundeen, bending over and scooping up both tourniquet and pen in the same hand, "and then continue on my rounds." He stood and crammed both items into his pants pocket. "Just let me know if you need anything."

"Thanks," Barb responded.

As he started out, clipboard and case in hand, Ellen Cherney shouted, "You liar, you were going to give me a big shot!"

The nurse turned to him and in a low voice said, "This one can be so difficult. Yesterday she accused me of stealing all her clothes, and today she thinks you're after her. Oh, brother. Sometimes I wonder why I just don't work at McDonald's."

"Because we need all the help we can get," replied Dundeen with his standard smile. "Thanks for taking her off my hands."

Taking a deep breath and then letting it slide out over his lips, Dundeen stepped into the hall. Ellen Cherney would forget the incident in minutes, but to avoid a similar episode he'd have to return later. He'd have to wait, perhaps until some evening this week. He'd order her sleep medications doubled. Then, with her responses thoroughly dulled, he'd be able to continue his research totally undetected.

# Chapter

# 10

"Nina?"

She looked up from the vinyl couch in the guest lounge where she had just finished feeding Jenny. He stood there, clipboard in hand.

"Dr. Dundeen." So he'd received her page. "Thanks for coming so quickly."

Though she was sure her eyes were still red, Nina had calmed down. Jenny, too, was quiet, having nursed to her fill.

"Your father's fine," said Dundeen, sounding weary. "They gave him a shot of Haldol."

Her poor father, she thought. Everything was out of balance. He'd been given so many sedative-hypnotics, so many antipsychotics, antidepressants, and antianxiety medications that it was a wonder he could talk at all.

Dr. Dundeen said, "Outbursts of this nature are to be expected, particularly in your father's case. There's nothing to worry about for now."

She wanted to believe him. If only she could. "But what if it gets worse? Will you be able to treat him?"

"Not, I'm afraid, without just knocking him out all together. He's getting some pretty potent stuff. Anything more and he'd be unconscious."

"Oh, God."

One of her largest fears was that some day they

wouldn't be able to control him, for it had become more difficult by law to administer drugs for violent behavior. If he became uncontrollable, Nina knew what awaited: a straightjacket and an all-male ward in Chicago. The thought alone was horrifying to Nina—she couldn't bear even the idea of him rotting away in such a hole.

She placed a cotton diaper on her shoulder and lifted Jenny and began to burp her. This is my anchor, she thought. This little person is all that is keeping me alive. What would she do without her?

"What happened?" asked Dundeen.

"I ... I ..." She caught herself, tried to keep from crying again and almost laughed hysterically instead. Control, she thought. That's it. Bite the lip, close your eyes. Suck it all back in. Just don't lose it. "My father didn't ... didn't know me."

"I'm sorry."

"Nothing. He didn't even recognize me. He was holding Jenny and he asked whose baby it was and then he wanted to know my name and then Jenny started to cry and he got all upset. It all happened so quickly. The only person he wanted was Brian. He just kept calling for him."

"Who's that?"

"My little brother." She squinched her eyes shut in pain. "He ... he died thirty-eight years ago ... just after his second birthday."

Yes, that was the horror. After all Bill had put her through, after all she'd done for him, her own father didn't know her. Her, Nina, his blonde little girl, his only child, the one whom he'd taught to fox-trot, the one he'd taken to Colorado skiing, the one he'd always been there for. How could it be that such a mountain of a person could be so quickly washed away?

"It's like that, you know. The slightest things can set them off."

"Why?" She looked up at him, her angular face begging a truth that had yet to be found. "Why? He knew me yesterday. He knew Jenny, too. He recognized her face and her laugh and that she belonged to him. Then . . . then . . ." She choked on her words. "I . . . I knew the day was coming when he wouldn't know me, but I didn't expect it so abruptly. Least of all today."

He rubbed his eyes, looked down, looked back up at her. "You know, my father died of Alzheimer's, and the only thing I can say is that for you it's going to get worse. I'm sorry to say that, but I want to always be direct with you. Nina, you have to be prepared for what is ahead. Sometimes, you know, it takes forever for the mind and then the body to go—ten, sometimes twelve or fifteen years." Obviously tired, Dr. Dundeen glanced around the room as if he were looking for something that couldn't be found. "Otherwise, we're working hard and learning a great deal." Only with effort did his words sound encouraging. "I can't say we're on the verge of a cure, but we're making progress. We do a great deal of research here at the Institute, observing the patients, seeing what works, what doesn't. There's a lot being done elsewhere, too— the pharmaceutical companies are spending millions and millions."

"Yes."

She'd read of the tens of billions being spent nationally on the care of Alzheimer victims and that that figure would escalate dramatically with the graying of America. Besides being a cruel tragedy, Alzheimer's was also big business, and whoever developed a treatment for the disease would reap an immense fortune.

"Dr. Dundeen, if there's anything at all you can give my father—anything—please do. You have my permission."

"All right, but—"

"You mentioned some new drugs. Would any of these

help? Or what about any new methods? His diet, perhaps. Or . . ."

He looked at her long and slow before saying, "There are some new things, a few developments that are beginning to pay off. Unfortunately, they're all still experimental, some even dangerous."

"Dr. Dundeen, please. I . . ."

What did her father have to lose? The progressive memory loss of Alzheimer's had already consumed so much of his mind. What could be worse? Besides, that was why they had brought him here to the ECRI— long-term care combined with research. Nina herself had signed the consent forms, stating that each drug, each theory and every prospect that was come upon could be tested on her father. She consented to this, not only praying for a cure for her father, but also realizing that her father wouldn't want his suffering to go in vain. However possible, he would want to contribute toward the search for diagnostic and genetic tests, as well as for any type of effective treatment.

Catching her off guard, tears swelled out of Nina's eyes. Shit, not now. Not in front of him, she thought, desperately dabbing her eyes.

"I'm sorry," she said. "It's just that . . . that I'm still trying to get over Alex's death and . . ." The truth, this was it. "I just need my father around for a little bit longer." She couldn't take another major blow, not yet. Her chin began to quiver and she said, "Please, I'd just appreciate anything . . . anything at all for him."

This wasn't her. She was the rock. The solid one. But, dear Lord, she felt so desperate, and here she was, eyes moist, staring at Dundeen, begging, pleading. Do something, please!

He glanced helplessly away. "I can't promise anything, but I'll thoroughly review your father's case and see what I can do."

"Thank you. I really appreciate it. It's all just so overwhelming."

Boundaries, she thought. That was the worst part about all this. She had to transgress every boundary between her father and her, slip into the hollow chambers now in his mind, make decisions she hoped he'd make for himself, then pray she decided on the best. What's more, she was doing it for someone who hadn't looked this well-rested in years. That was one of the odder quirks of Alzheimer's—a sufferer could be losing his mind yet on the outside appear completely normal. At least her mother had looked exponentially worse as her cancer progressed.

"As unfortunate as it is, it's good for us to note the difference in your father," said Dr. Dundeen. "I'll—"

He stopped mid-sentence and clutched his head with one hand. The always cool face grimaced in pain.

"My head," he said, rubbing his scalp. "Ah."

"Are you all right?"

He nodded and forced a smile. "It's been a very busy morning and I haven't had any coffee today. I get a bad headache when I don't get a dose of caffeine on the job." He seemed to shake it away. "Anyway, I have some time now, so I'll check his charts. Perhaps there was a change in his diet or medication. Perhaps he didn't sleep well last night or was up too early. I'll stop by his room and see if there's anything I can do. How's that?"

"I'm very grateful."

At some point, too, she wanted to ask him about Alex and if there might have been an autopsy. But not now. She'd asked enough for today. She'd secured preferential treatment for her father and she didn't want to push her luck. Besides, she had an idea where to start.

"Thank you," said Nina. "Thank you very much."

"I'll be in touch," he said, and headed out.

Sending all of her hopes with him, she watched him

leave, his white coat billowing out behind him. Thank God medical research was so thick in his blood.

Once Nina had laid Jenny down on the couch and changed her, she sat her back in the umbrella stroller. Then Nina took a deep breath. There was just so much going on in her head. A father whose mind was shrinking but whose body was in perfect shape. A husband whose mind had been at its peak but whose body gave out . . .

She rose, rubbed her head. The thoughts just couldn't be quieted. She was on a roll, a neurotic one perhaps. Alex, her father. Her father. Alex. Don't fight so hard, she told herself. One is gone, the other leaving. You can't do anything about it. But . . .

Pushing the stroller, Nina started out. As she neared the elevator, she heard music to her right and stopped. Peering into the common room, she saw that it was filled with perhaps twenty older adults, all patients. While Frank Sinatra's rich voice crooned "Witchcraft," they sat there solemn, vacuous. One woman wore a straw summer hat and blue-check dress, while the man behind her had the seasons confused and was wearing a scarf, gloves and hat. In the back Nina saw one woman who had just wet herself and was crying into her wrinkled palms.

Then one of the attendants turned off the stereo and wrote in big bold letters on a blackboard. All together they then followed her prompting and chanted: "Today is Monday. We are in a special class. It is a beautiful summer day."

At once it reminded Nina of both a zombie movie and a sci-fi horror film. She turned and nearly ran out, fumbling with the code at the security doors, then bolting for the lift. She had to get out of here, away. She'd done all she could for her father. And now she'd do what she could for Alex.

# Chapter

# 11

He would only do this for Nina Trenton. Dundeen sensed he shouldn't, but at the same time wanted to very much. After all she'd been through, it was the least he could do. Her husband, now her father. He knew what it was like to lose someone to Alzheimer's. God, yes. The meltdown of the mind. First they forget where they parked the car. Next they don't recognize their loved ones. And last they no longer remember how to smile. All you can do, thought the doctor, was stand by, hands folded. Be supportive. Be helpless. Not this time, though. Not today. Just this once he would do virtually all that he could. The Trenton family was his case, he had to look at them as a single family/patient unit. And they were in need, Nina as much as her father.

Dundeen had returned to his office and collected the solution from his safe. Now, his small leather case in hand, he pushed open the door to Bill Trenton's room. He found the retired stock broker lying on his bed, fully dressed and eyes closed. For an instant, Dundeen had a vision of Nina's former family life. Her father perhaps dozing on a Sunday afternoon while on TV the Bears played the Packers. Maybe her mother sat knitting in the same room.

As he pushed the door shut, the pain clawed its way up the back of his head. He froze. God, he wasn't going to make it through another half hour. Gasping, he held his breath, reached out and braced himself against the wall. This one was sharper, deeper, like a coagulating sinus attack that seized the rear of his skull. Just as quickly as it had struck him, though, it faded away. Blinking, he stood stunned. He knew what this meant. To thwart such withdrawal attacks, he was going to have to increase both the dosage and the frequency. As soon as he'd finished here he'd return to his office and take care of himself.

This time he pulled a chair in front of the door. That wouldn't keep anyone out, but it would certainly slow them down, give him enough time to put everything away. If only there were locks here. He understood why there weren't though. Mindless men and women inadvertently bolting themselves in, then screaming for freedom. Or doing it purposely in a fit of paranoia. No, the staff didn't need that aggravation. Just as they couldn't let the patients have telephones. They'd abuse that, too, calling the same number a hundred times a day, forgetting they'd just dialed the number two minutes earlier.

Dundeen leaned over Bill Trenton, checked the closed eyes, noted the breathing. The tranquilizer had worked well. He shouldn't have any problems.

He sat alongside the bed, placed the clipboard in his lap and on top of that laid his small leather case. Unzipping the kit on three sides, he opened it wide. He removed a fresh syringe, then took not the vial full of synthetic solution he'd tried to administer to Ellen Cherney, but the tube with the black top. The natural solution, fresh and potent, spun down in his home lab only last night. Nina will be astonished, he thought. Thankful. Relieved.

Dundeen pushed up Bill Trenton's left sleeve, then applied the tourniquet. Finding a nice rising vein, he checked his patient one last time. Trenton was out, eyes closed, body still. This was the way to do it. No protests from this one.

Quickly, he removed the syringe from its sterile plastic case, then filled it with the rich, syrupy liquid. Next he scrubbed the inside of Trenton's arm with an alcohol wipe. Slipping the tip of the needle into the man's arm was easy, like piercing the top of a buttery steak. As he pressed down on the Singlject's plunger, he studied Bill's face. Not a flicker of the eyes. Not a quiver of the lips. This would be over within—

"Oh, shit!"

A fist seemed to crash into the back of Dundeen's head, seemed to scrape up his neck, across muscle and into the back of his skull. Nails of pain drove into the back of his brain. This was the worst. By far. He bit into his lower lip. Let it pass, please. Stop. Oh, Christ. He clamped his eyes shut. Tried to take a deep, calming breath, but then another wave dug into his head.

"Ah!" cried Dundeen, falling over on the edge of the bed.

His hands shrunk in agony, twisted, as the mauling continued. His vision swelled and receded, and he could only faintly make out the syringe in his hand, the needle still piercing Bill Trenton's vein. Awkwardly, Dundeen slammed down on the plunger and shot the remainder of the solution into his patient's body. Then he ripped the hypodermic needle from the fleshy arm, which in turn sent a fine red mist into the air.

Gasping, Dundeen knew what this meant. His body had weakened yet again, become more needy, more desperate. He'd sunk another step closer. So what? So what? he thought. Just stop this fucking pain . . .

Hands shaking like an addict's, he struggled to tie the rubber tourniquet on his own arm. But he couldn't get the damn thing on. He tried once, it fell off. A second, it was loose. Then . . . yes, tight and firm. Good. He had to do it now. He couldn't make it back to his office like this, he couldn't let the staff see him. No. He needed it here, right away.

With a fresh syringe, he pierced the black-topped vial and sucked out the solution. He took a breath, aimed at a wormy vein and jabbed the needle through his flesh. With firm, hard pressure, Dundeen shot the natural liquid into his body. Just knowing it would soon take hold, soon soothe his screaming cells, enabled him to relax. He'd be all right. He'd worry about the ramifications of an increased dosage later. For now the pain would shrink and dissipate.

Dundeen sat back, his forehead beaded with sweat, the discharged syringe hanging from his arm. As if he'd just been running, he sucked the air in big gulps. Oh, God . . .

Then he saw something twitch on the bed. Bill Trenton—the fingers on his left hand began to curl inward. Dundeen looked up at his patient, only to see Trenton gazing at him and the needle stuck in his arm.

Dundeen lurched forward and seized the older man by the arm. "You're not to mention this to anyone," he snapped. "Especially not Nina."

Bill Trenton's brow pinched together as he drowsily replied, "Of course not, doctor."

# Chapter 12

Leaving the ECRI, Nina passed through the large glass lobby, then cut past the information desk and headed into Mendota General Hospital. Some twenty feet down the hall, she found the coffee shop, a large room with pale brown walls, a few green plants and a scattering of tables. A group of nurses was off to one side, and here and there lone people sat eating.

Nina had coffee and a bran muffin. Jenny sat in the stroller, at first fussy, then quiet as Nina rolled her back and forth. As Nina sipped her hot drink, she forced her father out of her mind. There was nothing she could do, not just now. Dr. Dundeen had promised he'd do all that he could. There was nothing more Nina could hope for. Clear your mind, she told herself. And hope for the best.

As for Alex . . .

She just wanted some clear, simple answers so she could lay him to rest in her mind. That was good, wasn't it? Didn't that show that the healing process was progressing? Yes, of course. In the last six months all she had wanted was to ignore what had happened, keep herself wrapped in a cloud of disbelief. Now, however, she was emerging, and although she still found Alex's death so improbable, so difficult to accept, it was time for the bare facts.

Her husband, she knew, had been brought here, to

Mendota General Hospital. He was D.O.A., but had they applied CPR or shocked him in an attempt to revive him? Or had they carted him into the emergency room and verified the medics' report? Or had they simply whisked him right on through to the morgue? It chilled Nina just to think of the night—she being wheeled into the delivery room while her husband was rolled into a drawer. Who would have thought . . .

There must have been some sort of examination. A coroner's report even. Right. At least that's the way these things went on television. She'd heard talk about all this, too, in the first day or two after Jenny's birth. She couldn't, however, remember any of the specifics. At the time, she had blocked all that she could, sealed herself in a cocoon of disbelief. She'd just held Jenny as close as she could, loved the baby, nursed her and cried. Somewhere, though, it had to be all recorded. That's what she wanted. The file that held all the answers.

Nina glanced across the broad, mostly empty room and saw the male nurse—the one who'd helped calm her father—sit down with a cup of coffee. Without a second thought, she gulped a last sip from her cup, stood, then pushed Jenny over to him.

"Hello!" called the young black man.

His Caribbean accent was rich and bright, like his infectious smile. Not particularly tall, he was thin, yet had a wide, rather round face and eyes that were eager to see and learn. Nina had seen him any number of times— working with patients, delivering food, handing out meds, helping in emergencies. Even bowling. With his help the patients loved to roll a plastic ball at large, soft pins set up in one of the corridors. Nina suspected that when the duties on the third floor wore down the other nurses, the staff turned to this young man to be cheered.

"Please, would you like a seat? My name is Marcel Dufour."

Nina introduced herself and pulled out a chair, seating herself on the very edge of it. She maneuvered the stroller right by her side.

He said, "You have no need to worry. Your father is fast asleep."

"Good, I'm glad."

She almost blurted it out right away, but she stopped herself, cut herself short. An awkward moment passed in which she felt suddenly hesitant. Now that she was going to ask someone, she felt grotesquely awkward.

"I . . . I have a question," she began.

"Please ask."

"It's not the most pleasant question, but when . . . well . . ." She looked away, then turned back to him. She had to know. Had to find out at least what was done officially. Then she'd know where to begin. "When someone dies and the cause isn't known, is the body examined?"

His eyes grew large and he rubbed his chin, uncertain why she would be asking such a question. Clearly this was something that he did not care to discuss.

"A body? Examined? If the cause is unknown, then yes, of course. Such is the law in your country." He shrugged and took a sip of coffee. "The medical examiner must be notified even when there is a broken bone or a cast."

"And would it be . . ." Nina's words trailed off. "You see, I'm asking in regard to my husband who died a few months ago. He was brought here."

"Ah . . . then this is where the death certificate was signed."

Certificate? She blinked, looked across the room. She'd never seen such a paper.

She turned back to him. "Does that mean he was examined?"

"Well, not necessarily, but I'm sure he was. This is not a big town, you know, and there's only one medical examiner. You see, there are two hospitals, here and St. Mary's, and—"

She interrupted, asking, "But if a death certificate was signed here, is this where he would have been examined?"

"Yes, yes, this is what I'm trying to say. You see, the town's only medical examiner doesn't work at Saint Mary's, but here at Mendota." His brow puckered up, making it clear that he did not like speaking of such matters. "But you shouldn't worry about such past matters." Shaking his head, he added, "It's not good to busy yourself with the dead. You have more important things now. Your baby and your father. No, it's not good to busy yourself with the dead," he said, superstition lingering in the darks of his eyes. "Not good at all."

"Well, I . . . yes, of course, you're right." As she had taken to doing lately when she was unsure of herself, Nina turned to Jenny and stroked her head. She rose. "Thank you. You've been very helpful." She stopped and turned to him again. "Thanks, also, for looking after my father. You do wonderful work up there."

Quickly she made her way out of the cafeteria and into the hall. Instead of turning left toward the main lobby and the exit to the parking lot, she cut right. Passing through another set of doors she entered the heart of Mendota General Hospital. With a new set of directions from a nurse, Nina made her way to the rear of the building, and then down.

Two floors below, Nina paused in front of a double door. She bent down and wrapped a blanket over Jenny, a feeble way of insulating her from what lay ahead. Without a second thought as to why she was doing this, Nina took a deep breath and went in.

"Hello?" she called.

The reception area of the morgue was bright and clean

and empty. A desk filled one corner, while against a wall a few chairs were lined up. Nina called out again, and again received no answer. Determined, Nina pressed on, passing through another set of doors. Still finding no one, she went deeper. And suddenly stopped.

A deep, entirely foreign smell—at once both dirty and antiseptic—washed through her senses and around her body. Directly in front of her lay a long, fat figure completely covered from head to foot with a white sheet. At once she jerked the stroller to the side, wheeling Jenny around and past the body. Then Nina looked up. Directly in front of her stood a large bank of square refrigerator doors, their surfaces bright and shiny as if they belonged in the cleanest of restaurants.

Nina tried to call out but couldn't find her voice. All at once she knew she had to get Jenny out of here. She steered right and the hall opened into a large room filled with six metal tables. On two of the tables lay naked bodies, one with its chest cut and split open, the other, the body of an old woman, with the top of her skull removed and her brains cut out. A man in a green gown was so busy working on the woman that he didn't notice Nina.

Something clenched her arm from behind, and Nina cried, "Ah!"

She spun around to find a short, stern woman staring up at her. Wearing a beige suit, a light blue blouse and thick heels that offered her a critical inch, the woman shook her kindly face.

"My dear, you shouldn't be in here."

"I . . . I . . ."

"Why don't you come with me? You look as if you need to sit down."

The woman, not quite of her father's generation, took her lightly by the elbow and directed her the opposite way. They passed through another door, and soon Nina found herself sitting in a chair, a glass of water in hand. She gazed down at Jenny, who slept in the stroller. Thank God those little eyes were shut, thought Nina.

"I'm Dr. Volker, director of this part of the hospital." She leaned back against her desk. "Are you all right?"

Nina nodded. It was just the smells, the sights. Stroking her baby's hair with one hand, with the other she took a sip of water.

"So what is it that brings a mother like you down here?" she asked, her face softened with wrinkles. "Are you lost? Is there something I can do for you?"

"Actually, yes." Nina took a deep breath. She had to force the words out. "I wanted to get some information. I was told the medical examiner's office was down here."

"That's right. That's just where you are." The woman's smile was as perfect as the reddish hair piled on her head. "You see, I'm also the medical examiner for the county. How may I help you?"

"It's . . ." Nina looked away, then back. "It's about my husband."

Finding her strength, Nina cleared her throat and recounted her husband's death and what little she knew about it. She wanted to know precisely, she said, what had happened, what could kill a man so physically and mentally fit. She wanted to know if his body was examined and what was found.

"Well, from what you've just told me of his death, I can say that his body was most definitely examined," said Dr. Volker. "Weren't you informed either by us or the attending physician? Didn't anyone tell you the results?"

"I . . . I don't know. It was a very trying time, you see. I . . ." She leaned over and rubbed Jenny on the back. "I had my baby that same night. The shock and all brought on delivery." Nina added, "Plus I had hurt my arm and ankle."

The doctor's eyebrows rose. "My word, how terrible. I'm sorry."

"I might have been told, but I really don't remember. There was so much commotion."

"Well, then, it's good you came here. You should know these things. That's part of my job. When you have all the facts, you understand. When you understand, you can lay people to rest." She smiled and stood. "So tell me his name. I'll dig out his file."

"Alex Hale."

She raised one finger, telling Nina to wait right there, and then picked up her glasses from the corner of her desk. Bustling out of the room, Dr. Volker's thick heels clopped as she went into another room. Then Nina heard the rolling of file drawers, the fussing of paper and finally more steps. Her feet moving slower, Dr. Volker reappeared, glasses on her nose, open file in hand.

"Here it is."

Reading as she walked, the doctor proceeded to her desk and sat down. She read a page, nodded, licked a finger and turned to the next page.

"Sure. I remember."

"You do?"

"Of course. I was the one who performed the autopsy, and it wasn't that long ago." She looked up. "Your husband—he was a handsome man. Dark hair, nice face."

Nina's heart thumped. "Yes."

Did she also know, wondered Nina, about the scar on his groin and that stupid toenail that would never grow back? Christ, this doctor had seen parts of Alex that Nina had never dreamed—nor had any desire—of seeing. At the thought of this person cutting open her husband, of her reaching literally inside of him, Nina wanted to run away as fast and as far as possible.

"Ah, yes," continued the doctor. "He was the jogger." She paused and put down the file. "This is not that large a town and we are not that big a facility. I have only one assistant. And, as I said, I was the one who performed the autopsy."

"So . . . so what did you find?"

Dr. Volker took another glance at the file, then, her voice and look touched with sympathy, said, "I remember noting how young he was, and, in fact, that saddened me. I figured such a handsome man as he had such a beautiful wife as you. Even children, though I didn't know how very young."

"Yes, but . . ."

"I wish I could tell you something that would ease your pain." She looked at the chart once again. "But your husband died of a myocardial infarction—a heart attack. Technically he died of an arrythmia, which is often associated with MIs. This means his heart didn't receive the proper electrical message, so it just stopped. Fifty percent of such cases never make it to the hospital."

"But . . . but isn't there anything more? I mean, why did it happen? What went wrong?"

"That I do not know. Some part of his body just malfunctioned or wore out. It doesn't happen often in relatively young people, but we see it." Dr. Volker shrugged. "Sometimes it's a jogger or a football player. Sometimes it's someone who simply pushes himself too far. Last year I had a thirty-one-year-old man who shoveled his driveway and then dropped dead in the road."

"Oh."

So that was it? Nothing more? Nina's eyes searched the patterns of the linoleum floor. Why was it that she felt such a loss of hope? What had she wanted to discover, anyway?

"I see." Nina pushed herself forward, readied herself to stand. "I don't know why I'm so disappointed."

"I have a half dozen or so people that come down here

each year, all searching to understand death. They want to know what happened, how it happened. Did their mother or their father or their spouse suffer any. Was the autopsy quick and simple or . . . In the case of your Alex, I can assure you that he died quickly and rather painlessly." Another soft smile spread across her face. "It's good that you came, it's good not to let questions fester."

"Now I know." Why don't I feel convinced? she thought.

"Exactly. It will help tremendously in coming to accept it. Is there anything else I can do for you?"

Nina pushed herself up, then reached for the handles of the stroller and hung on.

"No. I don't think so." Nina took a deep breath. "Thank you, Dr. Volker. You've been most kind."

"If I've eased some of your pain, then I'm glad I could help."

Nina made her way out of Dr. Volker's office, through the reception area and back upstairs. She emerged from the windowless lower floors of the hospital into a bright, perfectly clear summer day.

She gazed into the blue sky, felt the warmth of the sun embrace her and hated it all. That hadn't been at all what she wanted to hear. No. She wanted to turn around, run back downstairs and hear an entirely different story. Her dream. That's what Nina wanted. Her dream, the one that visited her almost every night. The one in which Alex was alive.

Dr. Volker folded the file shut and stood. She had heard the outer door close, but stepped into the reception area just to be certain. Nina Trenton had indeed left. Dr. Volker took a deep breath and sighed. Hopefully she had answered all of the young woman's questions. Hopefully she had gone into enough depth to soothe the widow's doubts and confusion. It was a terrible thing that had happened to her, terribly unfortunate that her husband had trespassed where he shouldn't have.

Dr. Volker turned and was startled by the figure of the black man in the door from the laboratory.

"Is she gone?" asked Marcel Dufour, his smile noticeably absent from his face.

Dr. Volker glanced over her shoulder to check yet again, then bustled forward and pushed Marcel into the back hall.

Her voice low, the doctor said, "Yes."

"How did it go?" asked the male nurse.

"Fine. If I do say so myself, I was perfect. You're a life saver, though, Marcel. I couldn't have acted at all naturally if I hadn't known she was coming."

"Then I am very happy."

"Yes," said the short woman. "I don't think she suspects a thing. And I think I settled her last doubts. She shouldn't be back to bother us."

"Good."

"That was a minor scare." More than she ever wanted, actually. "And if she comes back again—if she comes any closer—then I'm afraid we'll have to dispose of her, too."

"Absolutely," agreed Marcel.

But it was all right for now, thought Volker. Now at least they knew to keep tabs on her.

She looked up into his dark eyes. "And what about the solution—is it ready?"

"I'll finish it tonight. Don't worry, your Mr. Morton will have this batch in the morning."

"Good. Everything else is progressing as well as can be expected. Now hurry back to the Institute," she said, her small figure shooing him along, "before you're missed."

"No problem, dear doctor," laughed Marcel, his voice big and rich. "None of the patients are able to remember my name, let alone wonder where I've gone."

# Chapter 13

From the back of the former mansion's dining room, Morton stood patiently while a young widow dressed in black gazed a final time at her husband's body. A few short sobs rose from her mouth and she could be heard muttering something. Probably, Morton thought, an apology. Or perhaps an affirmation of love. The mourners were always like that. As full of words as they were of emotion. That, Morton believed, was the only tragic thing about death—people never said what really mattered until it was too late. I love you. I'm sorry. Why didn't we?

As Mrs. Sullivan, her hair stiff with spray, her face puffy from crying, bent over the coffin and pressed her cheek to her husband's, Morton flinched. Close moments like these drove him crazy. What if she sensed something?

Biting a fingernail, Morton stepped back into the next room. Mikey, clutching a miniature black and white television in his lap, was curled up in a big armchair. Earphones clasped over his head, he was intensely watching a cartoon. Then Morton glanced back at the widow, who still hovered only inches over her husband. He couldn't bear it.

He shouted: "Mikey, how many times do I have to tell you not to do that? Stop that right now!"

Mikey didn't even hear him, didn't even notice. But Mrs. Sullivan lifted her round face from the dead man's cheek and glanced back.

"Oh . . . Mrs. Sullivan, I'm sorry," mumbled Morton. "I . . . I didn't mean to disturb you."

She nodded, rose and wiped the tears from her eyes. Then with a deep breath she instantly regained her midwestern dignity, a martyr-like stoicism passed from generation to generation, from crop-shriveling drought to endless winter.

Passing to the rear of the room, a hankie to her nose, she said, "He was a good man and he worked hard. He was real proud of his business, and so am I. But he was much too young to go. Dear Lord, he was only forty-six."

"Yes, I know," responded Morton.

Morton knew practically everything else, too, from the moment Anthony R. Sullivan, a tad inebriated, swerved too far on the curve and collided with an oak. When it had happened three months ago it seemed a miracle that he hadn't been killed instantaneously; a week later it was a tragedy. Supported after that by an array of machines, his body functioned normally. His mind, however, registered barely any activity. When he was finally unhooked from the life-support systems just a week ago, it seemed he could go on living, a curled fetus, indefinitely. But then, thought Morton, they had changed things. Marcel had snuck in and injected him with that potion of his, and Irene Volker had seen to the rest. Mrs. Sullivan, unaware of course of their activities, had thought it all natural and nothing but a blessing from God Himself.

"I . . . I suppose this is better. The doctor said if he ever came out he'd never . . . never . . ." Unable to mutter the possibilities, her voice trailed away. "Oh, you don't know how unbearable the past few months have been."

"Well, it's all over now. I'm sure your husband's quite at peace," said Morton.

"Yes, let's hope. He was such a good man."

All the other visitors had already come and gone, and Morton followed Mrs. Sullivan to the entry hall. A half step behind her, he waited as she stood in the shadows of the gold brocade curtains and wiped her eyes.

"Is there anything else I need to take care of now?" she asked, carefully pulling a black lace veil over her face.

"Don't worry about a thing." Morton graciously bowed his head. "You have a very conscientious son and he's taken care of everything."

"Tom's a good boy. Young but so responsible. He's going to take over the dry cleaners, you know. Move back to town and everything. I don't know what I'd have done without him." She paused at the heavy front door. "The service . . . will the . . . the . . ."

"Yes, the ashes will be at the cemetery tomorrow afternoon. As I said, there's no need to worry. We'll see to everything."

"Th-thank you. You've been so kind."

Morton pulled open the door, and the bright August sun sliced into the funeral home. Like a mole scurrying to escape the sunniest of days, Mrs. Sullivan hurried down the front steps and into the car, where her son and youngest daughter were waiting. As young Tom drove his bereaved mother up Ridgewood Avenue, Morton watched in silence, then shut and locked the door.

To appease himself, the old man returned to the former dining room. He stared at the body of Mr. Sullivan lying there in the silky folds of the coffin, and was pleased by its still, sallow appearance. No, his wife couldn't have noticed a thing. With a deep breath, Morton realized how relieved he was that this one was almost finished. Tomorrow the body would be delivered, the remuneration received.

Morton returned to the main room, where Mikey, clutching the headphones over his ears, was still captured by the cartoons on the mini-TV. Suddenly his son started laughing, his voice rising loud and uninhibited in the stone-quiet mortuary.

Leaning in front of his son, Morton smiled, and said, "Mikey, would you like to help me?"

Obviously unable to hear, Mikey glanced at him, frowned, then stared back at the television cradled between his knees.

Morton leaned over and lifted one of the earphones. "There's some work to do. Will you—"

"Don't!"

Suddenly, Mikey swung out, batting Morton's arm. Totally shocked, the older man jerked back his hand. In doing so, Morton's thumb caught one of the long, looping wires, and the earphones came ripping off Mikey's head.

"Ow!" screamed the son.

"Oh, Mikey, I—"

"Ow!" he shouted, punching out again at his father.

As a heavy fist grazed Morton's side, he shouted, "Mikey!"

Lord, thought Morton, the scene flashing by before him, what was this, what was happening? This wasn't like his boy. Mikey was so sweet, so gentle. Always a smile. As he stared into his son's red and angry face, however, Morton feared the worst, feared the implications of what he was seeing. He'd been warned to expect such outbursts, he'd been told that as Mikey deteriorated the otherwise docile young man would be gripped by such fits.

His voice shaking, Morton said, "It's ... it's okay, Mikey. Just calm down." Morton sensed his own heart throbbing, dashing. "You like to help me, don't you, Mikey? Of course you do. Now come on, let's go downstairs and you can—"

"No!" he screamed, springing up from the chair. He raised the tiny television high overhead. "No, no, no!"

Morton ducked as Mikey hurled the little portable at the floor. With an enormous crash, it smashed against the hardwood boards, sending plastic and glass exploding. Dials and wires and shards of glass went zinging in every direction, flew and slid all the way into the next room.

Trembling, Morton glared at Mikey, who stood totally shocked. Oh, God, thought Morton, the noise still ringing in his ears. What does this mean?

"Oh, Mikey," moaned Morton.

Tears sprang immediately from Mikey's eyes and he whirled around and collapsed in the chair. His body shook with huge, gasping sobs.

"My TV!" he wailed. "My TV!"

Feet crunching over bits of plastic, Morton rushed to his son's side and lowered himself onto one knee. Nearly as frightened as his son, he stroked Mikey's straight brown hair.

"It's okay, Mikey. It's okay. We can go out tonight and get you another TV—a nicer one, maybe even color. You'd like that wouldn't you?" He patted him on the back. "Shh. Shh. It's okay," said John Morton, praying that help for his son wasn't too far off.

# Chapter

# 14

It was past eight-thirty and dark by the time Nina put Jenny down for the night. She had nursed her and rocked her and clung to her as the very last of the day had fallen away. Then she had carefully risen from the rocker in Jenny's room, separated the little body from her own and as gently as possible laid the sleeping bundle in the crib.

For some fifteen minutes Nina stood staring at the child, whose tiny rib cage puffed up and down with every breath. So uncomplicated. Nina wanted those days back, wanted those times when two years or five or ten seemed quantum leaps ahead, not just around the corner. Yes, she wanted to be at the bottom of the generational heap, not at the top. She wanted to have several generations ahead of her, there to care and nourish her, there to be an endless supply of love and support. Yet here she was at the top and in charge and alone. Jenny was just starting off and Nina's total responsibility. Her father had gone full cycle, from dependence to full independence to dependence again. Did that mean that in thirty or forty years—perhaps less—Jenny would be in Nina's present position? Would this infant before her have total responsibility for Nina's life sometime in the future?

A deep shiver shook her body, and Nina was roused from her trance-like fixation on the baby. She kissed Jenny on the head and turned on the intercom that sat next to the crib. She then took the receiver, a white plastic device that looked like a walkie-talkie, complete with rubberized antenna. In the upstairs hall, Nina flicked on the switch and the small speaker crackled with static. Turning up the volume, Nina could hear Jenny's clear breathing.

The reception was perfect in the kitchen as Nina poured herself a rare treat, a glass of mineral water with a bit of white wine. It was perfect as well in the den, where Nina sat at the small desk and reached for the phone. Just why she dialed the number of Louise, her close friend in Chicago, Nina didn't know. Just what she was reaching for was beyond her. But when Louise's answering machine picked up instead of Louise herself, Nina didn't know what to say and hung up.

Seated there, she spotted the red leather photo album propped up in the corner of the desk. She hadn't done any work on it since Jenny was born, and she was by no means going to start tonight. Not yet. She still couldn't look at photos of Alex.

Restless, Nina made her way to the front porch and stood in the dark night sipping her spritzer. She raised the receiver to her ear and heard nothing but peaceful sounds from Jenny. This gadget, she thought, was one of the more useful baby items she'd bought.

Impulsively, Nina locked the front door, left her wineglass on the porch railing and walked down the steps. On the sidewalk, she paused. The baby's breathing was as clear as if Nina were in the room itself. Nina glanced at Mrs. Larson's house—the older woman would be horrified, Nina was sure, to see Nina leaving the baby alone in the house—and then started walking. Suddenly a sheepish grin sneaked across her face. The length of the tether had just been dramatically increased and to her own surprise it felt wonderful.

She continued up Leaf Street almost to the corner of

Ridgewood, and the entire time she could perfectly hear Jenny's gentle sounds. She paused at the corner house, a yellow wood-framed structure, and gazed back at her own home. A faint nightlight glowed up on the second floor, up there in Jenny's bedroom above the kitchen.

Perhaps Dr. Dundeen was right. It was time to wean the baby, to start getting out, and . . .

Her eyes fell on the yellow brick structure across the street. So beautiful, so graceful there in the night with its stately white columns in front, its low majestic roof. What a fabulous house it had once been. What a terrible place it was now. The funeral home. Alex. He had been taken there while she and Jenny were still in the hospital. Taken there and pumped with some chemical that would keep his body as human-like as possible for as long as possible. She clenched her eyes shut. Alex abhorred the idea of being embalmed. When they'd first moved onto Leaf Street he had looked out at the funeral home and ranted on and on how he just wanted to be buried in a simple wooden box, no chemicals preserving his body. Cemeteries, Alex swore, were the largest chemical waste dumps in the country—all those bodies, all those cracks, all that formaldehyde leaking into the ground water. If only Nina had been more aware of what was happening in those days after he died. But she hadn't been, and Alex, not buried soon enough, was by law embalmed.

Staring at the large dark building, she now understood why Alex had never wanted to live across from such a place. Yes, it was quiet. Yes, Mr. Morton and his son Mikey were polite and helpful. It was, though, such a constant reminder. Death was never far away, and in this case it was right across the street. What had ever happened, she wondered, to the sale to the sorority? What had ever happened to the now-attractive idea of a parking lot full of kids and cars? Defeated. Yes, that was right. A neighbor down the street had vehemently opposed the sorority, lobbied the town council and the rezoning had been denied. Why in the hell had Alex and she ever opposed the idea of that big house full of lively students?

Alex. She cut across Leaf Street toward the funeral home. The warm, moist summer air faded away, as did the throbbing of the trees. Returning was the gray chill of that late winter night. The naked trees had been spindly and black, the ground gray and slick with ice. As he finished his run he must have come this way, up from the park on Ridgewood Avenue, then right on Leaf. When had his heart started to trouble him? Down below by the creek? Or up here? Had the attack been quick and ruthless? Or slow and painful? Had his been a terrified run home for help and comfort or had life simply ended without a moment's warning? She gazed up Leaf Street, saw that body sprawled all out again and . . .

Wait. Had he come running up Ridgewood and taken a right on Leaf Street he would have cut at an angle from his corner and across the street to their house. That was the most direct route, emergency or not. Who, wondered Nina, would jog or even walk up this side of Leaf until he was directly opposite the red Victorian, and then cross the street? It wasn't a matter of traffic. The road was a dead end and there weren't more than a dozen cars on it in an entire day.

No. Alex probably wouldn't have come this way. The image of him on the icy ground directly across the street from their house would be forever frozen in her mind. That meant he had to have come from some other direction.

She held the receiver to her ear and satisfied herself that Jenny was fine. Without a bit of hesitation, she continued down the hill and past the front of the funeral home. Alex always ran down to the park, along the creek, then back up to the house. Three miles. He had it figured as only a lawyer could. He even said he was going down there that night. So he'd headed down to the park, perhaps sensed trouble and turned back. Yes, that would make sense. He wasn't gone long enough to make the complete roundtrip. Then, either walking or running, he'd trudged his way up this hill. Yes, that and the cold could have intensified the attack.

Up Ridgewood, but then where? Nina turned back. She was just past the funeral home, and the most direct route from here to her house was not up the sidewalk and right on Leaf. No. It was a detour off the walk and up the small hill, then a path around the funeral home.

Yes, perhaps. With a rush of excitement, Nina trod up the slope. If Alex had come this way he probably would have been able to find enough traction in the crusty snow. Then maybe, just maybe, he'd hurried right through here, right along the side of the funeral home. He'd have passed alongside the funeral home itself and past the side door. Mr. Morton could have first heard him that way and . . .

Her mind raced forward and she wasn't able to keep pace with it. As she passed alongside the funeral home, she tripped on a rock and landed on her knees. The receiver tumbled out of her hand, spinning in the air and landed on the dirt some six or seven feet in front her, just past the building's massive chimney. Stunned, she sat back, brushed off her hands.

The side-door light burst on. Nina froze in the shadows. Had Morton heard her, just as he must have heard Alex? What would he think now? That she was a burglar? Although she was still, the rhythm of her body raced on as the door opened. Metal grated against metal as the spring on the screen door was pulled taut. Finally she saw shiny brown hair and a heavy-set figure. One step at a time, Mikey emerged. As carefully as he could, he eased shut the noisy door behind him and froze like a thief. He looked back through the door's window, then turned into the night. So, thought Nina, he wasn't supposed to be out here, either. He, too, was a stalker.

Suddenly the receiver crackled with static. Mikey froze and scanned the dark. Lying on the ground, seemingly miles from Nina, the receiver popped again. The air pushed in and out of her chest in panic. On her knees, there was nothing she could do without Mikey seeing her for certain. Her fearful eyes staring at him, she watched as he rotated in her direction, searching the bushes and the night.

Out of nowhere a man's long arm emerged from the other side of the chimney. In shock, Nina watched as the hand extended out and into the faint light, felt the ground, then picked up something and hurled it. A moment later a pebble landed in the bushes on the other side of Mikey. As if he sensed danger, the young man hugged the house and stared in that direction. Mean· while, the hand reached further, giving way to a shoulder and the outline of a man's head. Grasping the receiver the unknown person flicked off the switch, then picked up another stone and hurled it.

Mikey gasped. He stared into the woods, perhaps conjuring up some terrible creature that was about to jump out. With a little cry, he leapt for the door, yanked it open and flew inside. In the same instant, a dead bolt clicked and the light was cut off.

One threat was now replaced with another, and Nina wasn't sure which was worse. When she saw the full shape emerge, she decided. Mikey could not compare to this large man with the broad shoulders, long arms and dark hair.

He stepped toward her and she backed away.

"I don't think anyone heard us," he whispered, as if he were her conspirator.

Was that bad? She looked past him toward the side door, wishing only that Mikey would come back out. There was, however, nothing but dark silence.

"Who are you?" she asked.

"Shh."

Nina started stepping backward. "What are you doing here?" And why did he want her to be quiet? Louder this time, she said, "Who are you?"

"Quiet!" he hushed and took a step toward her. "I know you don't want Morton to hear us, either."

She hadn't wanted him to before, but now she'd welcome the old man. Nina glanced behind her, saw the front yard of the funeral home, the gentle slope down to the sidewalk. She could make a run for the streetlight, but this tall man with the long legs would be upon her within seconds.

"I live right there," he said, still in a whisper. With his empty hand he motioned back through the bushes. "I just moved into the garage apartment."

Her neighbor? Could she believe him? No, her Chicago instincts told her not to.

"Listen, just give me the receiver."

He looked at it, handed it to her. "We need to talk. Let's get out of here."

She took the device and started for the street. This was not the time nor the place.

"No, I have to get home." Don't, she told herself, let him know you're alone. "A couple of friends are waiting for me. In fact, they're right—"

"Wait." Raising his voice, he insisted. "You don't understand."

"Tomorrow." Nina was half trotting now. "We can talk tomorrow." She'd deal with this creep then.

He jogged up and caught her by the arm.

"Let me go!" she said, twisting herself free.

"You don't understand." The stranger glanced back at

the funeral home. Desperate, he blurted, "Listen, I just want you to know that I have a lot of questions regarding your husband's death."

His words took away her breath. Alex? His death? What could this guy possibly know about that? She shook her head, looked at him, looked at the big white pillars of the funeral home. Her finger hit the switch of the receiver, and over it came not Jenny's gentle breathing, but a tight cry.

"What?" said Nina, ignoring the baby and staring at the dark figure. "What are you talking about?"

# 15

This part was good, thought Marcel Dufour, turning up the volume of his boom box. It was great when the drums beat like a trio of fast hearts, the smallest and the highest pitched of them racing along, joined at intervals by the second. The third drum, the deepest, roared in and out, in and out, like thunderous waves pounding the shore. Showering over all this was a stream of rattles. And then came a brief pause, and a chorus cooed, "Hoo-ah, hoo-ah." Tiny bells next began to flicker, flicker like drops raining over all, until there was an entire storm of them. Suddenly a woman cried, "Make the magic!"

*Très bon*, thought Marcel, swaying in the basement of his rented house. Come *loa*. Make the magic. Make it strong and powerful. His body rocked, undulated erotically and his arms reached and pulled. The music flowed into his ears and filled every corner, overtook every thought. The singers' chants became his chants, their power his power and the pulse of the drums became his pulse, driving, forcing, pushing all.

*Oui, oui*, groaned Marcel. But louder. Louder still, because he liked this next part when the chorus stomped its feet and begged for the work to be blessed. Cranked up in volume, the music of his land poured into him, through his senses and out his limbs. Across the dirt floor of his basement he danced, his body swaying. He looped around, bent over like a goose and peered down. Beneath him, drawn with cornmeal in the dirt, was a cross with stars and circles. Marcel leapt to the side and now peered down at snakes and three-headed figures, also etched in yellow meal.

The chorus on the tape cried out, and as loud as he could, Marcel hollered, "Make the music! Make the music!"

Seconds later a voice shouted. What, he thought, is this? That's not on the tape. He glanced about, rocked his shoulders, touched himself. No, he was not about to be possessed, ridden by one of the gods. This . . . this . . .

"Marcel!" hollered a woman's voice.

He turned. There at the top of the white wooden stairs were the espresso-black feet of his wife, Aline. He could see the bottom of her aqua dress as well, but nothing more.

"Oh!" said Marcel, hitting the stop button on the tape machine. The silence that greeted him was frightening in its emptiness. His eyes blinked. "What is it?"

"I'm on the phone," she said, without bending into sight.

"So?"

"You were shouting out."

"I was? Oh, *excusez-moi, excusez-moi.* I'll turn it down—I'm about to start work anyway."

As Aline disappeared, he started the tape again, the drums and rattles softer now. Still, the rhythm and sounds filled him with such memories, such a sense of faith, that he knew he couldn't help but shout out sometimes. Back home in a hill of slums, his father had been a great *houngan,* a vodoun priest, and half of Marcel's youth had been spent in such spirit-cleansing ceremonies. Behind their house had been a *hounfor,* a temple, a round structure built of wood and topped with a thatched roof. Night after night it had been filled with worshipers—people chanting, dancing, praying, being ridden by the *loa*, the gods. He missed it. It was there, too, that his father had taught him how to make the powerful drug that the *blancs* wanted. All that, while here there were only endless cornfields, dull rivers, and black and white cows. This was such a spiritual wasteland, a flat prairie void of faith and power.

The basement Marcel danced in was old and rough, the foundation of a farmhouse built nearly a hundred years earlier. With a dirt floor and walls of rough field stone, it had been intended for little more than a cool place to store carrots and potatoes. But it served Marcel well now. While behind a curtain was his lab, on this side rose an altar, a riotous display of candles, herbs, colorful crosses, human skulls, dried fish, and a doll head and wedding veil. Yes, thought Marcel, all of him was down here. His history, his faith, his modern science.

Stepping over to the altar, Marcel bowed in front of a cross made of rooster feathers, then lit a fat candle and stuck it in the middle of a skull. It was time to begin work.

Marcel had begun this batch of poison for the *blancs* three days earlier, and he would complete it tonight, heating the last of the ingredients, then grinding them all together and adding the liquid. It was a lengthy and delicate process, one that had to be done just right. His father had taught him well, though, and Marcel had further refined the steps, combining his father's knowledge with his own as a chemist. That the ingredients came primarily from the hills outside of Port-au-Prince and from the waters around his country would also assure the poison's potency.

Marcel stepped to the rear of the farmhouse basement and pushed aside a heavy curtain. He pulled an overhead string, and a fluorescent light was brought to fluttering life. From a hook he lifted a white robe and white hat, both of which he put on. Then he took a mask and pulled it snugly over his face. He completed his dress by putting on a pair of safety glasses and a pair of tight rubber gloves. He would be working with the key ingredient and it was the most toxic.

Marcel sat at his work table, a long, clean surface with bottles and a series of clay pots at one end, a digital scale, test tubes and other measuring devices at the other. In the middle stood a gas burner and a mortar and pestle, all of which he would use again tonight.

Marcel's father had always made the poison in the summer when the heat was its strongest. His father would begin by throwing a handful of explosive powder into a flame, then, with a live rooster as a sponge, bathing himself with protective oils and herbs. A potion was next concocted, mixing the gratings of a skull with cornmeal, sugar, rum and herbs. Once his father had drunk this there would be a great cry for the magical forces of *Simbi*, the patron of powders.

Always the poison had been made in powder form, including in it an irritant that broke the skin and allowed the substance to be slowly absorbed into the body. Marcel, however, was a modern man. After many months of experimentation, he had adapted the old ways to new scientific methods. You had to be very precise, though, when making the poison in the liquid form demanded by the *blancs*. You couldn't just throw in a handful of this, a bit of that. Oh, no. When concocting the liquid version everything had to be heated just right, measured to the gram and mixed thoroughly. If the proportions were just slightly off and it was injected directly into the bloodstream, it would kill within seconds.

First things first, he thought. He crossed to a side table, where a clay pot sat some eight inches beneath a sun lamp. Marcel checked a thermometer leaning against the pot. Perfect, he thought. This was a warm spot, just as if this little container were baking in the strong sunlight of his homeland. Inside, ground together in a powder form, were three items, all valued for their pharmacological compounds. First was the skin of a white frog, which caused cyanosis and paresthesia. Second were the venom glands of a snake found in the hills beyond Marcel's home; the toxin contained bufogenin and bufotoxin. And from the swamps of his slave-ancestors came the salt toad, the skin of which held compounds that inflicted paralysis and pulmonary edema.

Marcel knew well that the final item, the puffer fish, was the secret to the poison of his homeland. While the puffer seemed a simple, even quaint creature whose only means of protection was swallowing water until it was ball shaped, the tissues of its body contained tetrodotoxin. A neurotoxin hundreds of times stronger than cyanide, tetrodotoxin was, Marcel had learned, one of nature's strongest poisons. But in order to work in his recipe it had to be handled just right, especially since his would be a liquid solution and not a powder. The *blancs*, of course, only wanted to go to the very edge. To go beyond would defeat their purpose.

Marcel lit the gas burner. Using a pair of tongs, he reached around in the largest of the clay pots until he found an organ and a chunky piece of skin. Careful to stand away from the smoke, he held the pieces of puffer fish over the flame, slowly charring them. This would be a good batch. One of his couriers had just brought this particular fish, and the ones from the summer waters, when they were breeding and passion was high—thereby creating higher concentrations of hormones—were always the best.

For thirty minutes Marcel held the bits of fish over the gas flame. Finally satisfied, he dropped them into the mortar and ground them while still hot. When the fish was a fine powder, he placed a small bit of it in a glass container, then set that on the scale. He added a little more of the ground puffer until the digital numbers froze at the exact amount.

Marcel took a deep sigh and sat for a moment. Dealing with the puffer fish always made him nervous, and his spine was a rigid pole. Eager to finish, however, he quickly rose, took the pot from beneath the sun lamp and from this container scooped a fraction of a gram. Adding this to the ground puffer fish, he then dumped all of it into an old mayonnaise jar that Aline had given him.

From yet another clay pot, Marcel carefully ladled a dark liquid extracted from a combination of bark, roots and leaves; boiled down to a concentrated syrup, it was used in the South Americas as an arrow poison. He added this to the jar, and the powders fizzed as the liquid engulfed and swallowed them up. Quickly Marcel screwed on the lid as tight as he could and swirled it around. The powders dissolved completely, leaving a nice dark brown liquid, clear and free of floating matter.

Marcel first removed his gloves and threw them away. He would take them outside later and carefully burn them. Then he pulled off his face mask. He took a deep breath, exhaled. This was good stuff he had made tonight, he thought with a big grin. Real good stuff. Perhaps he should ask for more. After all, the courier had brought such a nice fresh puffer fish.

He shrugged and removed his robe. Tomorrow. He'd deal with that tomorrow.

Stretching as he moved, Marcel stepped into the other room, pulling the curtain behind him. He popped another tape into the boom box and took a deep breath and tried to clear his head. The completion of his work called for different music—slower drums, delicate chimes, more-pleading voices. Yes, it was time to call out for *Guede*, the spirit of the dead, and beg his forgiveness.

# Chapter 16

In the front yard of her house, the man who identified himself as Bruce Fitzgerald told Nina that he worked for the local paper, the Mendota *Gazette*. He was a reporter, he swore, and she brusquely told him to wait right there. Then she came in and, the tension seizing her gut, she tore through the morning's paper. Who, she worried, is this guy? Some weirdo or—?

And then she saw it. There, his by-line above an article about the school board choosing a new director.

At the top of the porch, she pointed at the wrinkled paper and demanded, "Is this your piece about pollution?"

He stared up at her, the crow's feet around his eyes tightening in mild amusement. "No . . . I wrote about the school board."

Hesitating, she finally said, "Right."

She made him wait in the living room while she went upstairs and quieted Jenny. Then Nina, her mind racing, came down, baby in arm, and proceeded directly to the phone in the den. Just one precaution, she thought, albeit a weak one.

Her back to the living room, Nina picked up the phone and dialed the time and temperature number.

"Hi, Louise, it's Nina," she said into the recording. "Listen, Bruce Fitzgerald from the paper stopped by." She glanced over her shoulder to make sure he could hear her. "Could you and Tom wait a bit before coming over? Oh, great, thanks. About a half hour? Good. See you."

Not quite feeling so vulnerable, she entered the living room and studied him as he sat on her couch. A long face, moustache, dark brown hair with a bit of gray at the temples. Simply dressed in jeans and a blue short-sleeved shirt. About her age. Not, she had to admit, creepy in his appearance.

"What," Nina began, Jenny balanced on her hip, "were you doing sneaking around the funeral home?"

He blinked and looked at her directly. "Looking through the basement window and counting coffins. And you?"

"Looking for fossils," she tersely replied.

"I'm serious. That's what I was doing. I've been observing Morton for some time now and I . . ." He stopped, shook his head. "Listen, I'm not some sort of jerk."

She stared at him, not quite believing she'd let him in.

"I used to be a C.P.A. in Chicago," he continued, "but I did a little career switch—or rather a major one—and about eight months ago I was hired as a reporter for the *Gazette* and—"

"What in the hell do you know about my husband?"

He studied her, his hands, then cleared his throat. "I have to say that I'm sorry to meet you like this. It wasn't how I expected to. I wanted to contact you in a week or so—there were a just a few more things I wanted to check out first. Really, I was—"

"Tell me what you know," she demanded.

"Hale, Alex, age 43, of cardiac arrest." He paused briefly, staring at her with those simple brown eyes. "Survived by wife Nina Trenton, daughter Jenny Elizabeth, and parents Pete and Carol Hale of California."

Nina held her breath, tried not to let her shock show. He hadn't said anything of importance—it was just so horribly odd to hear a complete stranger talk about her life in such simple, factual terms. Partly cloudy and warm today, he could have said.

"So?" said Nina, sucking in her emotions.

"I know that from the newspaper because . . . because I wrote it." Bruce shrugged and rubbed his brow. "The *Gazette* isn't that big of a paper. We all do a lot. You know, double duty. Even the editors. I cover news, high school sports, weddings. And I write the obituaries."

"Go on."

As he talked Nina stepped into the den. Cradling Jenny in one arm, Nina opened the red photo album. In the back, carefully pressed between the plastic pages, she found the obituary, four paragraphs long and with a photo, the headline reading, "Alex Hale, Lawyer from Chicago." Bruce Fitzgerald's by-line was there, too, right above the text.

"Well," continued Bruce, "your husband's death caught my attention because he was about my age and also from Chicago. So I decided to do a longer piece on him. I even sent a messenger over to get a photo."

Yes, that made sense. Alex's parents were staying at the house then. Didn't she remember Pete Hale mentioning that he'd given his son's picture to someone at the paper?

Nina laid the obituary back in the album and returned to the edge of the living room, saying, "But I don't get what any of this is leading up to. What's your point?"

He eagerly sat forward. "You see . . . you see, I've been doing the obits ever since I came to town. And I've noticed something."

Oh, Christ, she thought. Fact or fiction?

"Every person," began Bruce Fitzgerald, "younger than sixty-five who died of heart failure at Mendota General Hospital and who was to be cremated was sent right across the street to our Mr. Morton. If the person was older than sixty-five or wasn't to have been cremated, they were most likely sent elsewhere. Likewise, if they died of other causes most did not come to Ridgewood Mortuary."

Who, Nina thought, was he? Some unstable guy playing investigative reporter or someone who had some legitimate insights into Alex's death?

She said, "I'm not quite sure I understand what you're leading up to. I really don't see what this has to do with my husband's death. Listen, I—"

"Believe me, there's something going on, whether it's a case of malpractice at the hospital or some kickback scheme or . . . or just what I don't know. But something's wrong." He turned and nodded out the window. "That's why I rented the garage apartment over there. To keep a better eye on Morton. He's the one person linked to all the deaths. You see, patterns like that just don't happen. I know that from accounting. If something odd turns up regularly then someone's been messing with the books."

But who and why? All along she'd wanted desperately to discover some reason or some concrete cause for Alex's death. Now her mind searched every angle for a way to apply what Bruce Fitzgerald was saying to her situation. But she couldn't.

She turned back into the den, shut the window and laid Jenny down in the portable crib. Once the child was settled and covered, Nina made her way through the arch and into the living room. Standing there next to the fireplace, she didn't know what to say.

Bruce pressed on. "I know this all sounds kind of crazy and it has to be difficult for you to hear."

Absolutely, she thought. "I'm sorry, but this just doesn't sound like any of my concern."

In defense, the words and statistics came blasting out of him. "A man, forty-six is in an auto accident. He is in a coma for months and finally the family issues the orders: Do not resuscitate. A few days later the man dies of heart failure, his body is brought to Morton and he is cremated. A boy, sixteen, runs into a tree on his motorcycle. He is in a coma for two months. The orders: Do not resuscitate. Finally he dies not of malnutrition or brain damage but of heart failure. He is brought to Morton and his body is cremated. A woman, fifty-two, is in for a tricky liver operation. She lives through the operation but is expected to die within a few days. That night, however, she dies not of complications from the operation, but from heart failure. Her body is brought to Morton and is later cremated."

"Please, I really don't . . ."

Sitting on the very edge of the couch now, Bruce said, "What I'm suggesting is that there's something going on here that isn't immediately apparent. Either a doctor is guilty of malpractice or Morton is paying someone off at the hospital for the business, or he has some sort of profiteering racket up at the crematorium. It has to be something like that. Something like that fits, too. Besides, how does Morton make a living over there? He just doesn't have enough business. He has to be making money on the side."

"Maybe . . . I just don't know."

Nina paced to the other side of the room. She didn't like this conversation, didn't like where it was going. How Morton made his money was of no interest to her.

"Listen," said Bruce, "your husband ties into all this, too. He fits the pattern. He was relatively young, he died of a heart attack, he passed through Mendota General and—"

"Jesus Christ," snapped Nina, "you're talking about my husband as if he were a dirty sheet being taken to a laundry service!"

"Sorry," said Bruce, sitting back. "I suppose I am getting a bit out of control. It's just that there are so many coincidences." He hesitated, then added, "Listen, I know I might be way off track, but I have a book of some clippings. If I dropped it off tomorrow, would you take a look at it?"

No. No, she thought. "I don't—"

"Please, I haven't talked about any of this with anyone else. I'd just like to hear your opinion. After that I'll leave you alone."

She stared at him, suddenly angry. She had no choice, she realized. Right then Nina knew that if she didn't pursue this and convince herself that this guy was nuts, then she would soon start wondering, doubting and, of course, growing suspicious of everything.

"Well, all right, but . . ." She sat down on the arm of a stuffed chair, yet was unable to look at Bruce. "But what you're talking about is . . . is a link of some sort between my husband's death and Morton, right?"

"Exactly."

This was too weird. Morton? No, she told herself. Don't bring it up. Don't contribute to this man's theory.

"What is it?" he coaxed.

Suddenly worried, she said, "There's something else. Something you probably don't know. I wasn't the one who found my husband. Not really. I was on the phone and the doorbell rang. I opened the door . . . and there was Mr. Morton mumbling on. He was very nervous and pointed across the street. Alex was in a heap, already . . . already dead in the snow."

Bruce sat forward. "A connection, then, between the two."

The rims of Nina's eyes reddened. "God, are you suggesting that Alex might have been . . . been . . . ?"

"Yes, I am."

Nina nodded and put her hand to her forehead. "That was my first reaction when they told me Alex was dead. Alex couldn't have just died, I thought. He was in such good health, we were going to have a baby any day. He couldn't have died just like that. He wouldn't. No, Alex would have to have been . . . been murdered to leave me."

"Sometimes," said Bruce, "your first reaction is the one to trust." His voice gentle, he asked, "So you'll take a look at that book of clippings?"

Her eyes full of tears, she nodded, then said, "Would you leave now please?"

## Chapter

# 17

The next morning Nina fed and dressed Jenny, made decaf coffee and toast, then glanced at the paper, all as if she were in some sort of unpleasant hangover. She wanted to move on, to dive into this day, but she couldn't. Along with her own thoughts, Bruce Fitzgerald's words and suspicions kept pulling her back to Alex's death.

What had been said kept reverberating and circling in her mind without coming to rest in any one corner. It was impossible. She wished she hadn't gone outside last night, hadn't snuck around the funeral home, and most of all had not met the drop-out accountant who thought he was working for the Chicago *Tribune* instead of the Mendota *Gazette*.

Shortly before nine she heard a car pull up out front and, hiding upstairs behind her bedroom curtain, she caught a glimpse of Bruce. Jenny in her arms, Nina sat in the rocking chair in her room and listened as he bound up the porch stairs two at a time, then rang and eventually knocked. Rocking as she sat, she stared out the second-floor window, willing him to go and not return. When she finally heard his car start up and pull away, she still didn't move.

Almost ten minutes later Nina went down. She hesitated at the door, hoping there wouldn't be anything left on the porch. But there was—a black, three-ring notebook. Taking a quick glimpse inside, Nina saw that it was filled with clippings, all obituaries. An attached note read:

> Nina,
>     Thanks for listening to me last night. I know this must be hard for you, but I'm curious what you can make of it.
> Thanks,<br>Bruce Fitzgerald

Without a second thought, Nina took the notebook and dropped it in a corner of the front hall. No, she was certain of it. She wasn't going to look at it, wasn't going to entertain the reporter's theories. She was going to give the notebook back to him as soon as possible. Thanks but no thanks. This morning it just sounded all too weird. A stretch of imagination she could not make.

Trying to put it all out of her mind, Nina slowly went about her daily routine. She changed the baby, picked up around the house, sorted bills and threw in a load of laundry. It was after eleven when Nina and her baby reached the ECRI for their daily visit. Passing through the third-floor security doors, Nina took a deep breath and headed directly for the nurses' station.

"Good morning, ladies," said Barb, the broad-smiling nurse at the desk.

"Hi," began Nina. "I have a favor to ask. Would you mind watching Jenny for just a few minutes?"

"Oh, you bet. I'd watch this kid any day."

"Thanks. It's just that after yesterday . . . she started crying and my father got all upset." Realizing what that portended, Nina sighed, "I suppose I'm going to have to start getting a sitter when I come here."

"Neah. You don't want to do that." The redheaded woman stepped around the desk and bent down to Jenny.

"Trust me. He's going to have more than his share of bad days, and the best thing you can do is still share this kid with him. Your dad's world is shrinking all the time and the last thing you want to do is make it any smaller."

As Barb scooped Jenny out of the stroller, Nina said, "I suppose you're right. Any idea how he's doing today?"

"Really well, I think. Dr. Dundeen spent some time with him yesterday and then this morning, too."

"Great," said Nina with a rush of relief. "Is he still on the tranquilizer?"

"Nope."

That was good, too, wasn't it? Didn't that mean he'd calmed down totally? Of course. She just hoped there was no repeat of yesterday's scene.

As Nina passed the lounge, she saw two women and a man playing Scrabble. Up until last month, her father had likewise been ordered to play the game twice a day. Reminded by one of the nurses, of course, he did so obediently, racking his mind to spell *and* or *but* or the almost impossible *telephone*. Now instead her father was led down here in the evening, where with a group of others he watched an old Cary Grant or Ingrid Bergman or Humphrey Bogart film on the VCR. Although he couldn't follow the story line because he had trouble tracking the scenes, he was enraptured by the clothing, the cars, the sets—the patina of his virile days.

Nina hesitated outside her father's room. She took a deep breath, clenched her fists. Could her father have recovered from yesterday's low notch or had he sunk too far?

*"Nina, I'm ready to go home now."*

*Frying pan in hand, she leaned around the corner of the kitchen in her condo.*

*"Dad," she said, a cheerful lilt to her voice, "you're living with Alex and me."*

*"I am?"*

*"Yes, you moved into the den last week."*

*He looked at her. "What? Oh, yes, I'm living here now. Sorry, I forgot. I forget sometimes, you know."*

*"That's okay, Dad. You're doing great." She served up their dishes, and added, "It's just the two of us for dinner. Alex won't be home until late."*

*"Oh." Bill sat down and took a bite. "Nina, I'll be ready to go home after dinner."*

*"Dad, you live here now."*

*"I do?"*

*Patience, Nina told herself as she looked across the glass-topped table. He's trying. It's not his fault.*

*"Yes, you live here. We sold the house, remember?"*

*He dropped his fork. "What? But I want to go home. Home, to my house! Why did you sell the house? I didn't give you my permission. You're after my money, aren't you?"*

*"Dad, don't be silly."*

*"You are. You want all my things, all my money. You even took my own house and sold it out from under me!"*

*"Dad!"*

*"You and Alex are just after my money!"*

*Horrified, Nina sat there as Bill shoved back his chair and stormed over to the balcony doors. Please not again, she thought. Please don't let him kick and scream and cry out.*

*Nina took a deep breath. Control. Just maintain it. You have control and the power to help him, calm him. He can't help it, she thought, as she stood and walked quietly to him. Reassure him, touch him, tell him you love him. He understands all that, needs all that. Yes, she thought, wrapping her arms around him from behind.*

*"I'd never do anything to hurt you. You're the best father. I love you. Everything's going to be okay." She kissed him on the back of his neck. "Shh."*

*She felt the tension in his body drip away, sensed his muscles relax, soften. As she held him, he turned around and wrapped his arms around her. There, thought Nina. Crisis averted. He just needed to know he was loved. And she needed this, too. A good hug from her father.*

*Then suddenly she felt his arms tighten around her. This was more, she realized, much more than a parental embrace. Was he going to burst into tears? Or, dear God, was he still mad? Was he going to attack her?*

*"Dad, what is it?" she said, trying but unable to move.*

*She raised her head, and as she did so, he caught it with one hand. She felt his fingers sink into her chin. Just as quickly, he moved his head. And then his lips were upon hers, firmly, directly. Something warm and moist darted between her lips. Christ, she panicked, that was her father's tongue inside her mouth. He was kissing her!*

*"Daddy!" She brought her arms up between them and hurled him back against the glass door. "Stop it! Stop it!" she shouted, wiping her mouth with the back of her hand. "That's disgusting!"*

She quietly pushed open his door and saw him sitting and staring out the window. As if he actually remembered what he'd worn yesterday, he had changed and today wore perfectly pressed khaki pants and a light blue oxford shirt rolled up to his elbows. That's what he always wore to the club—the stockbroker relaxing on the weekend. Oh, God, thought Nina. If only he were sitting around the pool in the warm summer air instead of gazing out his hospital window.

She squeezed the words from her throat. "Good morning . . . Daddy."

His head slowly turned. As handsome as ever, he stared at her as if vaguely recognizing an old stranger, and Nina almost couldn't bear it.

His lips parted and he spoke the one word she was certain he'd never be able to remember again: "Nina."

As if she were the one who'd been lost, she ran to him, ran across the linoleum, dropped to her knees, kissed his hand. He sat there still, motionless, as she clung to his arm, and then with his free hand he started stroking her hair.

"Shh," he whispered.

She kissed him on the arm, and as she did so she noticed a bandage where he must have had a shot. Thank God. He'd been given some powerful drug. Some brand-new medication that had brought him back.

Tears came to her eyes. This was her father, the one with the sharp wit and warm heart whom she'd thought she'd lost forever. Like an alcoholic who'd been on an endless binge and then suddenly stopped, her father was back. But for how long?

This might be the last time he'd ever be able to hear and accept her words, and she blurted, "I love you, Daddy." She stumbled on emotion. "Just always keep that in your heart. Please, don't ever forget that. I love you."

"I . . . I . . ."

He pulled her closer, bent his head over her and hugged her. He nodded, and Nina knew that was him echoing his affection for her.

They sat like that for a long time, the two of them not wanting to let go. Finally, he pulled back. Nina looked up and saw the tears in his eyes, and nearly broke down herself. In all her life the only other time she'd seen him cry was at her mother's funeral. Yes, deep within himself her father knew what was happening to him. He was aware that his mind was crumbling.

Stuck to the wall next to the chair were a bunch of Post-It Notes, tiny slips of paper with adhesive on the edge. He took the first one and read it slowly and thoroughly.

With each syllable carefully formed and paced and thought out, he said, "I am sorry. About yesterday. I remember and I am sorry."

"That's all right. Don't worry." Her teeth pinched her bottom lip shut and she struggled to control the emotion that swelled in her chest. Fearful that she had spoken too fast, she repeated herself. "It's all right. Everything is all right."

He took another slip, and half reading said, "When it is my time . . ." He stopped and touched his head as if it hurt. "When it is my time let me be like a balloon."

She nodded but couldn't speak. How many hours had it taken him to compose this speech? She was shocked, too, not only by what he spoke of, but also because her businessman-father was speaking not in profit margins and book values, but in metaphors.

"Hold me like a balloon now. Cherish me." He stopped and collected his thoughts. He touched his head again and, struggling, continued with his idea. "But . . . but when it is time, let me go."

The tears could no longer be held back, and they came freely from her eyes and flowed down her cheeks. "Sure, Daddy. Sure."

He squeezed her hand. "Don't worry."

"No. No, I won't," she lied. "I promise."

"Let me go and I will fly." He stopped to form the thought. "I will fly into the sky high above. Perhaps my head first . . . and then the rest of me. But I will fly up." His hand drifted upward. "And when you can no longer see me, just remember. Remember. I will always be up there." He pointed straight up. "Like a balloon in heaven."

"Yes," she sobbed. "And someday I . . . I will be there, too."

Crying out of gratitude, she let herself fall into her father's arms and be rocked. Dear Lord, she wondered, what had happened? What had he been given?

He pulled the last note from the wall, and said, "Where is my granddaughter, Jenny? May I see her?"

Gasping, Nina scrambled to her feet and was out the door. Thank God, she thought, for Dr. Dundeen. Thank God for the treatment that had given her back her father.

# Chapter 18

Nina had so many thoughts that her head ached. Seated in the rocking chair in her bedroom, she looked out the bay window and into the dark. There was Bruce's notebook and all that he had said last night, there was the possibility that Alex's death had truly not been a simple heart attack and there was the miracle she had witnessed today. Her father, returned to lucidity.

Jenny slept soundly, cradled between two pillows on Nina's bed. Nina glanced at her and envied the child's peace. So calm, so simple. If only she could reduce her life to such a pure state.

But how could she? What was she supposed to think? In her lap was Bruce's three-ring notebook. When he'd called late this afternoon he'd asked if she'd looked at it yet. She said she couldn't talk now, the baby was hungry, and asked him to pick up the notebook tomorrow.

In truth, however, she'd broken the promise to herself, had been halfway through the collection of obituaries, and didn't know what to make of it. She hadn't intended to study the clippings, hadn't wanted to note who died at what age and where and what happened to their remains. But she couldn't help herself, and she was forced to admit there was something oddly repetitious about not one or two alone, but the way all the deaths were strung together. There was indeed a pattern in the ages and causes of death of those who came to Mr. Morton. But what did that mean? One large coincidence?

What, she asked herself, was she doing? What? Why was she listening to some reporter and his ideas? Why was she indulging in some bizarre theory?

Oh, crap, she thought. Of course she was going to talk to Bruce Fitzgerald, perhaps even in a few days. She knew she would, that she had to. But was it because he was the first and only person here to talk about Alex's death? Or was it simply because she needed to talk to someone, anyone? God, I'm lonely, she thought, sitting there in the dark. The best part of marriage was the constant companionship.

While her mind skipped from thought to thought, her eyes remained fixed on one thing. As if in a trance, she stared at the yellow brick building across the street. Ridgewood Mortuary. Huge and solid. Only a few lights burned in the windows. Mr. Morton and Mikey were home, she had seen them pass from room to room. What could be going on in there? Could Alex have stumbled onto something? But how and when?

Several lights in the upstairs apartment fell dark. A stairwell light was flicked on. The back stairs. As clearly as if in a fishbowl, Mr. Morton walked by an uncovered window. He stopped, called back, and Mikey came bounding down, a jacket in hand.

Nina's hand reached for the telephone. In the dark she strained to read a number on a piece of paper. Balancing the notebook on her knee, Nina dialed. The phone on the other end hadn't finished even the first ring when it was picked up.

"Hello?" said the deep voice.

"It's me, Nina."

"Oh, hi."

She looked behind the funeral home and across the black parking lot. On the other side of the lot was a band of trees, after which stood a row of houses with their large garages, some even with old servants' quarters above. She couldn't see much, yet knew that a pair of eyes in one of these garage apartments was now upon her.

"Listen," said Bruce, "I'm sorry if—"

"They're getting ready to leave."

"What?"

"Morton and his son. Aren't you watching?" she asked, almost able to feel his gaze swing from her and back to the funeral home.

"Of course. But I can't see them from this side. Where are you? I have a pair of binoculars but I can't see you, either."

"Upstairs in my bedroom. The big bay window. The lights are off."

"How long have you been watching?"

"I don't know. Awhile. But listen, from over here I just caught a glimpse of the two of them coming down from their apartment. Mikey was dragging a coat. I couldn't see what—" She leaned forward. "Wait, another light just went out downstairs. Look, the back light. They're going somewhere."

"Thanks for the tip. I'll talk to you later."

"Hey, wait a minute. What are you going to do?"

"Follow them, see if I can learn anything."

Before she realized what she was doing, Nina blurted, "I'm coming with you."

"What?"

"Listen," she said, sitting forward, "either I'm coming with you or I'm following them in my own car."

Without a pause, Bruce asked, "You got a car seat?"

"Yeah." God, was she really doing this? Yes, absolutely. "As soon as they pull out I'll run across the parking lot and through the trees. You just have the car ready and going."

"Right."

She hung up, only now captured by a moment of hesitation. Then, however, she glanced out and saw Morton and Mikey emerging. She had to go. She had to find out, and the sullenness of the night was instantly gone. Snatching Jenny from the bed, she bolted downstairs. In her bouncing arms, the baby woke and began to cry.

"Shh, baby. It's okay. We're going for a ride."

With an experienced hand, Nina grabbed the car seat that sat by the front door and strapped Jenny into it. As she fastened the belt, she glanced out and saw the lights, not of Morton's hearse, but of his big Oldsmobile parked behind the mortuary. At first the rear lights burned red, then they flicked white as he backed around. Finally he shifted into drive and slowly cruised out of the parking lot—the plane of flat black that had once been a garden—and onto Leaf Street. Before he reached the end of the street, Nina was out the door, Jenny and car seat in hand. She carefully made her way down the front porch steps, then charged across the parking lot, certain that Morton hadn't seen her in his rearview mirror.

On the other side of the parking lot, she cut through the bushes and trees and found Bruce in his idling Honda. The passenger door was open, and she quickly made her way into the back seat. Without turning on the lights, Bruce stabbed the car into reverse.

"His right blinker was on," said Nina, over Jenny's cries.

He hit a bump and the car shot upward. Nina caught the car seat a few inches in the air and Jenny screamed. Then Nina buckled in the molded plastic seat as Bruce twisted the wheel, hit the lights and took off for the main road. Jenny's wails reached higher decibel levels.

"Shit," said Nina, searching her pockets. "I never have a pacifier when I need one." At last she felt one in her shirt pocket. "Here you go, kiddo. Look what I found.

Come on, it's okay. I'm sorry. There. There. That's it."
To Bruce she shouted, "He's in his brown Oldsmobile."

"I know," responded Bruce, calmly. "License plate
RBG 674."

She braced herself as he drove swiftly onto Ridgewood,
then swerved around a truck.

"There he is," said Bruce, slowing. "He's three cars
ahead of us."

Maintaining a distance, the gold Honda Accord followed the brown Oldsmobile as it skirted the western-
most edge of town. Morton drove the speed limit, nothing
more, nothing less as he headed toward the countryside.

"What do you think of what we talked about last
night?" asked Bruce, glancing at her in the rearview
mirror.

"I . . . I don't know."

It all sounded so absurd—ill-doings at the funeral
home, mysterious causes of Alex's death—yet she had
been up there staring at the funeral home and she was
here in the back seat of a near-stranger's car. She sensed,
though, that this was right. It felt good to be doing
something, to be out actively looking for the truth rather
than sitting at home. Even if they found nothing,
wouldn't that help her lay Alex to rest in her mind?
Absolutely.

Bruce said, "My guess is that someone's doing a little
bribing—maybe Morton's offering someone at the hospital a little kickback in exchange for the business. Or
maybe it's more serious. Perhaps he's smuggling something."

But what, she wondered? Drugs? Nina pushed herself
up against the right window and caught a glimpse of
Morton's car.

"He's turning right up at the next road."

The town was fading fast, melting from the closely
packed Victorians of the older part, to scattered split-

levels, to this area of fast-food restaurants and cut-rate supermarkets. The dense maple trees gave way to sparse saplings and finally no trees, just fields of blacktop. The road was high and wide with special turning lanes for all the daytime traffic. Tonight, however, it was not heavily traveled.

Bruce realized where the Oldsmobile was headed, and mumbled, "What's he doing here so late?"

Slowing, Morton turned left into the parking lot of The Omelette House, the town's only twenty-four-hour restaurant. What was this, a late-night snack? Perhaps, thought Nina. Or perhaps something not so simple. This could merely be their first stop.

As Bruce drove another hundred yards down, Nina stared out the back window, keeping her eye as long as possible on the brown Oldsmobile. Then Bruce pulled a U-turn and headed back toward the restaurant. They were wordless as he steered into the parking lot and drove to the far side. They parked, half hidden by a van, and watched as Morton and his son made their way to the front doors.

She reached between the seats and touched Bruce on the shoulder. "They might be going on after this—to meet someone or . . . I don't know. Can we wait?"

"Yeah, I think that'd be a good idea." He shut off the engine, then turned around and offered an enormous grin to the baby. "Hello, kiddo, how ya doin'?"

Nina studied Bruce and couldn't help but smile. All right, she thought. Admit it. He's tall, broad shouldered. Yes, handsome. And, obviously, good with babies. Of course, she surmised.

"You're divorced, aren't you?"

"What? Oh, yeah."

She knew it. "And kids?"

"Two—a boy and a girl."

He's probably a good dad, thought Nina. But where

were his children? Still in Chicago? And why the divorce?

His voice low, Bruce looked at Nina, saying, "You know, if we discover something and Morton gets hauled in, the only person who's going to suffer is Mikey."

That's right, she thoght. Mikey would probably be placed in an institution of some sort.

"Poor kid," she said, thinking of her own little brother, who'd died so long ago. "You know, he really doesn't have much longer."

"What are you talking about?"

"Mikey has Down's Syndrome."

"Obviously."

"Well," began Nina, recalling what Dr. Dundeen had told her, "do you know what happens to virtually every Down's person if they reach their thirties?"

Bruce glanced toward the restaurant. "No. What?"

"They develop Alzheimer's disease."

"What?" he said, turning back toward her. "You're kidding?"

"No, they get plaques and tangles—the whole bit, all the trademarks of the disease. The main hypothesis is that they both have something to do with a defect on the twenty-first chromosome. That's what my father's doctor believes, too."

When her father had first been admitted to the ECRI, Nina had been required to complete a full family history. Noting the Trenton family's, Dundeen had explained his theory and told Nina how Down's Syndrome and Alzheimer's tended to run in families. That's when he'd strongly advised Nina to obtain genetic counseling should she ever become pregnant.

And Dundeen, thought Nina as she sat in the car, had to be right. He always was. After all, both tragedies had plagued the Trentons. Her father had Alzheimer's now. And Brian, little Brian, her parents' only son, Nina's baby brother, her only sibling. He'd been a Down's baby, a severe case, and he'd died of an enlarged heart not long after he'd turned two.

"That's incredible," said Bruce. "I never—"

Looking across the lot, Nina suddenly said, "Oh, my God."

"What is it?"

Staring out over the hood of the faded gold Honda, Nina spotted a short figure. It was a woman in her sixties, her hair neatly coifed, her steps direct. She no longer wore a suit, but Nina recognized her immediately.

"Nina, what is it?"

"That woman right there, the short one. That's . . . that's Dr. Volker. She's the medical examiner from the hospital, the one I talked to about Alex's autopsy."

Silent, she and Bruce watched as Volker, purse in hand, strode directly into the restaurant. I can't believe it, thought Nina.

Bruce smiled. "Now isn't this interesting. I hadn't considered the medical examiner being involved, but . . . of course she's going in there to meet him. Of course they know each other." He added, "She does the autopsies, he buries the bodies."

"Yeah, but . . ." What did this mean? How far could they realistically take this? "This is really odd, but it doesn't necessarily prove anything."

It could be a coincidence. Maybe Volker was going in there to meet a cousin or a brother or anyone else. Or maybe she really was joining Morton.

"You know," said Nina, "they might be just friends— and that's all."

Out of the corner of his eye, he stared at her. "You really think so?"

"Actually . . ."

No, she didn't. This was something, she sensed, that would lead somewhere, to an answer of some sort. But to arrive at that point, to ascertain the nature of their relationship, they had to test the connection between Morton and Volker. Quickly, Nina voiced a plan of action that was based on nothing more than intuition.

"Seeing Volker go in there doesn't tell us much except that we might possibly, maybe, perhaps be on the right track," said Nina, touching Bruce on the shoulder. "But tomorrow I could go back down to the morgue. And if Morton and Volker are indeed up to something, I bet I can stir it up."

Bruce laughed. "I bet you can, too."

# Chapter
# 19

It was past two in the morning when Dr. Gregory Dundeen opened his office safe and again withdrew the synthetic solution. Placing the vial in his small leather case, he extinguished the lights and eased open the door. The outer offices were dark and the main corridor dim. Aware that the janitorial services had completed their work and that the night watchmen had recently swung through and returned to Mendota General, Dundeen proceeded directly to the rear staircase. Using a passkey, he opened the security door and started up the cold concrete stairwell.

He found the second floor empty, calm. Slipping from the stairs, he pressed himself up against the wall and was still. No one. In the dull light, he could distinguish neither nurse nor pacing patient. If he were spotted, he could say he'd merely been working late in the lab and had come to check on a patient. It was far better, though, to avoid such a situation.

His feet padding over the soft carpeting, he reached the room, glanced in either direction, then entered room 212. Ellen Cherney was there, her body motionless in the blue glow of the nightlight.

With both hands, Dundeen slowly shut the door. As he proceeded to her bedside he saw her shift slightly beneath the white sheets. It didn't matter if she woke, though.

She was much too heavily sedated to be any problem.

Standing next to her, he opened his case and tore a large piece of tape. He stuck that on her bedside table, then stood hovering over her. She was on her side. He just needed her to—

As if answering his wishes, Ellen Cherney rolled over on her back. Her breathing was quick and short, her eyes weary but open.

"Who . . . who . . ." she muttered.

No. No sounds. Dundeen had had enough of her ranting earlier. In an instant he dropped over her bed, clamped his hands over her mouth. She squirmed, bit into his palm with slimey lips. With one hand he reached back, grabbed the thick tape, then slapped it over her mouth. He pressed it firmly in place. Yes. That would keep her quiet.

Into her ear he whispered, "Everything's all right. I'm a friend."

He smiled when he saw her eyes swell wide. Sorry, he thought, but you don't know how much you are helping, what you're doing here for your fellow patients.

"Just relax," crooned Dundeen. "You're in a special home. And I'm a friend."

He pushed up her sleeve, spotting her dark veins at once. A good one she was. With her high blood pressure she was perfect for his purposes. He reached into his kit for the tourniquet.

"Don't worry. This won't hurt."

At least he hoped it wouldn't. He just needed to ascertain the effects, to learn if he had successfully corrected the problem.

He wrapped the rubber cord snugly around her arm. Then he felt for a vein. Good. Right there. This would only take a moment. Almost working on automatic, he cleaned her arm then readied the syringe. If only it works . . . if only . . .

She lifted her arm, twisted slightly.

"Be still!" he snapped, holding her down.

He wouldn't tolerate her resistance a second time. No. He was just going to give her the damn shot and then . . . There. Yes, he thought, gliding the needle into the old woman's body and pressing the synthetic solution into her system. That's it.

Within moments, though, he sensed the first tremor. Oh, shit, he thought. Jerking the needle out of her, he reached for her neck, found her pulse. Abruptly, he sensed a blip of sorts. Again it seemed to skip. Hesitate. And then almost at once her pulse started gathering momentum, charging ahead faster and faster. The old woman gasped, and stared at him with small, hateful eyes. When her heartbeat reached that of a drum roll, he knew he had failed again, this time critically. Furious, he watched her tiny eyes suddenly swell in her head.

He looked over, saw her right arm trembling, curling. Shit. A stroke. What was wrong? Which of his calculations were off? If anything he thought he'd mitigated the chances of this type of reaction.

He had to get out of here. Quickly he stowed his things in his case, then reached down to her again. He picked at the end of the tape, then ripped it off. Immediately, a deep scatching noise clawed its way out of her throat.

Furious, he stormed off. He'd made an incorrect assumption, proceeded in the wrong direction. This was worse than before. The balance of synthesized gangliosides was all wrong, out of proportion to what could be tolerated. What did this mean? How many months more work?

At the door, he glanced back once and saw the old woman's body jerk and convulse with the last energy of life. Crazed with frustration, he slammed his fist against the wall.

"Damn it!" he cursed, for he had no time for failure.

# 20

The difference between yesterday and today was shocking. The next morning when Nina found her father in the common room, he looked at both Jenny and her and gasped as if they were mere images from a dream. Then he rubbed his forehead and stammered out Nina's name. He recognized Jenny, but when he couldn't pull out the name, Nina coaxed him along. At once he was on his feet, seizing Nina by the arm, his face flushed with frustration and anger. Nina tried to pull away but he wouldn't let go, and she was instantly transported back to the night when the horrors of Alzheimer's had delivered its harshest blow.

*"What's wrong with me?" sobbed Bill.*

*"Everything's all right."*

*In the living room of her apartment, Nina hugged her father, his tears dampening her cheek. She patted his back, rocked him as if she were comforting a child. She wanted to be there, to help him, to care for him, but that was all. No more incidents.*

*Bill said, "I . . . I think you're beautiful."*

*"Now, Daddy . . ."*

*She brought her arms up between them and pushed him away. Just as quickly, Bill caught her with his left hand, his fingers clutching her wrist. With his right, he started massaging his crotch. She glanced down.*

*"Oh, shit!" she gasped.*

*Straining against her father's khakis was the outline of something large and swollen.*

*"I love you. I want you," he moaned.*

*Nina jerked to the side, tripped on her father's foot and fell to the floor. She rolled over, only to see her father reaching into his pants and freeing an organ that stood hard and fleshy.*

*"Oh, my God!" she screamed. "No!"*

*Scrambling to her feet, she punched him in the gut and sent him hurling backward. Then she turned and ran, charging down the hall and into the bathroom.*

*And there she stayed, locked in, until Alex came home an hour later. Sobbing and crying, she could take no more. The time, she knew, had come.*

Whatever Dr. Dundeen had done for her father, Nina thought, it had worn off quickly, much too quickly. She had to find him again, beg him again. Obviously, Dundeen hadn't visited her father yet today or he would have seen the difference and done something. Whatever he'd given Bill the other day had worked miraculously, but now Nina's father needed more. More.

Desperate, Nina looped her arm in her father's and, pushing the stroller, started into the hall. Perhaps Dundeen was already up here, maybe he was just visiting one of the other patients. Nina could show him what her father was like today and . . .

They hadn't gone but twenty feet when they came to the nurses' station, where, just arrived and sitting on the counter, was the morning snack, small cartons of milk and a tray of Snoopy bars. Spotting the food, Bill shook off Nina's arm and ran toward it, as if it were the first food he'd seen in days.

Yes, sweets, said Nina to herself. Crazy about sweets. As she watched, her father bypassed the milk and grabbed one, then two of the rich peanut-butter and chocolate bars. Clutching them in his hands, he rushed away before the nurse's aide saw that he had taken more than a single serving.

Scanning the hall for Dr. Dundeen, Nina trailed her father to the TV room. Pushing Jenny ahead of her, she found Bill sitting on a blue couch, cramming the candy into his mouth. He glanced at her and kept chewing, crumbs tumbling out of both ends of his mouth.

"Slow down," said Nina. "No one's going to take it away from you."

He looked at her distrustfully.

"Are they good?" she asked.

He nodded.

"Just eat slowly, okay Daddy?"

Jenny slept in the stroller, and Nina rocked her back and forth as Bill gobbled down the second Snoopy bar. She glanced around. There were three tables in here, a TV, a couch, some chairs, a few ashtrays. On the wall was an old-style etching of a girl with an umbrella and a dog. Long ago Nina had stopped wondering if her father was happy here, if this place nourished his soul.

She looked over at him. There were crumbs on his lips, on his lap. He was clutching his head.

"Daddy, are you all right?"

"My head . . . it's pounding."

"That's because you ate too fast. And all that sugar." Nina rolled her eyes and rose. "Come on, let's go get you some milk. That'll make you feel better."

And, she thought, let's find Dr. Dundeen. If nothing else, perhaps he could explain her father's sudden deterioration.

At the nurses' station, however, Nina was informed that Dr. Dundeen was in conference. Discouraged, she led Bill back to his room, nursed Jenny and then headed down to the hospital cafeteria. There, as scheduled, she found Bruce Fitzgerald, sipping a cup of black coffee and eating the last of a roll. Wheeling Jenny alongside the table, Nina sat down in the orange plastic chair across from him, looked at the brownish crumbs on his plate, then stared out the window.

Bruce took another sip of coffee and finally asked, "So?"

Nina gazed away and shrugged. As wonderful as her father's lucidity had been yesterday, now she felt cheated.

"Worse?" said Bruce.

Nina nodded. "He recognized me. Jenny, too. But . . . I could practically see him slip away."

"Sorry."

Nina shrugged and brushed back her thick blond hair. "I guess that's the way Alzheimer's goes—the days can differ so dramatically."

While yesterday she'd hoped for a miracle cure, today she realized that even if there was one it might come too late. Her father's condition was deteriorating. She could foresee the final stages of the disease when her father would be incontinent, when he would have to be tied in a wheelchair or to a bed because he had lost his motor abilities and when his speech would be reduced to but half a dozen words.

Nina closed her eyes and out of nowhere said, "I'm glad you're here. It's . . . it's just nice to talk to someone after seeing my father."

"I bet," he said, his voice soft with sympathy.

A bit embarrassed by her confession, Nina looked at her watch, took a deep breath and said, "I should get down there."

"You sure you want to do this? You don't have to speak with Volker, you know. We can think of something else."

"It's okay."

She wanted to. It still felt right to be pushing, looking, testing. Yes, trying to find out instead of sitting and wondering. On the way over Bruce and she had gone over what she would say. Now she just had to go downstairs and present it convincingly. Then they would watch . . . and see what Volker might do and if she would draw Morton into some course of action. If so, then at least their connection would be confirmed.

"Jenny should be okay," she said, kissing her on the top of her head. "I just fed her. And there's an extra diaper in the bag. You sure you can watch her?"

"Don't worry, I can handle it," said Bruce, leaning over the child. "She's the baby and I'm not."

"Well, at least you know that role." Nina looked at him. "Thanks, I . . . I . . ."

Not sure what it was she wanted to say, Nina turned and quickly left the cafeteria. She was glad Bruce was here, she was glad she had someone to talk to but what else was it she felt? Guilt? Could that be it? In any case, she thought, she was glad she was going back downstairs. It would force her mind off her father.

As if in a trance, Nina descended to the basement, where she looked for and found Dr. Volker. As before, she followed the doctor to her office, where Nina was again seated.

"I can see you're still upset." Dr. Volker sat on the edge of her desk and motioned to a chair for Nina. "You have that distant, preoccupied look in your eyes."

Nina nodded, willing herself to speak. "Something has come up."

"Oh?"

"My husband's doctor . . . there's a problem."

The other woman's face puffed in a frown and she cocked her head to the side. "I'm sorry to hear that. Is there something I can do?"

"Actually, it is a bit serious and you might be able to help." Nina cleared her throat. Just say it, she told herself, the way you rehearsed it with Bruce. "You see, we ... we might be in a lawsuit with Alex's—my husband's—doctor."

Nina watched as Dr. Volker's eyebrows went distinctly upward. What did that mean? Could the doctor be afraid of something?

"Oh, I see," said Volker. "Is it someone from ... ah, from here?"

"No. From Chicago. Alex was put on some sort of medication last year and now there's a question of what that might have done to his heart. My lawyer wants me to sue him for malpractice."

"How terrible."

"Awful, isn't it?" She shook her head and continued. There wasn't too much more—she'd make it. "Incredible, really. I can't believe any of this. I really don't believe in suing people, particularly doctors, but if it really is a case of blatant malpractice ..." With sad eyes, she looked directly at Volker. "My lawyer wants to come up next week from Chicago and talk to you, since you did the autopsy. Would you mind? He's still checking to see if there are grounds for a lawsuit."

Nina's blue eyes settled on Volker. At first the other woman seemed at a loss for words. Was it shock? Nina couldn't tell. But searching Volker's face, Nina sensed something. Something the older woman wanted to keep in the shadows.

Dr. Volker finally said, "Of course not."

"Thank you. It's all so dreadful. Apparently it could go to court, which might mean the ... the body would have to be ex ... ex ..." Even though she'd thought the word, Nina couldn't bring herself to say it. "You know, brought up. I just hope that doesn't happen. I'm hoping we'll be able to settle out of court."

"Certainly." The doctor pulled on her gold necklace. "But trust me. I'll do what I can. And thank you for giving me some advance warning. It'll allow me to go over the file more carefully. Just have your lawyer telephone and we'll set something up."

As Nina stood, she studied the other woman, strained to discern what transpired behind those eyes. Were there truly some ill-doings going on and was Volker in on it?

Nina extended her hand, perhaps a little too directly, smugly. "Thank you. You've been very kind."

"Just doing my job." The short woman added, "You have enough things to worry about with your father."

"I know. I just want this to be over as quickly as possible."

"I'm sure you do." Volker looked at her directly, and said, "I would hope so, also."

Some ten minutes later, Irene Volker still stood in her office, still held her hands in tense fists. She'd telephoned him right away, telling him only that Nina Trenton had just been there. That was enough to frighten him, and he was on his way down to learn the complete story. Damn it, she thought. This was exactly the situation she wanted to avoid. Now, however, they could not.

Volker fiddled with the gold necklace around her neck. It wasn't supposed to be complicated, but now that it was they'd just have to simplify it again. There was no other way, and she was sure he'd agree.

She heard the rear door open. Good, she thought. He's here. Quickly, Volker made her way around her desk and into the back hall. A tall, solemn figure stood there, his face stiff with tension.

"What happened?" said Dr. Gregory Dundeen, his voice hushed.

"It's serious," said Volker, staring up at him. "She came down and asked more questions about her husband."

To a totally silent Dundeen, Volker related in detail all that Nina Trenton had said about the lawsuit. When Volker mentioned the possible exhumation, she could see Dundeen's face deepen in color. So, she thought, he's as afraid as she is.

Volker nervously said, "She's getting too close. You know what this means, don't you?"

"Of course I do." Dundeen slid his glasses down and rubbed his eyes. Then he reached out and slammed the wall. "Shit. There's no other way."

"Of course there isn't."

He took a deep breath and turned away. "All right, then get Marcel on it immediately. And tell him not to waste any time . . . or he'll spend the rest of his life in an American prison."

Her eyes on Dundeen as he started to leave, Volker said, "Don't worry. He's good at this sort of thing. He'll take care of it right away. Tonight, if he can."

# Chapter
# 21

"More wine?" asked Bruce, holding up the bottle in the dark.

"No, I've had my half glass." Although she'd have loved more, she wouldn't let herself. "I'm a nursing mom, you know."

They sat in the dark in her bedroom drinking the cheap wine and looking out at the funeral home. They'd started off downstairs, Bruce coming over around seven and sneaking in through the back door. Then as the sun set and Jenny fell asleep in her crib off the living room, they'd come upstairs for a clearer view. It was almost eleven now and so far there'd been no strange activity nor had Morton even left his house.

Over the intercom's receiver Nina heard a rustling of clothing and small noises. She lifted up the plastic device and listened to her daughter, who stirred in the portable crib downstairs. Could she be cold? No, she shouldn't be. Nina had closed the den windows. Then the child was quiet again, obviously having tumbled back into sleep. Satisfied that Jenny was all right, Nina placed the receiver back on the floor, leaned back in the wooden rocking chair and took another tiny sip of white wine.

"I've never known anyone to make a half glass of wine last two hours," said Bruce.

"I'm tempted to wean Jenny completely just so I can have coffee and chocolate and booze."

"No cigarettes?"

"Don't smoke. Do you?"

He shook his head. She really knew very little about him, but at the same time she understood him. It was partially, she assumed, because they were both from Chicago; the lake to the east and the prairie to the west always gave one such a centered perspective. Flat waters, country plains and city grids. Wasn't that how she felt put together?

"Do you miss your kids?" Nina asked.

"Yeah," Bruce said, still staring out the window. "A lot. They're coming up for Labor Day weekend. You'll have to meet them."

"I'd like that."

She'd like to learn more about Bruce, too. She'd like to learn about his former life—why he quit accounting and went into journalism, how he liked being up here and . . . But there was time. Maybe even a lot of time. In him, Nina recognized that it was in fact loneliness they had in common.

Bruce asked, "How did you and your husband end up here?"

"Too many furs in Chicago." She smiled and shook her head. "One day it just struck me how much we'd not only left behind, but lost. Alex and I used to be into all these causes, and then we both gradually settled into our careers. I was in advertising, he in law. In no time we were awash with bucks. Then one day I was at a restaurant and the cloakroom was overflowing—I mean really overflowing because there were so many big, bulky furs. And I just stopped and said, what happened to granola, what happened to the idea that wearing an animal's skin is repulsive, what happened to a social conscience?" She shrugged. "Dad was much worse by then and we had to do something about him. We wanted out, too, so we came up here because there was an opening for him at the Extended Care Research Institute. Then by some miracle I got pregnant."

They sat there for a long time, staring not really out at the funeral home but into the night. Nina forgot about Alex, forgot about the doubts lingering like ghosts around his death. For the first time since his death she felt relaxed, and she wallowed in it. It was so pleasant to be with someone and not have to say anything. Bruce seemed like an old friend, and she liked that.

Up and down the street lights popped off like squashed fireflies. Only a few on the top floor of the funeral home remained lit until shortly after midnight, when they, too, abruptly went black.

"Guess they're going to bed," said Jenny.

Bruce checked his watch. "Morton stays up on the late side." Bruce stretched and edged himself to the front of the chair. "Guess that's that. We certainly didn't discover anything devious tonight, did we?"

"No, we didn't."

That was good, she thought. Maybe they'd be lucky and they wouldn't find anything. A new friend and a return to normality sounded very inviting.

"It was nice having you here, though. You know, just sitting around."

"My pleasure."

"You'll have to come back for more spying."

"Sure. When?"

"Tomorrow night. I'll even cook some real food."

Only after she extended the invitation did she realize what it sounded like. Might not dinner twist things in another direction? Probably. But did she want that? God, she didn't know, and she was becoming stupified by the awkward silence.

Finally Bruce said, "Guess I should be going."

"Yeah."

Nina set her wineglass on the floor by the intercom

and stood. Bruce rose, too, and followed her lead to the door. Only steps from the hallway, she felt a hand reach out from behind her.

"Nina."

She hesitated, then turned. Bruce stood before her in the dark, a large figure, warm and friendly. She didn't know what to do or how to act, and she was motionless as he stepped forward and wrapped his arms around her. Then she saw her bed in the background and she wanted to give in, wanted to let a first kiss lead to many more. He bent over and his lips brushed through her hair, grazed her ear, pressed finally on her mouth. Moaning, Nina rubbed her hands up his back and thought how wonderful it was to have someone so warm so very close.

Then suddenly Bruce's moustache tickled her nose and Alex came screaming out of the grave. This man kissing her now wasn't her husband of fourteen years. This man desiring her was a stranger. Nina pulled her hands up between them.

"Bruce, I . . ."

"What?"

She twisted aside and started out of the bedroom. Flushed with confusion, she stood in the darkened hallway unable to look at Bruce. Then she sensed him approaching and she twisted inwardly. Just leave, she thought. Alex is still with me, his spirit still embraces my dreams. Please, just leave.

"I . . . I . . ." she began.

But before she could say anything, Bruce came up behind and kissed her on the back of her head. Just as quickly, he moved on, brushing past her.

As he headed down the stairs, he said, "Dinner tomorrow night?"

Nina watched him go down, watched him sink away and responded, "Sure."

She trailed him to the back door, then twisted the bolt and watched as Bruce made his way across the yard. It seemed rather foolish, his sneaking out the back, cutting through the neighbor's yard, then looping around to Ridgewood and back to his garage apartment. Could Morton really be watching them watch him? No. And there probably wasn't anything for Bruce and her to discover, either. Perhaps she'd simply been grabbing at things, desperately searching for some real reason why Alex had died.

Once Bruce's large figure had melted into the dark, Nina turned off the overhead light in the kitchen. She passed into the living room, turned left into the little den. Asleep in the portable crib beneath the closed windows, Jenny had barely moved since Nina had put her down. For a moment Nina wondered if she shouldn't just leave the baby down here rather than wake her; with the intercom Nina could hear virtually every move Jenny made. She thought better of it, though, and scooped up the little child in her arms. At once the baby began to turn and fuss, all of which eventually turned into a healthy howl.

"It's okay, Jenny. It's okay."

Kissing her, Nina again thought how lucky she was to have such a healthy child. Such a beautiful baby. Pressing her cheek against Jenny's, Nina felt silky warm skin. Oh, baby, she thought. What a wonderful baby . . .

Rocking her child as she walked, Nina turned off the last of the lights downstairs and headed up. Instead of putting Jenny down in her crib, Nina carried her into the master bedroom and sat down in the chair in the front window. She glanced out, saw a light in Bruce's garage apartment turn on, and then she unbuttoned her blouse and raised the baby to her breast. In the dark, Nina felt the hot little body snuggled up to her, take hold and nurse.

Some ten minutes later Nina had burped Jenny and rocked her back to sleep, then placed her in the crib in the back bedroom. When Nina returned to her own darkened room, she looked out and saw that Bruce's light had gone off. There was no sign of life across the street at the funeral home, either.

Wood scraped against wood, a deep screech as a layer of splinters rubbed together. Floorboards. Nina's eyes rolled open like window shades sprung loose. Was that a footstep on the hardwood floor? Was someone in the house?

She rolled her head to the side, glanced back at the digital clock on the bedside table. Three thirty-three, and she was still lying on the bed fully dressed, just where she'd dropped herself hours earlier.

She sat up and looked around. So what had she heard? Something from outside? She glanced into the summer night, saw only the street lights, heard only a lone, distant car. No. Whatever had awakened her had come from inside. Or had she been dreaming?

Then she heard it again. She froze, listening to the long, slow squeak of the wood floor as someone walked across it. But it was so close. Nina spun from side to side. Jesus Christ, she thought, someone's in my bedroom!

But there was no one. Confused, she started to get up when the sound came again. She looked at the floor. There, by the chair. The intercom. That's what it was. She'd left the transmitter on downstairs and the noise was being broadcast up here. An intruder was walking carefully through her house and the sound he or she was making was being picked up by the intercom.

Nina was on her feet instantly. The baby. Nina grabbed the intercom receiver and started out of her room as quietly as she could. She dialed up the volume, pressed the speaker to her ear. Nothing but crackling. That meant whoever was here had either left . . . or was in some other part of the house, away from the intercom.

She paused at her bedroom door and peered down the hallway. The shadows seemed solid, not made of living flesh and bone. She took a step. Another. The stairs looked empty. But what if the intruder had a knife or a gun? Christ, he could bolt up the stairs, slam her against the wall.

She moved a little more. The air held a deep, musty scent. Up on the left the door to the empty bedroom was open. Could someone have snuck in there, could someone be lurking?

Suddenly something cold and sharp dragged across the back of her neck.

"Ah!"

She jumped forward, swung her fist around, saw it was only the chain to the overhead light. Catching her breath, Nina peered into the empty bedroom, saw no one but again smelled something heavy and coarse. Then she turned slowly around toward Jenny's bedroom and saw something far worse.

"Oh, my God!"

The soft beams of a nightlight illuminated the front of Jenny's room, and Nina was able to see what looked like steam dancing on the floor. It rose through the cracks in the wood, swirled and wound itself upward. But that wasn't steam. It was smoke.

"Jenny!" screamed Nina, throwing the intercom to the floor.

She bolted forward, hurling the door to Jenny's room open. There was smoke up to Nina's knees, rising through the floorboards from the kitchen below. Yes, that's where it came from. From the kitchen.

"Jenny!" cried Nina again.

At the sharp pierce of her mother's voice, the child woke up in terror. The baby's lungs emptied themselves in a long, shrill cry. And Nina was glad. She was glad her baby could scream and shriek, and Nina grabbed Jenny out of the crib, turned and ran through the hall, and down the front steps two at a time.

At the bottom of the stairs, Jenny looked around, saw

no intruder, and assumed that it was the sounds of the fire she'd heard over the intercom. She looked back through the dining room and in the kitchen saw yellow and red flames slithering up the walls, gobbling everything they could. Clutching Jenny, Nina cut through the smoke toward the phone in the den. She dialed the operator, screamed her address and the emergency, then turned and jogged to the front door.

The smoke was thinner up here, not bad at all. She unlocked the door, grabbed Jenny's car seat and ran out on the porch. Outside the night was deathly at peace and every single house on the block was black with sleep.

She glanced back inside and saw the flames growing stronger and brighter. Everything that was left of her family was there inside the brittle, dry walls of this Victorian house. Fearful that the fire department would be too long in getting here, she strapped Jenny in the car seat and rushed her down to the car. Quickly but carefully, she placed Jenny in the front seat, rolled down the window and then went back into the burning house. The former owners had left a fire extinguisher near the entrance to the kitchen, but Nina hadn't noticed it in weeks. Was it still there? Did it contain anything?

Every few feet Nina glanced back through the entry hall and out the front door at the car. As the smoke grew thicker, she lifted up her sleeve and covered her mouth. Passing through the dining room, she reached the edge of the kitchen, and in the reddish, gray light that filled the room, saw the fire extinguisher. She grabbed the canister and instantly her hands burned with heat and fire. She dropped it on the floor, turned, yanked the table cloth from the dinner table and wrapped it around the tank.

The spray came out of the black nozzle in big white clouds, spitting and sputtering over the fire. Standing on the edge of the kitchen, Nina shot fire retardant on the breakfast table, the blue curtains that were nearly devoured by flames and on the cabinets that smoldered alternately black and yellow. Wallpaper curled up in great big sheets, then caught fire and disintegrated into smoke.

Panicking, Nina sprayed foam over the stove and across and up the walls. Then the canister began to spit and sputter. Fifteen seconds later there was a burst of air. The thing went dry. Nina shook it. Nothing.

She turned and out the front door saw the street flashing red and yellow and heard the screaming cries of a siren. Dropping the fire extinguisher, Nina started out, but just as quickly stopped. The entire house could go, but she wanted just one thing. The photo album. The one that held the last pictures of Alex's last year. No one else had any copies of these. There were even a couple of Alex kissing Nina's very pregnant stomach; she had to save those for Jenny.

She spun around and dashed into the den. From the desk she snatched the red leather photo album. As she again started out, however, Nina saw that one of the two windows was halfway open. She glanced down at the intercom that sat on the floor, then heard the rumbling of steps charging up the front porch.

Coughing on smoke, Nina stumbled outside, made her way down to the car, took Jenny and made her way across the street. As the firefighters extinguished the blaze and as her sleepy neighborhood poured into the street to observe the tragedy, Nina thought not of fire or the damage or their near deaths. Rather, she thought of that window in the den, certain that she had closed it earlier that evening when she'd put Jenny down to sleep.

A hand came up around her. "My God, are you all right?"

Nina looked at Bruce and said, "I don't know."

# 22

Morton gazed across the large room, the very heart of the hospital morgue, and saw a woman so short that she needed a footstool to perform her work. He cleared his throat with a coarse cough, and she paused in the midst of the autopsy and looked his way. Her face blanched as she realized who he was, and she set down her knife, stepped from her stool and stormed his way. She held her rubber-gloved hands—red beads of moisture on the tips—stiff and still and away from her body as if they were plaster casts attached to her diminutive torso. Across her green apron were slashed red, modern artlike streaks of blood.

Morton shifted from foot to foot. "I need to talk to you."

"You shouldn't be here," said Dr. Irene Volker, her voice stern and the wrinkles in her face tight.

"I know that. But it's very important. Besides, it looks official."

She hesitated, then sighed, "Go into my office. I'll be right there."

Glad, at least for a moment, to be told exactly what to do, Morton left the main room and proceeded to her office, where he settled his lanky frame in a chair. He was so tired. He hadn't been able to sleep at all last night.

What had they gotten themselves into? Anxiously he rubbed his long face, ran his hand through his very thin hair. Things had gone from bad to worse to terrible. This shouldn't be like this. It all should be progressing smoothly. They'd spent so much time hammering out the exact details and . . .

He heard voices in the hall and froze, holding his breath. It wasn't the police, was it? No, of course not. Just don't panic, he told himself. Don't panic. There still might be a way.

"There's some problem with a death certificate," said Dr. Volker to one of her assistants in the hall. Her voice was as big as ever, reaching out and way beyond her small stature. "Mr. Morton from the funeral home is here—I just have to fill out a new certificate and I'll be right with you."

Morton sat still as Volker, having shed her rubber gloves and green gown, came in and carefully shut the door. He stared at her, this woman with the fine wrinkles and the auburn hair that was glossed with gray. For fifty years they'd known one another, and he was still attracted to her.

"I'm sorry, Irene."

"Dundeen would be very disturbed if he knew you were here. I wish you hadn't come," she said as she proceeded around her desk and sat down. "I wish—"

"It's an emergency. It didn't go right."

"What happened? Where's Mikey, John? He's all right, isn't he? Dear God, nothing happened to him, did it?"

"No, he's okay. He's in the car. He'll be fine for a few minutes." Morton shook his head, rubbed his brow, then whispered, "There was a fire—but they got out. Now what? What if she suspects something? What if—"

"Calm down. Just tell me what you know."

He closed his eyes and rubbed his worn face. He'd been

awake, of course, worrying about it all and whether or not it would be successful. Then he'd heard all the commotion and . . . and . . .

"There was a fire. It . . . it started in the kitchen. She caught it early somehow. She even managed to put some of the flames out herself. One of the neighbors told me the only real damage was to the kitchen itself. She and the baby are fine."

Morton looked up from wrenching his hands. Irene was there, calm, pensive, as calculating as ever. Wasn't that, he wondered, how she had been when she decided to leave town for medical school some forty-five years ago? Always so rational. The best education, that was what she was after. And she'd found it, too, entirely at the expense of their relationship. Perhaps some of it had had to do with their age difference—seven years—perhaps she just couldn't make the commitment he'd wanted back then. Whatever the reason, he'd taken it as rejection. By the time she'd decided to return to her hometown over a decade later, he'd already given up and married someone else.

"Well, you weren't right there, were you?" she asked, and glanced toward her door to make sure no one was lingering.

"No, of course not. Not when it happened. I was in bed."

"Did you hear any sirens?"

"Certainly. That's what got me up. Then Mikey and I came running out in our bathrobes, just like everyone else in the neighborhood. She looked over and saw me, too."

"Well, she can't possibly suspect you."

Morton twisted in his chair. "No, I suppose not. Not directly at least. But . . . but we can't leave a loose end like this. We just can't."

She nodded, her expression as serious as a smooth lake

before a storm. "Of course we can't. I spoke with Dundeen just yesterday, and he feels the same. He wants this taken care of right away."

"We have no other choice." He shook his head. "It wasn't supposed to become ugly like this—destroying innocent people. I just wanted to help Mikey. Help find a cure. But look at what I had to do to her husband and now . . . now . . ."

"John, we both knew the risks. And we've both waited too long." She gazed across the table. "I don't think we can put this off, do you?"

"No. Absolutely not. We have to finish what we've started. It would be too dangerous otherwise."

He folded and twisted his hands together. There was just so little time for their lives, their hopes. Most importantly, all the while this thing was eating away at poor Mikey. There was no other way. They had to act at once to protect themselves.

"Then you'll get it started?" he asked. "It just makes me so nervous."

"I'll talk to Marcel."

"Good."

He reached forward, stretching his gnarled hand across her desk. She jerked herself back.

"John, no."

"But . . ."

"No. Not here."

He pulled back, closed his eyes. Now that it was growing close, he could barely stand the wait. Once the three of them were in Mexico—Irene, Mikey and he— once all of this was far behind him, then life indeed would be good. Not only would they have a drug that would protect Mikey, but Morton would have corrected a mistake of a lifetime. If only Irene hadn't left town so very many years ago, if only he'd have waited just a bit longer . . .

"Irene . . . I love you."

She nodded. "Soon."

Saying nothing else, John Morton grabbed the arms of his chair and raised himself to his feet. He was just so tired, his body so stiff. He stopped at the door, his hand on the knob, and turned slowly.

"Do you know how he'll do it?" asked Morton, dreading any more shocks.

Irene Volker stared at him. "She only has one vulnerable point left."

Right, thought Morton, letting himself out of the basement office, then heading for the elevator. And they had but one option.

# Chapter

# 23

Nina inhaled, the dead scent of fire and smoke filling her lungs. Had this really happened? It barely registered that again flashing lights and screaming sirens had charged through the night to a tragedy that had vexed her life. Stunned by the sight before her, Nina stood in the dining room, staring at what ten hours earlier had been a pleasant, slightly run-down kitchen . . .

She glanced at the cabinets that hung charred and blackened, at the countertops that sat shattered like cracked windowpane. The walls were entirely black except in a few places where the paint had blistered into brownish scabs. Hearing a steady drip, Nina gazed upward at water that oozed from the bubbly-black ceiling. The firefighters, wanting to be certain that there were no smoldering boards that could reignite, had drenched the back of the house with a swimming pool's worth of water. Most of that, of course, ended up in the basement, and Nina dreaded facing the sea of things floating down there.

Her eyes fell to the kitchen windowsill where a lone, undisturbed banana sat, its black color making it appear as if it were the perfect ripeness for use in a banana bread recipe. With the window behind the piece of fruit entirely knocked out—as were all the windows in the kitchen and Jenny's room above—the scene was all the more odd.

"I can't believe this. Oh, God. I just can't believe this."

Thank God they'd made it out in time. "What a mess. What a complete mess."

In the dining room, Bruce unfolded a huge role of heavy plastic. It was Saturday, and he showed no sign of doing anything but helping her.

"Yeah," he said, "but you're alive, and it's only the back of the house."

Leaning against the smoky door frame, Nina clutched a fist to her mouth and tried to block the huge sob that was rising from her stomach. Eyes closed, she thought she was going to collapse, right here, into a puddle of misery. This . . . this was too much. But then an arm wrapped around her waist and steadied her. No, don't, she thought to herself. Don't lean on him. Don't grow to depend on anyone ever again.

"Are you all right?" asked Bruce.

"No. No . . . I'm not."

First a small cry bubbled out of her mouth, then a long deep one. She slumped her body against his. This was her life. Charred, dampened, smashed. Ruined. All of Nina's strength ran away, and she fell into him, sobbing against his chest. Bruce was the only thing that kept her upright, and her body shook as all the frustrations and hurt came rushing out of her eyes and mouth. Then she tried to mutter something, but it came out a garbled mess of tears and sobs. She attempted the words again.

"Th-thank God J-Jenny's all . . . all right."

"Right. She's fine. She's next door at Mrs. Larson's taking a nap and she's just fine."

But suppose she hadn't woken? Suppose she hadn't gotten her baby out in time? The thoughts flashed through her mind, and she cried all the harder out of fear of what might have happened.

And then she stopped.

She pushed herself away from Bruce, wiped her nose

and eyes. That was it. No more. Whatever you do, don't fall apart, she told herself. There was Jenny, her father. She took a deep, unsteady breath. The kitchen was ruined but Jenny's room was only smoke damaged.

"I think the smell will come out of most of Jenny's things, but this," said Nina, peering into the kitchen, "is a real dump. It'll have to be gutted."

"Look on the bright side. Your insurance will pay for a new kitchen, and at least it's summer and you can have the windows open." Bruce turned back to the dining room table. "I got the plastic up on Jenny's door upstairs. Let's get what you want out of the kitchen, then put the plastic on this door and get out of here. You must be exhausted."

Yes, she was, Nina thought. Exhausted, almost to the point of hallucinating. She'd only dozed those few hours after Bruce had left and before the fire. Then the fire department and, it seemed, the whole neighborhood had been there for hours, first extinguishing the blaze, next staying to make sure there were no further problems. By then it was dawn, and Anna Larson, the grandmotherly woman next door, brought over coffee and muffins and took Jenny to her house for a nap. The insurance investigator was out there by nine, anxious to check the scene before anything was disturbed. He was thorough, too, checking the kitchen wiring, searching for cigarette butts, asking about oily rags. He took every measurement of the house that could be taken, and inspected the rear of the house from the basement to the kitchen and on up to Jenny's bedroom, which was lined with great streaks of black smoke.

Finally with an initial damage report and a partial listing of damaged goods, he left, saying, "You can't always say for sure, but the fire marshal and I both suspect the toaster."

"The what?" Nina had said. "You must be kidding. That thing can barely brown a bagel."

"Well, it must have had faulty wiring. What I suspect," said the large man with the billowy eyebrows, "is that one of the elements heated up and caught the paper towels above it on fire. You know, you should never have had them so close together."

"But I didn't. The toaster was by the refrigerator and—"

"Well, you better look again because it's sure not there now."

"But—"

Shocked by his words, she dashed into the kitchen. Looking like the burnt ruins of an airplane, the toaster was right where he said it was, right beneath the melted plastic paper towel holder. Once that was pointed out, she could see how the investigator had reached his conclusion. The counter, the cabinet and everything nearby were the deepest black, the deepest charred.

Fifteen minutes later, Nina and Bruce had the plastic in place over the doorway, thumbtacked, then taped, in an effort to seal off the kitchen. They had salvaged a few cans of tuna fish, a jar of peanut butter and a handful of canned vegetables, placing all of these in a stack on the dining room table. Though they were smoky, Nina had also brought out some glasses and dishes, cups and flatware.

Next, they went around the house opening windows, and a gentle summer breeze flowed through and began to clear away the heaviest of the odor. In the den, Nina stood staring at the two windows. One of them, the one she was certain she'd closed when she'd put Jenny down last night, was still cracked open.

Bruce came in and nudged her. "Nina, you need sleep."

She couldn't move. She couldn't stop staring at the

open window. Nor could she stop thinking about the placement of the toaster beneath the paper towels. And the noise. What about the noise? Just what had she heard over the intercom?

"Nina, come on, let's get Jenny and head back to my place. You really need to lie down."

"Yeah, sure."

Overwhelmed and confused, she let Bruce lead her out and down the front steps, the bright, fresh morning as sharp as vinegar on her senses. Wordlessly, they went to Mrs. Larson's next door, where they collected the sleeping Jenny, her portable crib and two grocery bags full of freshly laundered baby clothes. The three of them headed off like a normal family, Bruce cradling Jenny in one arm and a bag in the other, Nina carrying the collapsible crib.

"I almost feel like we're coming back from a picnic," said Bruce, as they shuffled across the street toward his apartment.

"I wish," sighed Nina, looping her free hand in the crux of Bruce's arm.

They proceeded directly across the parking lot of the funeral home, and Nina didn't care whether or not Morton saw them. If he was even interested in her and Bruce's relationship, there'd been ample evidence all morning.

Bruce's apartment was a rustic place built over a garage behind a large dark-brown house. Coming up the old wooden stairs attached to the side of the garage, they entered a medium-sized room with heavy pine paneling that had darkened over the years. Old, tattered furniture filled the place, making it look like a lake cottage. Windows lined three sides of the living room and looked out toward the rear of the funeral home. The middle of the living room was broken by a bar-height counter, with a small galley kitchen behind that. Nina glanced down a narrow hall and saw the bedroom and bath.

Some fifteen minutes later, Nina had fed Jenny and put her down in her crib in Bruce's bedroom. She came out, the exhaustion eating at her like a bad hangover, and found Bruce's long body sprawled out on the couch, his feet dangling over the end. She glanced at him and sensed her heart tense and release.

"You must be tired, too," she said, steering herself toward a chair. "Thank you so much. I don't know what I would have done without you."

He raised a hand toward her. "This way. Come on over here."

"What?"

"What do you mean, what?" He stretched his hand farther. "Come on and sit down by me."

She froze and glanced out the row of windows and into the bright day. God, she still felt married. Yes. That was it. So many years with Alex.

"If you want me to spell it out I will," said Bruce. "I just want to hold you. It would be nice."

Yes, it would be, she thought. After all this time, after all these traumas, it would be nice to have something other than cotton or wool warming her shoulders. Still, it was much easier to stay just where she stood, easier still would be to cross the room to that ratty chair.

"Nina . . ."

She took several steps forward and then his hand closed around hers. She felt him gently pull down on her arm, and then things began to fall away. Alex retreated to the shadows of her memory, if only briefly.

"Bruce, I—"

"Shh. Can I spoon you?"

She grinned. "Sure."

That's what Alex had called it, too, lying side by side, closely pressed together like a pair of friendly old spoons. It was all the encouragement she needed. She slumped down, stretched out on her side next to Bruce, her back to him. He nudged a pillow under her head, then wrapped an arm around her stomach, tucking his fingers beneath her.

"Comfortable?" he asked.

"Uh-huh."

"It's not so bad, is it?"

"No. Not at all. It's nice."

It was actually very nice, she thought. It felt so good just to be so close to someone. Then suddenly a sob began to rock her body. Just as quickly she caught it. Don't give way, she thought. Not yet at least, because if you do you're never going to get up again.

Bruce kissed her, his firm lips pressing against her neck. "I like you, Nina."

She reached over and patted him. "Thanks. I . . ."

There was more she wanted to say, but couldn't. Not now, not yet. Still, she was glad to be so close to him as she drifted away into a soft sleep.

Nina woke to the sound of water splashing against a wall. Still lying on her side, Nina opened her eyes and peered around the room and searched the dark pine panels for some meaning. The sun streaked into the room at a high angle. What time was it? Where was she?

The shower stopped and she rolled on her back and pulled up a cotton blanket. Down the hall she saw Bruce step carefully out of the bathroom, naked except for a white towel around his narrow waist.

"I'm dressed and you're not," she said. "Did I miss something?"

He glanced into the bedroom where Jenny still slept, then moved into the living room.

Smiling he said, "Unfortunately, no."

"Oh. What time is it?"

"Just after one."

She shook her head. "I can't believe it. I haven't slept so soundly in months. You're a good sleep, Bruce."

He laughed. "Gee, thanks."

Her eyes followed Bruce as he crossed the edge of the living room and ducked behind the kitchen bar. Admiring his thick chest and long arms, she watched as he, half-hidden behind the counter, started to dress.

Pulling on his jeans, Bruce said, "Jenny woke up about a half hour ago."

The baby, thought Nina, bolting upright. "Is she all—"

"Don't worry. She's just fine. I changed her and she's back there in her crib hanging out with a rattle."

"Oh."

Nina swung her legs to the floor. She really must have been out; never before had she slept through one of Jenny's cries. Particularly after last night, Nina never could again. Never.

"I'd better check on her."

Bruce looked over the kitchen bar as he buttoned his shirt. "Hey, relax. She'll screech when she needs you."

Against her own judgment, she sat back down. Even so, the tension that had seeped away now came rushing in, filling her pores like a fast-rising tide. With startling clarity, she recalled it all. The footsteps. The toaster. The fire. Damn it all, what was happening? Who was—

"So what is it?" asked Bruce. "Is there something I don't know?"

"What? No. Nothing," she brusquely said.

"But what's—"

"Bruce, this isn't the time for an interview."

Wanting to block him out, she bowed her head and covered her ears. A bomb of anger, she thought. That's all she was. A mad bomb eager to explode, to vent itself of its pent up fury. There was so much ruined around her, but who could she get mad at? A baby who couldn't understand? A demented father whose mind was shrinking to an infant's level? A junior journalist?

Nina looked up and saw Bruce, his back to her,

standing at the window. Oh, great, she thought. Just slow down. Take it easy.

"Bruce . . . I'm sorry," she said, rising.

"That's all right."

She was the one who broke the boundary, traversing the small living room that seemed so broad, skirting the coffee table that was so awkwardly placed. Without hesitation, she went up behind Bruce and wrapped her arms around him.

"I'm sorry. Really, I am."

As she held him, he spun in her arms, and she kissed him on the chest, on the neck, on the cheek. She felt his hands and arms rise up and around her, and pressed herself into him. Their mouths met, lips that weren't the least bit frightened, but sure and confident and eager. Although Nina couldn't make sense of the world around her, this, she felt, was right. Completely right.

The baby began to cry.

"Shit," laughed Nina.

"My wife tried to claim the reason we didn't have sex more often was because of the kids." Bruce rubbed his hands up and down her back. "I think she just hated me."

Nina parted his shirt and kissed the hairs on his chest. "She must have been crazy."

"Still is, if you ask me."

Nina broke away, retreating to the back bedroom and taking the baby in her arms. Once she'd nursed Jenny, she came back out, child in arm and ready to tell Bruce.

"You're right. There's something you don't know," she began.

Her eyes ran over the dark wooden walls of the garage apartment. She glanced out the window, then dropped herself onto the ragged couch across from him. Balancing Jenny on her knees, she told Bruce about the noises she'd heard over the intercom and about the open window she was sure she'd closed.

"And that stupid toaster—I sure as hell didn't move it," she said. "I *always* kept it by the refrigerator."

"Yeah, but—"

"I know. The fire marshal found it all the way over at the other end of the counter, beneath the paper towels. But I didn't put it there. I never would have. Never."

"Oh, man . . ."

Her own words firming her suspicion, Nina said, "Someone snuck in and started that fire, didn't they?"

Bruce spent a long time pondering his hands. "Maybe."

It was a gentle way of saying probably, and Nina knew it. And she was also aware there was nothing they could do. It looked like a common kitchen fire to both the fire marshal and the insurance investigator. This was just like Alex's death, she thought. A tragedy with an entirely simple and natural explanation that just didn't make sense—to her.

"We have absolutely no evidence that there's been any kind of wrong-doing," said Nina.

Bruce puckered up his lips so that the ends of his moustache curled into his mouth, then said, "What's worse is we don't even have a motive. I mean, why would someone want to set your house on fire? What would that keep you from discovering? Are we that close and don't know it?"

"I . . ." Her eyes closed and she shuddered. "I don't know. Maybe it's like what you said. Maybe Morton has a deal on the side. Maybe he's getting the bodies from the hospital and . . ."

"It has to be something like that. You just saw Volker yesterday, and now this. You must have hit some kind of raw nerve."

Her face tensed with distress. "All I really said was that there might be a lawsuit and . . . and that Alex's body might have to be exhumed."

He stared at her, then finally said, "I hate to suggest

this, Nina, but it seems someone wants to stop you from doing just that."

Her stomach suddenly turned sour. "I . . . suppose. But—"

"Nina, where's Alex buried?"

"At Riverbluff Cemetery. You know, out on the edge of town."

"I think we'd better take a look, don't you?"

Full of dread, Nina said, "Yes."

It was, she thought, the only logical thing to do.

# 24

It took a day for Bruce to arrange it all. He spoke with a couple of guys out at the cemetery and set it up for the following evening. On the way out, Nina thought how good it was they were doing this. If she had seen Alex's body before, perhaps she wouldn't be having such a hard time letting go of him. If she had seen him lying there lifeless, then perhaps she could have believed in his death. In the end, that was the real reason she had agreed to go through with it. She'd never been able to visualize Alex as dead and hoped after tonight she'd be able to. She hoped it would offer her peace of mind as well as help explain some of the recent and odd occurrences.

Mourning, thought Nina. Perhaps that was the problem she was having with Alex's death. She'd never mourned him. Not really. But how could she? Alex had lain dead in the basement of the very same hospital where Nina had given birth to Jenny. And at the very same time. He was in the ground and buried before Nina could even walk. In an attempt to make it real, she'd tried over and over again to picture his body trapped in that coffin. What did he look like? Peaceful? Placid? Bland? Pale? Green?

"Nina," said Bruce behind the wheel of his Honda, "you don't have to be there."

"Yes, I do."

Bruce had already offered to go alone to the cemetery,

but Nina wouldn't let him. He'd said she could stay home with Jenny, but Nina wouldn't do that, either. She had to see for herself. She wanted the reality seared into her mind, branded there for the rest of her life.

Nina glanced out the car window, her eyes skipping over the still waters of the river, the bank of greenery on the other side, the blue twilight. It was a pleasant Sunday evening, and Nina was more sure than ever. She just wanted to discover the truth, then, yes, move on. Move into the future.

In the backseat, Nina noticed that Jenny was fast asleep, her head dropped to the side, one arm dangling in the air. Good, thought Nina. She's conked out. Maybe she'll sleep through this whole thing.

When they reached Riverbluff Cemetery—which had closed just an hour earlier—they were met by one of the groundskeepers. The young man swung open the gate, let them in, then jogged behind the Honda as Bruce steered toward a sloping stretch of earth. There, sticking up above the ground like a giant mechanical mosquito, was a large yellow excavator, its scoop ready to carve out the earth. Another man in jeans and jeans jacket stood alongside it.

Bruce stopped the engine. "One last time: Are you sure you—"

"Positive. I have to see for myself."

Leaving Jenny asleep in her car seat, Nina climbed out and walked directly up the hill. Bruce caught up with her and, as they neared the excavator, called out to the older man.

"This is Nina Trenton, the woman I spoke to you about," he said. "Uh, she was married to Mr. Hale."

"Pleased to meet you. I'm Tom Barlow and this is Chris Granger," he said, referring to the younger man. "I just want you to know that me and him . . ." He glanced away, his eyes following the pencil-line horizon for a long, even time. "Well, we haven't ever done anything like this before."

"I appreciate your help," said Nina.

Barlow looked at her with a directness that Midwesterners usually find impossible. "This is serious, you know. We'd really be in a mess if—"

"No one will find out. You can be done in an hour or so, can't you?"

"Sure, we can do it that fast. This is what we do all day." He glanced at his young partner, then scratched at the earth with a heavy boot. "But that's not quite what I—"

"So there you go." Cutting him off, Nina reached into her pocket and pulled out a roll of hundred dollar bills. "I'm willing to pay three hundred each if you start right away. You see, if we were to do this officially, it would take weeks or maybe months. And I've got to know much sooner than that. I'm very impatient and I'm willing to pay because of that." She took a deep breath and clenched her fists. Just keep it together, she thought. Just keep it together. "What do you say?"

Barlow glanced back at the young Granger, who bowed his head and rubbed his mouth to hide a grin.

Barlow turned and slowly said, "We'll get to work right now. Won't take too long."

"Ah, well, good," said Bruce. "We'll just wait down by the car."

Nina turned and started down the slope. Behind her, she heard the diesel engine of the excavator chug to a roaring start.

"Jesus, Nina," said Bruce, catching up with her and placing his hand on her elbow, "that's a lot of money. I told them a hundred each. They would have done it for that, too."

"I don't care. I just want them to do it and do it fast."

Without another word, Nina went directly to the car, checked on the still-sleeping Jenny, then leaned against the front fender. A moment later she felt Bruce's arm on her shoulder. She shrugged it off, and they watched in silence as the two men started to carve the coffin from the damp Wisconsin ground. Just hurry, thought Nina, I want to get this over with.

But the time dragged. The excavator seemed slow, an old, out-dated monster that grudgingly clawed the earth over and over again. Clods of dirt were pulled into the air, then plopped to the side. The diesel engine churned, strained as the machine dug a little deeper each time, a little closer to the mystery of Alex's death.

Finally the steel tip of the machine's claw scraped along concrete, a sound like monstrous fingernails upon a blackboard. Nina shivered, wrapped her arms more tightly around her waist. They were very near now. She leaned against the car's hood. Very near, for they had reached the concrete burial vault in which lay Alex's coffin. She was well aware of the vault. The month after her husband's death she had stumbled across the materials from the funeral home. Included in the papers was a color pamphlet showing that not only did the vault keep the earth above from sagging, but it also kept out moisture, thereby preventing the coffin from floating in a pool of water. In simpler terms, the body of Alex, Nina could be assured, was dry.

Nina took a step forward and Bruce caught her by the arm.

"Not quite yet," he said.

Paying him no attention, she twisted her arm free, brushed her hair out of her face and marched forward. Tom Barlow, at the controls of the machine, took one more scoop of earth and dumped it to the side. No sooner had he quieted the belchy diesel, than Chris Granger jumped into the hole, stood on top of the vault itself and pulled a shovel in behind him. Nina marched on like a numbed soldier about to meet her fate.

Alex? Alex, can you hear me? she called in her mind. I'm here, above. Are you there? Her mind went blank, stayed blank, remained open, but nothing came back. It startled her, this emptiness.

Bruce stood behind her, close but not too close and definitely not touching her. Her lungs in a tight mass, Nina barely breathed as she watched the young Granger shovel away the last of the dirt. Why is this taking so long, she thought. A small shovel full of dirt flew up, spread in the air, then landed to the side. Then another. Fifteen or twenty at least.

Bit by bit the brown dirt gave way to gray concrete and the large rectangular shape of the vault. Pushing the shovel in front of him as if it were a large broom, Granger walked back and forth over the vault and gathered the last of the dirt. He tossed that up and out along with the shovel itself. Without a cue or even a look, Tom Barlow immediately lowered a pickax from above. Granger took that and jammed it into the tar seal that connected the flat top to the box itself. Rocking the long wooden handle of the ax, Granger worked his way around until the seal was broken.

Nina gasped audibly when the lid moved. Tom Barlow glanced over, then slid down through the dirt, a second pickax in his hands. Together the two men edged in the tools, then began to pry. In a matter of seconds, one side of the top began to rise.

"Nina," said Bruce, his voice low and from behind.

She needed no further encouragement. Turning around, she grasped Bruce by one arm. He moved closer as if to hug her, but she pushed him away. Just a crutch, that's all she wanted. A little support and nothing more. Christ, she thought, here I am digging up my husband's coffin,

Bruce close by my side. She felt nauseated with guilt. What right had she to be living? Why couldn't she be dead, too?

"Bruce . . . just tell me what you see."

"Sure. Anything you say."

She flinched as something soft tore, something hard scraped. The ground quivered with a heavy thud.

"They just flipped back the top of the vault," came Bruce's soft voice. "They dropped it to the side. It won't be too long now."

Nina sucked the life into her, filling her lungs with air. She wanted to run away crying and screaming, kicking, shouting, tearing her hair. Oh, God, what was he going to look like?

The two men grunted behind her. She stiffened. Was that the coffin? She started to turn around.

Bruce stopped her, "Not yet."

Half turned, she froze. She swallowed, or at least tried to, as her head began to pound. Would everything she had been trying to deny now become a reality? God, what would he look like? Would she even be able to recognize him? Would these months have worn on his embalmed body as much as it had on her living one?

She heard groaning and movement from the grave, and asked, "Is it open?"

"Yes."

Turning around, Nina couldn't see into the very bottom of the grave. Automatically, she searched the faces of Tom Barlow and Chris Granger, who stood in the hole, leaning against their shovels, their heads bowed. From their lack of reaction, she understood at once. Alex was in there and had been in there the entire time. She took a step over. She had to see. It was either that or a lifetime of regret.

"Hold me, please," she asked Bruce. Yes, it was time for that now.

His long arm wrapped around her back, around her waist. She leaned into him and moved forward. Her eyes were wet—how that had happened she didn't know. Her body was shaking.

Where the grass was cut to dirt, where the dirt was cut into a hole, she first saw the gray sides of the vault, then the dark wooden coffin. Finally in the box itself, feet. Brown shoes, actually. Wing tips. And brown pants.

"Ah . . ." she whimpered, then stumbled slightly.

So he was dead. He was really dead. And there he lay. Now she knew the truth, now she had to . . .

She froze. Whose shoes were those? Not Alex's. Certainly not. He hated wing tips, refused to own a pair. Joked about them. And those pants, where did they come from? God, his parents didn't bury him in those, did they? They didn't go out and buy all new clothing for Alex? But they must have.

No, they hadn't. Alex's brother had told her what he'd taken to the funeral home. Sleek black Italian shoes and a navy-blue suit. Yes, Nina remembered. She was with Alex when he'd bought the suit at Marshall Field's.

Out of control, Nina lurched forward. A waist appeared, much too large. Was he bloated? And then an unfamiliar coat, a strange tie, and a chest that was too thick.

"No . . ." she cried.

She rushed to the very edge of the grave and peered down at the chalky gray face of a man nearly her father's age. The cheeks were swollen and wide, the scalp mostly bald. This was a dead man but . . .

She screamed, "No! No, that's—"

Before she could finish, she was gripped and spun around, her sobbing face pushed hard into Bruce's chest. She tried to resist, to pull away, but his strength overpowered her horror.

"Thank you," called Bruce to the two men.

He began dragging her away and she began beating on him. She opened her mouth to scream out the truth and he wrapped his palm over her face. She kicked, cried. No, this can't be, this can't be! Christ, listen to me! Something terrible has happened!

"Stop it!" he shouted in her ear. "We can't let those two know!"

She grabbed his hand and ripped it from her mouth. What was happening? What had happened?

"Bruce—"

"I know, I know. But we can't tell anyone. Not yet. We have to—"

"Bruce," she sobbed, horrified by the sight of the dead stranger in the coffin, "where's my husband? Where's Alex?"

# 25

It was decided that he and Mikey should leave at once. But there was so much to do and no time. No time at all. They should be on the way by now, never to return. Yet while most of what they could take was already in the car, there was more to pack. Just a bit more, and then they had to be out of here. Now. Right away.

Oh, thought John Morton, trembling, I didn't want it to end like this. I didn't want to have to run out of town. I wanted to sell this place, have a nice estate sale, pack the special things and then move on. I wanted to close this chapter of my life without this pressure. I wanted to bid farewell to those I've known for years and years—many for over half a century. I wanted to have the drug for Mikey and then leave—Mikey, Irene and I. Instead I'm being run out of town. Instead I'm being forced to escape.

"Daddy, where bike?" asked Mikey, the small brown eyes staring up from a frightened face.

"In the garage."

"Oh."

Morton said, "But, Mikey, we don't have time for that now. Go back and watch TV like I told you."

The young man turned and headed back to the living room, where the television blared with some soap opera. Poor boy, Morton thought. He has no idea what's taking place, that they would now be lucky if they made it away safely.

Morton went to a closet, pulled out the last suitcase, and laid it out on the bed. Then he went down his dresser drawer by drawer, and pulled out socks, underwear, T-shirts. From the top of the dresser he took a picture, one of his wife taken some twenty-five years ago, and wrapped a T-shirt around it. That's just about it, he thought, packing the photo. Just about everything.

Suddenly he sensed a figure hovering right behind him. He spun around. Mikey stood there, biting his lower lip and rubbing his hand over his chest.

"Mikey!" shouted Morton. "You've been following me around like a dog all morning!"

The young man glanced away, then back. His hand rubbed the left side of his chest, stroke after stroke after stroke. His eyes bounced from side to side as if he were watching an imaginary tennis match.

"Where bike?"

"For the hundredth time, it's in the garage!" Morton reached out and pulled Mikey's hand from his chest. "And how many times do I have to tell you not to rub yourself like that!"

Mikey's lower lip rose and swelled out. His eyes fell to the floor and he started twisting from side to side.

Oh, thought Morton, now I've done it. But I've no time for this. They should have left half an hour ago.

"Listen, Mikey, we're going on a long trip, a very long trip. Do you understand?"

He frowned. "Bike?"

"It's in the garage by the car." He reached out and touched the boy. "We'll put it in the trunk and take it with us."

"Good," Mikey pronounced.

Morton closed the suitcase. "You can take this downstairs now."

Eager to help, Mikey grabbed the suitcase with both hands, dragged it off the bed and headed out of the room.

Morton shook his head. Mikey was like a thermometer, picking up exactly on Morton's mood. If he was happy, Mikey was happy. If he was sad, Mikey was sad, too. But the worst was today. Whenever Morton was nervous and anxious, Mikey not only gleaned that automatically, but magnified those emotions tenfold. Anything that negatively affected the atmosphere of the household would put the boy in a tizzy.

Moving his tall, lanky frame from his room to Mikey's bedroom to the living room, Morton was filled with sadness. There was Mikey's bed, Mikey's toys, his wife's mother's china, a high school trophy for a track event Morton had won in the thirties. Yes, and there was the TV and the big old chair he loved to sit in while he and Mikey, curled up on the floor, watched their favorite programs. So much of his life would be left behind. Abandoning virtually everything except warm-weather clothes and a few pictures, it appeared more as if Mikey and his father were simply leaving for a long weekend.

Stop filling yourself full of regrets, Morton told himself. There would be time for those later. Now it was just important to get away, to make this first step on their trip to Mexico. And at least they were doing just that, getting away in time. Perhaps there was still hope for the drug. Maybe it could be sent later. Maybe there was still a chance to treat Mikey.

On the ground floor of the funeral home, Mikey and his father went through the entire building and closed all the curtains. Then they took the suitcase and headed to the back of the big yellow-brick structure. Yes, thought Morton, I should have sold it to that sorority. If only the neighbors hadn't objected so. If only . . .

No sooner had they stepped into the attached garage than Mikey bolted past Morton.

"Wait!" Morton shouted.

Mikey froze, then turned around. As his father laboriously unlocked the trunk of his big Oldsmobile, Mikey rocked from side to side. Then Morton loaded the last suitcase, made his way around the car and climbed in. Mikey started swaying faster and faster.

"Okay, Mikey," he called as he started up the engine.

The overhead motor kicked in and the door started to rise. Just as quickly, Mikey bolted for the door on the passenger side, jumped in, opened the glove compartment and snatched the remote control.

"Just wait, just wait," said Morton. "Don't push anything until we're outside."

Morton looked ahead into the daylight, into the broad, empty parking lot. There were no police cars, no team sent to arrest him, no TV camera crews. With a sigh of relief, he put the car into gear and started to roll out.

"Okay?" asked Mikey.

Morton glanced in the mirror and saw the end of the trunk emerge from the garage. "Okay, now."

Biting his tongue, Mikey began to push the button on the remote control over and over. Behind him, the garage door began to jiggle, then slide back down. Then stop. Then raise. Then start down again.

"Just hit it once!" ordered his father.

The door cranked its way down, and Mikey began to giggle. Giggle just as if this were the first time he'd done this, not the hundredth.

"Off we go," sighed Morton.

Morton pulled away from the funeral home, Mikey unaware that he'd never be returning to the only home he'd ever known.

"Bike?" asked Mikey.

Morton closed his eyes for an instant. Oh, damn, he thought. Should he go back? No, there wasn't time.

"Don't worry," he lied to his son, "it's in the trunk."

"Oh."

# Chapter

# 26

The miles from the cemetery passed like a slow, very bad dream from which Nina was struggling to wake but could not. The green hills, the placid dairy farms, the white cows with the haphazard black splotches. All this she saw. But was it real or was it an illusion? Certainly nothing was as it looked. She knew that for certain now. If you have learned one thing in life, she told herself, believe that, live by that. She thought of her father who looked so healthy but was so sick.

She sat in the back seat, stroking her baby's head, hugging her. Glancing up at Bruce, Nina saw his face stiff with thought, his hands tight on the wheel. Who was he? Why was he helping her? What did he want? Oh, she thought. Just my baby and I. That's all I want now. All I can trust and rely on.

She shivered in the warm air. Little bumps rose on her skin. What she always had feared was now true. Incredible. She felt the wind bursting in through the window, spreading lavishly across her face. She closed her eyes, tilted her head and let the rush of air brush her mind. Yes. She had known it all along. Alex was not buried in that grave. Never had been. So where was he? Was he even dead? Lord, alive? Alex alive? And who was that big man in Alex's coffin?

They rode in silence, neither Bruce nor she daring to

venture even the most minor hypothesis. She studied him again, saw him driving hard and heavy as if he were not steering on a wide road but on a fixed railway, so focused was his mind. She could practically see the ideas formulating in his head, sense him trying to construct the death of Alex.

But, really, why was Bruce here? A good story? Something shocking to write about? And what was she to do now? Where was she to turn? Why should they wait at all to tell anyone? Why couldn't they inform the authorities or even those two men back at the cemetery? Now there was proof at least that something criminal was taking place. A body was missing. Her husband's body. Oh, God, thought Nina. Could his fate in some way be more horrific than absolute death? This can't be, can't be . . .

The questions pounded her mind, and they scared her, for she felt that some great fissure within herself was about to rip open, to lead to many more cracks. And all of this, she knew, would cause great chunks of herself to then fall and crumble away, be torn apart, worn down and eventually reduced to shifting sands. This, she knew and feared, was her fate now.

She began to sob. Alex? Alex, where are you? Are you alive after all? Or dead and far away?

Bruce turned onto Leaf Street, and Nina saw the big red Victorian sticking up like some great ship. He passed her house, then pulled a U-turn, stopped and reached to turn off the motor.

"Don't," she said, wiping her eyes.

He looked back at her, his confusion more deep than ever. "But . . ."

"Please, I . . . I . . . just want a little time." She needed to be alone for a while. To fall apart. Hug her baby. Be scared. "Oh, God, I can't believe it."

"Nina, don't you think we should—"

"Bruce . . . I'll . . . I'll call you." She unbuckled Jenny

and lifted her up, then began pushing her way out. "I just . . ."

Clutching her baby in her arms and nuzzling her head against Jenny's, Nina slammed the car door and rushed off. She wanted nothing but escape. Escape from all this. This couldn't be true.

Making her way across the gray porch, she glanced back. Bruce was there, just sitting. His car sputtered but didn't move. Go away, she thought. Please. Just go. Can't you see I mean it?

Oh, God, Alex. Poor Alex.

She fumbled with her keys, crammed them into the lock, then left them dangling in the door as she burst inside. From the front hall, Nina went directly into the dining room and ran right into another horror. Water stains. Singed cans on the table. The heavy translucent plastic over the kitchen door. And that smoky smell. She cried, sucked in more air, felt the stale odor fill her lungs. The fire. Not even forty-eight hours ago.

"No!" she cried.

She spun, passed through the den and into the living room. Was there no escape? No relief? Her house charred, her father crumbling, her husband gone . . .

A board creaked. Nina stopped. Was someone here?

"Bruce?" she called, glancing into the front hall. "Bruce, is that you?"

When no response came, she crossed to the front window and saw an empty street. Bruce had left. How stupid. Why had she sent him away? She shouldn't be alone. She needed him, now wished he were here.

Jenny started shaking. She sucked in a couple of big gulps of air, her lower lip started quivering and then a deep howl came bellowing out. Nina hugged her, rocked her. Then she felt the baby's bottom. Warm, wet.

"Okay, okay, baby."

Diapers. Where were the diapers? Crying baby in arm, Nina went into the den. No. No big box of disposables. Without thinking, she headed toward the kitchen, passing through the dining room and . . .

I'm nuts, she thought, stopping in front of the plastic curtain. There was no extra box of diapers in the pantry. All that went up in smoke the other night. She raised her eyes. Now, where—

"Ah!" she screamed.

Just on the other side of the foggy plastic was a dark figure, the features wavy and obscure. Still and unflinching, the person stood staring at her. Oh, Christ, wondered Nina. Am I going crazy? Is that really someone or is this an hallucination?

The figure flinched, and Nina asked, "Who . . . who is that?"

The head flew back, the mouth opened. Dark skin. White teeth. A rolling laugh.

"It's me!" pronounced a man's voice.

Nina pressed Jenny closer to her chest and stepped back. She knew that voice, that odd accent.

The intruder said, "It's me, Marcel!"

Marcel? Who? Her mind strained, tripped. Marcel? The male nurse from her father's floor? Staring at the black outline of the man, she relaxed a bit. So she wasn't going crazy. So there really was someone. But . . .

"What . . . what are you doing here?" she asked.

He laughed again. "I came back to finish what I missed the other night."

Other night? What night? "Wha—"

From behind the plastic, he lunged forward. Abruptly a long blade stabbed through the folds of plastic and began slicing downward.

Leaping back, Nina shouted, "What in the hell are you doing?"

Marcel's smiling face poked through the hole. "The fire—it should have been much bigger. Know what I mean?"

Oh, God. Fire. What did he know about the fire? Unless . . .

Her thoughts stumbled, lurched. Fear started to pulse through her veins. All her big city instincts clicked into gear.

Sternly, Nina said, "I don't want you in here. Please . . . please leave!"

As easily as if he were unzipping a pair of jeans, his knife slid down through the plastic and all the way to the floor. Grinning, Marcel then jumped through the gaping hole.

"Leave? *Moi?* But I've only just arrived!" he pronounced, holding the knife high.

When he took his first step, Nina was on her way into the den. She darted to the phone on the table, picked up the receiver, dialed the operator. Just as quickly, though, she saw Marcel charge after her. Nina twisted to the side, shielding Jenny with her body. And then Nina heard it over the receiver. A voice.

"Opera—"

Marcel's knife came hurling through the air. Nina ducked and screamed. Jenny howled. But the knife wasn't aimed at either of them. Instead, it sliced through the telephone cord, then dug its blade into the wooden table top.

"Uh-oh!" laughed Marcel. "There's no one to call for help. Too bad!"

It all flashed before her. The fire. It was meant to kill her. Of course. And Marcel had set it. Somehow, too, Alex fit into this. Alex who was missing!

Rage taking over, Nina spun around, bashing a surprised Marcel in the face with the receiver. Blood splattered from his lip, he stumbled back. Was this one man, wondered Nina, responsible for all the ruin in her life? Yes! She was sure of it, and she felt a surge of animal anger shoot through her body.

"You?" she screamed. "You?"

As Marcel's hand tugged to get the knife from the table, she raised the receiver back again and bashed his knuckles. He cried out and his fingers popped off the handle. Alex. The fire. And now this blade . . . No, she wasn't giving in.

She screamed and hurled the pointed tip of her foot into Marcel's crotch. He cried out, fell back and Nina grabbed the knife, tearing it from the table top. Then she ran into the living room, howling baby in arm. Racing, Nina wedged Jenny between two pillows on the couch, then spun around. Knife tight in her fist, she started after him. Coughing for air, Marcel stumbled back into the dining room, grabbed a chair and lifted it in front of him.

"My . . . my," he said, forcing a smile over his bloodied mouth, "but this isn't a very nice welcome, is it?"

Nina stared at him, at his round black face. She had to find out. Here at last was someone who knew, who could tell her.

"What the hell is going on?" she demanded. "You know what happened to my husband, don't you?"

He clicked his tongue and puffed his face in an exaggerated frown. "Oh, yes. Of course I do. But you mustn't ask me things like that. No . . . no!"

"Tell me!"

She lunged forward, and he swung the chair at her. Wooden legs and dowels smashed into Nina's arm, hurled her to the side. She screamed, but her hand held tight on the knife. She had to get the truth!

"Ohhhh," goaded Marcel, rounding the dinner table. "You're so mad. You mustn't be so mad!"

With the table between them, Nina shouted, "Where's my husband!"

"Oh, no, no, madame. You don't understand. I mustn't tell you those secrets. I must kill you. And I will!"

From the table top he picked up the jar of salvaged peanut butter. Nina watched as he examined the singed label, then suddenly hurled it at her. The jar flew over her left shoulder and smashed into the wall.

"Oh, look, I made a mess!" giggled Marcel.

Blade held ahead of her, Nina charged around the table. He jabbed the chair at her, but Nina caught it by one leg. As she pulled on it, he grabbed a can of tuna from the table and threw that. It hit her on the forehead, metal digging into her head with a deep, painful thud. Dazed, Nina stumbled back, tried to focus, attempted to maintain her balance as Marcel threw another and yet another can at her. One struck her shoulder. The next her cheek. Pain exploded in her jaw, radiated through her head and a warm dribble of liquid curled down her face.

"Oh, did that hurt?" shouted Marcel. "I'm—"

"Ah!" she screamed, throwing herself into him.

The anger exploding out of her, Nina seized the chair and hurled it aside. With strength never tapped before, she lunged into him, plunging the knife deep into his left arm. Nina heard muscle and bone squish and scrape. Marcel screamed out and fell to the floor, the knife poking out of him. Nina leapt on top, grabbed at the handle sticking from his limb. As she tried to pull it free, his right fist came smashing into her chin. Nina tumbled to the side, batted her eyes heavily. She tried to push herself up off the floor. Don't pass out, she told herself. You can't. Jenny's in the other room. You can't . . .

A voice in the distance calmly called, "Nina?"

She tried to form his name. "B-Bruce!"

Steps trod her way, at first slow, then quick. She raised her head, faintly saw Marcel writhing on the floor, saw Bruce standing there, car seat and pacifier in hand.

"Oh, my God!" gasped Bruce.

All at once, Marcel curled over, grabbed the knife with his right hand and yanked it out of his other arm. Not missing a beat, he whirled around.

"Look out!" screamed Nina.

Bruce jumped back into the front hall as the knife whizzed past at knee height. Just as quickly, Marcel scrambled to his feet and darted into the den and around the corner. Oh, God, thought Nina. He's heading for the living room!

"No!"

She jumped to her feet and tore through the den. Just as quickly, Bruce came around through the hall. But it was too late. She froze.

"Oh . . . oh, please!" gasped Nina.

Marcel had thrown himself on the couch, streaking it with blood. He now leaned over the crying baby, tickling Jenny's stomach with the tip of the bloody knife.

"Yes, you're a cute baby, aren't you? And you have such . . . such a nice little tummy," said Marcel, gasping with exhaustion. "You know what, I don't think your mother or her friend are going to come any closer. No. They better not because this is a very long knife and all I'd have to do is—"

"No!" Tears gushing from her eyes, Nina dropped to her knees. "No, please don't hurt her! Please! Oh, God!"

Standing absolutely still in the entry hall, Bruce said, "What is it you want?"

"Well . . ." began Marcel, clutching his wounded arm. "Seeing how there are two of you and one of me . . . and I have this unpleasant wound . . ." Weakened, he blinked heavily, shook his head, took a deep breath. "No, I cannot handle all of you. You *blancs* would trick me, oh, yes. So . . ." He wiped one bloody hand on the upholstery. "My . . . look at what a mess I'm making on this nice divan. Oh, my."

"We'll do anything," pleaded Nina. "Anything. Just don't . . . don't hurt her."

As Jenny continued to cry, Marcel bent closer to her and said, "See, you'll be all right. You'll be fine just as long as your mommy does exactly what I tell her."

"Yes . . . yes, anything."

"Anything," echoed Bruce.

Her hands crumpled into fists, her body as rigid as wood, Nina watched in horror as Marcel dangled the long shiny blade over Jenny's stomach. Please don't let him hurt her, she thought.

"What is that door under the stairs?" asked Marcel, looking past Bruce.

"A closet," gasped Nina.

"Does it lock?"

"Y-yes."

"Where is the key?"

"In . . . in the door," said Nina. "A skeleton key."

"Then you two shall please to enter it."

"W-what?" asked Nina.

"The closet—get in," ordered Marcel from the couch.

"But my baby! What about Jenny? Please!"

Bruce took a half step toward her, saying, "Nina, I—"

"No, no!" barked Marcel. "You wait right there. She will come to you." Waving the knife, he ordered, "Go on!"

Nina bit her lip, bowed her head. Her body heaving with fear, she crawled across the living room floor, one arm, one knee at a time. Finally she felt hands on her. Bruce. Bruce . . .

"Now do as I say," called Marcel.

Nina reached back with one hand. "My baby!"

His face beaded with sweat, Marcel grinned. "If you want her back, you'd better keep moving!" He clamped his arm. "Oh, this is nasty. *Ce n'est pas bon du tout!*"

Bruce helped her to her feet and the two of them made

their way to the small coat closet. Opening the narrow door, Bruce pushed aside a rack of rain and winter gear.

"Go on!" shouted Marcel.

Bruce stepped over boots and shoes and pressed himself in. Nina stopped halfway.

"But what are you going to do? What about—"

"If you get in there and stay in there, then," said Marcel, "the baby will be fine. But you mustn't tell anyone. No, no. You must wait for me to call you."

Nina threw her hand to her mouth. "Oh, God!"

Bruce reached out. "Nina . . ."

She stumbled in, falling over a tennis racket, tripping over a boot. Tears rushed from her eyes.

Marcel, his strength fading, forced yet another laugh. "Now close the door!"

As Bruce pulled it shut, as the light slipped away, Nina cried deeper, harder. They were packed in there, the two of them, and her baby was out there, out there all alone with that crazy man!

"Jenny!" sobbed Nina in the black hole of the closet. "Jenny!"

"Now, now," called Marcel. "Do as I say, and she'll be fine. Do something else, and well, maybe I kill her or maybe I send her far, far away."

"Ah!" sobbed Nina.

Bruce whispered, "We'll get her back."

Out there, Jenny's crying continued, but now grew closer.

Marcel said, "Don't try anything because I have the baby in my arms. You stay nice and still in there and I won't hurt her."

"Oh, please!" begged Nina.

Nina clutched Bruce, was unable to see anything but a band of light at the bottom of the door. A coat hung over her left shoulder. Something else poked in her side. And she sensed Marcel coming closer, still closer. Finally she saw a shadow at the bottom of the door. Then there was fumbling and metal scraping as Marcel twisted the old key.

"There!" he proclaimed. "All locked in now!"

Nina pawed at the door. Her baby! Jenny was just on the other side!

"What are you going to do? Don't hurt her!"

"I won't if you're good. Will you be good?"

"Yes, yes!"

"All right," came the weak voice. "Then don't call the police. Don't contact anyone. You must wait. You see, I have this nasty wound and I must have it taken care of. Then I will get ahold of you. Just remember—we'll be watching and listening. We'll know exactly what you're up to. Do you understand?"

"Yes," said Bruce. "But if you harm her, I'll rip you apart."

"Okay," he laughed. "And if you tell anyone, I'll chop her to pieces."

"Oh, God!" cried Nina. "No!"

"Good. Then just wait . . . just wait."

"Yes, I promise! I promise!" cried Nina.

Huddled in the dark closet, she hung on to Bruce as Marcel started off. She heard his steps drift toward the dining room, heard Jenny's cries grow fainter and fainter. Then came the sound of plastic crinkling and being heaved aside, next faint steps, a distant cry. And at last nothing, as Marcel made his way out of the back of the house, taking the baby with him.

"Jenny!" screeched Nina, beating on the door of the locked closet.

# Chapter

# 27

Manila envelope in hand, Dundeen stood in the front hall of his large stone house. He had just parked his black Mercedes out front, entered through the heavy oak door and found his mail neatly stacked on a silver tray. And what he now held was nothing ordinary. These were the results he had been waiting for. Now if only they confirmed his hunch . . .

He quickly crossed through the dining room, swung open the kitchen door and called to his housekeeper, the only other inhabitant of the sprawling structure. He couldn't see her through the pantry, but he knew she was back there, preparing as usual his dinner.

"Martha, I'll have dinner in an hour."

"Yes, sir," came her voice.

Dundeen returned to the front hall, passing across the slate floor and to the basement door. He took a key from his pocket, opened the way, entered and tightly twisted the lock behind himself.

It had been over a year, Dundeen realized while rushing down the stairs, since he had discovered what no other scientist had yet to find: a genetic test that identified early-onset Alzheimer's disease. He had, however, chosen not to make his findings public. What good would it do if there was no way to prevent the disease? What benefit would a boy of ten derive from knowing that he

181

had a 100 percent chance of developing Alzheimer's in his forties? How would people just entering the prime of life react to knowing they only had ten or fifteen years before they lost their minds? No, the responsibilities and ramifications of predicting a disease as terrible as Alzheimer's were far too great. For now he had to keep his findings secret.

All, Dundeen thought, making his way into his office, except this one case. At least, that's if he was lucky.

He crossed directly through his office, a large, windowless space with blue carpeting and sleek chrome furniture. His desk was long and black—a computer terminal was at one end—while one wall was filled with black file cabinets and the opposite one lined with metal cabinets that held specimens. In the next room, just behind a door, sat his laboratory, which contained, among other things, a host of sophisticated testing equipment, from microscopes to a centrifuge and chromagraph. Still, he did not have all that was needed, and so over a week ago he had sent the samples to a research chemistry lab in Milwaukee.

His hands ripped open the envelope and pulled out the two computer printouts. The protein from the blood samples had been purified and then run through an amino acid analyzer which had digested the samples into fragments. Now studying the protein fingerprints, his eyes went down the complete list of amino acids and their sequence. In the course of his studies, he had found that amyloid protein production was adversely affected when the amino acid serine was replaced by arginine. This in turn altered the architecture in the middle of the brain, leading to sub-type 2R of Alzheimer's disease, a particularly virulent form of early-onset that Dundeen had identified.

He carefully studied the protein fingerprint of Nina Trenton and her daughter, Jennifer. He looked at one, then the other. And smiled. He found what he'd hoped not in both test results, but definitely in one. How misery loves company, he thought. Here was yet another person who would be as desperate as he had been these past years.

Quite pleased, he stuffed the printout in the envelope and leaned back in his chair. This was surely his most powerful tool yet. Perhaps, just perhaps, this information alone would be enough to guarantee that his work could continue uninterrupted.

# Chapter

# 28

Somehow the shower was running full blast. The bathroom fan was on, too. And through the closed door of the upstairs bathroom Nina could hear the stereo blasting.

She was wet. Not from the shower, but from tears of anger and fear. Here she sat, the bath mat tangled around her feet and a pile of towels in her lap. If you need to scream, Bruce had told her, scream into the towels. Bury your face in the folds of cotton and yell. Just stay here, he said. For Jenny's sake, just stay here and try not to let any of the neighbors hear you. We can't let anyone know, not yet.

It hadn't taken them long to break down the closet door; Nina could have done it herself, so full of rage was she. Bracing themselves in the tiny closet, Bruce and she had rammed their shoulders against the door and broken out within a matter of minutes. However, they found nothing but a dark, empty house.

Now the panic had exhausted her. Nina sat, her back against the toilet bowl, not able to comprehend. No, this was impossible. Jenny. Her baby. Gone. Alex gone. Her entire family ripped away. God, no . . .

The music downstairs abruptly ended and a moment later a hand rapped gently on the door. She looked up but did not speak. Bruce twisted the handle, then slowly stepped in.

"Hi," he said, towering above her. He turned off the shower and knelt down to her. "I brought down your bedroom phone and hooked it up, but there hasn't been anything."

"Marcel . . ." she muttered, looking into Bruce's deep eyes. "He was so wonderful with my father. He was so nice to me."

"Well, he's totally deranged." He reached for Nina's hand and held it in both of his. "It's after ten. I don't know what we can do now . . . unless you want to call the police."

"No!"

Shooting through her head was a vision of that long knife dangling above Jenny. Repeating in her head were Marcel's words. Yes, she believed him. If nothing else than to spite her, Marcel would do just as he said. Their only hope was to do exactly as he'd ordered. Maybe then he'd spare Jenny.

"We have to wait," said Nina. "You saw him, you saw what he was like. We just have to sit here, Bruce." She grabbed him. "Promise you won't call the police. Promise? Not yet. If we do anything, he'll kill her, I know it!" Suddenly there were tears again. "Oh, God, what if he's hurt her already? You don't think he has, do you? What if . . . what if he's . . ."

"Sh-sh," said Bruce, wrapping his arms around her. "She has to be all right."

Yes, she has to be, prayed Nina, because there's nothing that can be done now. Nothing except wait inside the house. Her body shaking, she collapsed onto Bruce, and at the same time felt her breasts press achingly against her clothing. Lord, thought Nina, I'm all swollen with milk and my unweaned child must be screaming with hunger.

Near one in the morning, Nina sipped at some bottled water while Bruce ate bread and cheese salvaged from the singed refrigerator. They'd been sitting in the living room all night, hoping for some news. A phone call. Something, anything. But they'd heard nothing. So should they call the authorities? No, insisted Nina. That might only further endanger Jenny. Just a bit longer, she said. They'd wait a day. A full day. Then somehow they'd quietly contact the police—yes, Bruce could do it—and seek help.

Bruce rose and went to the front windows, then pulled back a small corner of the drapes. Outside it was dark, void of life, a nightscape of peace and rest and horror.

"Anyone out there?" Nina asked.

"No. Not that I can see, anyway."

"What about . . ." Could Jenny simply be there? "What about the funeral home?"

"Nothing. No lights or anything."

There had been so sign of Morton or Mikey all evening, no movement of car or bike. Usually, Morton made an appearance after dinner of some sort, whether to pinch off some geraniums or search out his son. And Mikey was out as much as he could be, riding his bike with training wheels in the broad parking lot. But tonight there was no life. The big yellow brick structure stood as sturdy and quiet as a deserted office building.

Nina said, "He has to be connected somehow. Morton's always around. I mean always. God, maybe they even have her."

"I wouldn't doubt it from what you've told me." He dropped the curtain. "Listen, I have something I should get at my place."

Nina slowly turned to him. "Really? Is it important?"

He nodded.

Nina shrugged in response. She didn't move from the couch as the front door opened and then softly closed. She heard Bruce's feet tread across the wooden porch and down the steps. Could someone be out there, watching as

Marcel had threatened, now spying on Bruce as he passed beneath the yellow haze of the front light? Perhaps there was someone crouched behind a bush, perhaps someone in a parked car, watching, waiting, judging. But how could that be? Perhaps they were being observed by other means. A phone tap. A listening device in the house itself. A neighbor . . .

Minutes later, Bruce returned carrying a red toothbrush in one hand and a fresh blue shirt in the other. Nina stared at him, surprised.

Without a word, Bruce checked to make sure the drapes were still closed, then sat down next to her. He placed the toothbrush on the coffee table, then unfolded the shirt. From inside the soft pile of material emerged black wires and a small plastic box. A micro tape recorder.

"I forgot about this—it's hardly been used. I bought it when I was in journalism school to record some interviews." First he untangled an AC adapter, then he held up a small wire with a suction cup on the tip of it. "You put this little sucker on the phone and it records everything."

"Good."

While he hooked it up to the phone in the den, Nina went upstairs and gathered some blankets and pillows.

"I suppose we should get some rest," she said, returning, "but I don't think I'll be able to sleep."

"Try. For Jenny's sake, try. You don't want to be a total wreck tomorrow."

Nina shrugged. It didn't matter. All that mattered was her baby. Where was Jenny? Where was she sleeping? In whose arms was she resting, if she was resting at all? God, this was impossible. Unimaginable. Nina touched her breasts. The baby must be starving by now.

Bruce lay down on the living room floor and dozed off. Nina stretched out on the couch and stared for hours at the ceiling. Sometime later she felt her eyes slip shut and then the pain in her mind began to fog over in darkness.

But there was no escape. Nina slept for a while until she saw Jenny. Jenny floating around in her mind, in her dreams, right there, but so far away. The little baby with the blue eyes, the fair hair, the dimply cheeks, the harsh cry. Just like any other baby, but totally unique. When Nina tried to reach out for her, to take her in her arms, Jenny simply smiled and floated away. Nina woke with a gasp and could not go back to sleep. Rest, she told herself. You need rest. No, I need Jenny. I need Jenny, my daughter, my child, my baby. Nina rose and started pacing. Insanity was sucking at her mind. She couldn't take this.

Fearful of losing her milk, sometime near five she went up to the bathroom. From the linen closet she took a breast pump and then, leaning over the sink and with the tears pouring down her cheeks, she expressed away the milk, watching it swirl down the drain. This would keep it coming, she told herself, this would . . . When she was empty, she returned to the living room, sat upright, numb and in shock. She stared straight ahead, unable to move or think. Her eyes fluttered shut.

The phone rang.

"Oh, my God!" she said.

Bruce, his eyes swollen with sleep, sat straight up. He looked around, turned from side to side.

"The phone," he mumbled.

Nina lurched from the couch and jumped over him. She glanced at the clock on the mantelpiece. It was seven-thirty. So she'd slept. She'd slept and really she shouldn't have. Had she missed anything?

She grabbed the phone, and demanded, "Hello?"

A hand reached around her. She looked down and saw Bruce turning on the tape recorder.

"Hello!" she shouted.

Across the wires came a tiny gasp, a gurgling, then a twisted, unformed voice in miniature. Nina caught her breath, clutched the phone.

"Jenny? Jenny!"

Clothes rustling, bodies twisting. And then a cry. Her baby's cry, tight and high.

"Jenny!" she screamed.

But the little voice was already growing fainter, already melting into the background. And over it Nina now could hear breathing, deep and coarse.

"Is . . . is she all right?" begged Nina.

Nothing.

"Please . . . is she all right?"

A rich, cackling laugh burst over the lines, and Marcel sang, "Don't worry, be happy."

"But—"

"Have you been quiet?"

"Yes!" She could still hear Jenny's cries. She was hungry. Alive and hungry.

"Then don't worry, be happy!"

There was a click and Nina cried, "Wait!"

But it was too late. The line was dead.

Nina slammed down the phone and leaned over the table. She took a deep breath. She couldn't start crying, not yet, not so early.

Quickly Bruce removed the tape and played back the conversation. Nina clutched her hand over her eyes as Jenny's cries came clear and strong, as that obscene voice—

Nina blurted, "I don't know how long I can stand this."

She wouldn't have made it through these past months without Jenny; she wouldn't make it in the months ahead without her, either. She and Alex had waited so long for a child. And now Alex was gone. What if Jenny, the only living part of him left on earth, were gone, too?

Bruce shut off the tape player and placed a hand on her

knee, saying, "That's a pretty healthy cry, so at least we know she's okay. That was a good connection, too, which means Marcel must still be in town."

"What's this all about?" moaned Nina. "What's going on?"

"I . . . I don't know, but somehow it's connected with what happened to your husband."

Nina caught her breath. Through her mind shot the vision of the strange man in her husband's grave.

"Yes, but . . . how?" She shook her head. "Oh, God."

"Listen, I'm going to the police if we don't hear anything else by this afternoon." He rose and started massaging her neck. "Nina, we just can't sit here."

"But you heard him—we can't do anything. He might hurt her!"

"Yes, but—"

"Bruce, we have to wait. We have to."

He was silent for a moment, and finally said gently, "Nina, why don't you go take a hot shower and then we'll eat."

"Food just doesn't sound—"

He kissed the back of her neck. "You have to keep your energy up until Jenny's back. You have to eat for her sake, to keep yourself sane."

"Yeah."

"Now go get cleaned up and we'll eat. We have some things to talk about, too." He added, "Don't worry. I'll get you if the phone rings."

Numb with disbelief, Nina stood in the shower, letting the pulse of hot water beat down on her neck and run in warm rivulets over her body. The outer tenseness softened a bit, melted like a fresh bar of soap. She turned around, braced herself on the wall of the shower, and the water pounded on her forehead. Closing her eyes, her mind echoed with Jenny's cries.

By the time she had dressed and come back downstairs,

Bruce had plates and glasses set out on the living room coffee table.

"There's cheese, some tuna and more bread." Under her silent gaze, he said, "No, no one called."

They sat down on the couch and ate in pensive silence, each pondering the possibilities. Finally Bruce rose, searched out a piece of paper and pen in the desk in the den, then sat back down.

"Let's go over everything we know. Chronologically."

Nina nodded. They had to make some sense out of this.

"We went to the cemetery yesterday afternoon," she began.

"No, no. From the start. From the very start."

Not able to eat much, Nina rubbed her forehead. "I just can't stand this. I can't stand not doing anything."

"Do you want to go to the police?"

Yes, yes, she did. She wanted to turn all this over to some authority, some organization bigger and more powerful than she. But they couldn't. Not yet. She saw the knife. She heard Marcel's words. He'd do it, she knew he would. Yet . . .

"Soon."

Sitting there, Nina went through everything from the time Alex and she had moved to town to the present. She told Bruce about placing her father at the ECRI, about Alex's work, her pregnancy and the cold night when her husband had died and Jenny had been born. She repeated everything she could remember about Alex's death and his burial, and then went through the following months, trying to pick out any odd occurrences, any strange incidents. Nothing stood out. That time, Nina said, had been spent in shock over Alex's death, in dampened joy over Jenny's birth and in a desperate attempt to deal with her father's illness.

Bruce listened, nodding his head and taking notes. He was writing all this down, trying to anchor memories and ideas so that there was something concrete to work with. He stopped once and looked over at the fireplace in silence. Then he talked about the dead being funneled through the Ridgewood Mortuary and the things he'd noticed as writer of the obituary column.

"And the fire," said Nina with a glance back toward the kitchen.

"Right. That came right after you went and talked with Dr. Volker."

In the end, they came up with very little. All they were certain of was that Morton, Volker and now Marcel were involved. Just in what, however, they didn't know.

Nina glanced yet again out the front windows, and said, "There's still no one over at the funeral home."

Shaking his head, Bruce took another sip of coffee. "The only thing that's obvious is that someone's trying to stop you from finding out something. Well, we already know Alex isn't buried where he's supposed to be—but what else is there? Whatever it is has to be big. First your house is nearly burned to the ground and then Marcel tries to kill you. Next, just to keep you quiet, he takes Jenny."

"But why?"

"Drugs, mercy killings, malpractice. I don't know."

But what, thought Nina, could they have done with her husband's body? And where did they have Jenny? Nina put her head in her hands. Please, she prayed, oh, please, God, keep my baby alive.

By two that afternoon, some eighteen hours since Marcel and Jenny had vanished, some seven hours since Marcel had called, the anxiety was boiling in Nina's veins. She jumped from the couch and started pacing.

"I can't take this," she said, chewing her knuckle. She turned to Bruce, who sat in a chair by the fireplace. "I can't stand it anymore."

"Nina . . ."

"Listen, there's one person who knows Dr. Volker and Marcel—my father's doctor, Dr. Dundeen. He might be able to tell us something."

Bruce rubbed his chin and stared pensively at the floor. "Maybe."

"I don't know if he knows Morton, but maybe he has some ideas on Dr. Volker." Nina knelt next to the chair and, almost begging, said, "I'm sure he's at the clinic. Would you go see him?"

Bruce said, "That's not a bad idea."

"You could tell him what you've picked up from the obituaries and that something quite unpleasant might be happening at the Institute. He'll help, I know he will. The ECRI is everything to him."

Within twenty minutes Bruce was on his way. As he was leaving, Nina embraced him and kissed him.

"Just be careful, all right?"

"Don't worry," Bruce responded. "I'll be back in a couple of hours at most."

# Chapter
# 29

Bruce parked his Honda in a far corner of the hospital parking lot and made his way into the lobby. He turned immediately to the right and went directly toward a bank of pay phones. Before he spoke with Dr. Dundeen, there was one thing he wanted to check. He called information for a number, which he in turn dialed.

"Yes, I'd like to speak to Dr. Volker," Bruce said, shifting on his feet and glancing about the lobby.

"I'm sorry, she's not in."

"She's not?" So it was all fitting together neatly, he thought. Quickly fabricating a name, he said, "Ah, this is Charlie Collins calling. I was supposed to stop by and see her sometime today. Do you know when she'll be in?"

"No, I'm sorry I don't."

"Would you know where I might reach her?"

"Sorry, I don't know that, either. Dr. Volker's been out since yesterday afternoon. She left word this morning that she won't be in today," said the receptionist. "However, she'll probably be calling in shortly. Is there a message I can give her?"

"No, I'm in town on some sales calls and I'm calling from a pay phone. I'll try back later."

"All right. I'll tell her you called."

Bruce hung up. Not in today. Not in since yesterday afternoon. Dr. Volker was in effect missing. This made

Nina's and his suspicions all the more credible, the possibilities of who had Jenny all the more clear. Later on, he thought, he would call again. If Dr. Volker wasn't in, then he would somehow find out where she lived and drive by. If she was gone, if the house appeared as empty as the funeral home did, then the link would be that much stronger.

Entering the Institute, he made his way down the hall and tried to formulate the questions he would ask Dundeen. Bruce needed to know if the doctor had noticed anything about Volker or Marcel, and if there had been any strange occurrences at the hospital or Institute. Perhaps Dundeen might have some tips on where Volker might have gone. Perhaps he knew of something that might later help the police find Jenny. And, of course, Bruce was quite curious whether Dundeen could offer any insight into Morton's connections with the hospital.

Halfway down the corridor, Bruce passed a group of Alzheimer patients who, hand in hand, were being led along like a train of kindergarteners. Was one of these, he wondered, Nina's father?

Entering the main office area of the ECRI, he was greeted by a receptionist, a brown-haired woman with round glasses. At once he surmised that she had been chosen because she could smile at whomever—half-crazed patients or distraught families—came through the doors.

"Dr. Dundeen, please," said Bruce. He knew, however, that there was a problem when she didn't even look down at his appointment book.

She blinked and with the same smile that showed her nice white teeth, said, "I'm afraid he's not in."

"He's not?"

"No, he's never in on Mondays."

Bruce glanced from side to side. "But . . . but I had an appointment with him."

For the first time her smooth forehead creased with wrinkles. She looked down at the book, checked the blank page.

"There's nothing down here, Mr. . . . ."

"Fitzgerald."

She looked up and apologized with her smile still in place. "There must be some mistake, Mr. Fitzgerald. Dr. Dundeen always works in the lab at his house on Mondays." She turned the page. "And I don't see anything down for tomorrow, either. Can I tell him you stopped by?"

"Please do."

A few minutes later, Bruce made his way through the lobby to his car. From the parking lot he turned left and headed north. At least Dundeen wasn't out of town, Bruce thought. At least he now knew where to find him. Bruce checked his watch. Good. He still had time to go directly up there and see what he could learn.

The town fell away, first the businesses, then the white clapboard houses and finally the suburban ranch houses. The road twisted and turned, cut through corn fields lush with deep green stalks and then passed over a creek. As he crossed the bridge, Bruce glanced out the window and up to his right. The Dundeen estate, the largest in the county, was right up there. When driving by, everyone pointed it out.

The road started up again and near the top of the hill curved left. On the right Bruce spotted a stone wall with a black iron gate. He turned into the short patch of pavement in front and stopped the Honda next to an intercom box. As he pressed the call button, he glanced up and saw a video camera aimed in his direction. A minute later, Bruce was all set to buzz again, when a voice broke over the speaker.

"Hello, who's there?"

Bruce leaned toward the small box. "My name's Bruce

Fitzgerald. I'm a reporter, and I need to speak to Dr. Dundeen. It's very, very urgent. Would you tell him it's an emergency and that—"

"Please, Mr. Fitzgerald. There's no need to sound so desperate."

Puzzled, Bruce frowned and glanced at the camera that was trained on him.

The voice continued, saying, "This is Gregory Dundeen speaking. What is it you want? If it's an interview, then—"

"No, it's not." Bruce took a deep breath. "I need to speak to you for just a couple of minutes. It's very important. There's an emergency and we need your help." He added, "Dr. Dundeen, it concerns Nina Trenton."

A moment passed before Dundeen asked, "Nina Trenton, the woman whose father is at the Institute?"

"Exactly." Aware that there was no time to waste, Bruce said, "Her daughter has been kidnapped, Dr. Dundeen, and we have reason to believe it's connected to the hospital."

Seconds later, the gates before Bruce automatically swung open, and he let out a sigh of relief. Heading into the estate, Bruce followed the long drive, a narrow band of pavement that hugged a wall of bushes on the left, while on the right spread a broad field of corn. The road passed over a hill, sloped down, then curved to the right and passed through a thick forest. Finally, the trees gave way to a beige stone house with a dark roof and a variety of chimneys poking skyward. Immediately Bruce was reminded of an English country house—leaded glass windows, slate roof and all.

The drive circled a fountain, and Bruce parked and climbed out. Almost at once the heavy oak front door opened and Dr. Gregory Dundeen stepped into the late afternoon light.

"Thank you for seeing me," began Bruce.

"Of course."

The two men shook hands, and then Bruce followed the physician through a dark entry tiled with large slabs of stone. Entering the den, a room with heavy oak beams and clubby-looking furniture, Bruce glanced briefly out the expansive windows and at the river valley beyond.

"Please, sit down," said Dundeen, indicating a tall chair. "I'm shocked to hear about this . . . this kidnapping. Tell me everything you know."

"Well," said Bruce, not quite sure where to begin.

He closed his eyes and took a breath. He began with yesterday's attack and kidnapping, including in particular Marcel's warning not to tell anyone.

"How terrible," said the doctor, seating himself across from Bruce. "I'll do anything I can. But if you're supposed to keep this confidential, why are you here?"

"Because we . . . we have reason to believe that this might tie into the hospital—Mendota General Hospital— as well as the ECRI. We were hoping you might be able to tell us about a few people who work there."

Bruce spoke to a stoney-faced Dundeen. He told the doctor about the mysteries surrounding the death of Nina's husband and his missing body, and then explained the troubles Nina had encountered when she started making inquiries. Specifically, Bruce explained, there was the fire and now the kidnapping of the child. He further elaborated, stating that somehow this had to do with Marcel, Dr. Volker, as well as John Morton, whom Bruce had been observing for the past few weeks.

"You've been observing him?" asked Dundeen.

"Yes, noting all his comings and goings."

"So . . . what . . . what is all this about?" asked Dundeen. "What are they doing?"

"I'm not sure. Perhaps we've stumbled on to some sort

of scam." Bruce paused, looked at his hands. "But I think actually it's something much more. Why are all the bodies cremated, effectively destroying the evidence?"

Bruce watched as Dundeen rose and began pacing back and forth.

"I'm horrified to hear all this. I'm fond of Nina Trenton," said Dundeen. "But what can I tell you about Dr. Volker? I'm not sure. Actually, it might be a good idea if you brought in the police or the FBI."

"For the child's sake we haven't gone to either yet. But if there's no word by tonight we'll have to contact the authorities."

"Of course." Dundeen cleared his throat, then gazing firmly at Bruce, said, "It's a shame about the child, but I don't think she'll come to harm." He waited a moment before adding, "There are, after all, more important matters."

Perplexed, Bruce looked up at the doctor. "What are you talking about?"

Dundeen shook his head. "You have no idea what you've become involved in, do you?"

"I beg your pardon?"

"This involves years of research, of hope."

"What?" Bruce sat forward, totally confused.

"I'm referring to my research, of course."

What, wondered Bruce, is this man talking about?

"Oh, come now," chided Dundeen. "Don't play ignorant."

"I'm sorry, I . . . I don't understand."

"Do you know what gangliosides are?"

"No, but—"

"They're carbohydrates—quite fascinating ones—that are composed of complex sugar and fat. Amazingly, they promote lengthening and branching and even—"

"Dr. Dundeen, that's all interesting, but I—"

"God damn it, man, listen to me. I've discovered a treatment for Alzheimer's disease. I'm surprised you don't know any of that." He smiled. "After all, you're almost dead-on about Dr. Volker and Mr. Morton. They have been dealing, per se, in bodies. That's how I get what I need for my experiments."

In shock Bruce watched as Dundeen stepped over to a cabinet by the bookcase. This can't be, he thought.

Dundeen continued. "I knew they should have been much more direct in disposing of Nina Trenton. I shouldn't have felt sorry for her."

Bruce was on his feet. "Wait a minute. What are you—"

From the cabinet Dundeen quickly pulled a dark black pistol, the barrel of which he now trained on Bruce.

"I'd sit back down if I were you. And those questions about Volker and Morton—why don't you ask them yourself?" Dundeen called, "John, Irene, would you come in here please?"

From a side door emerged the short woman and the lanky, elderly John Morton. Bruce's eyes darted from them to the windows, then to a syringe held in Morton's hand and finally back to Dundeen's gun. This was impossible. This was crazy. This couldn't be.

Bruce lunged toward the windows. Almost at once there was an explosion from behind and then a figurine on a shelf dissolved into shards. A warning shot. Bruce knew the next would also be carefully aimed. He stopped, stood still and slowly turned around.

"Please, Mr. Fitzgerald," said Dr. Dundeen. "Hunting is my only sport, and I guarantee you I'm a good marksman. I'd advise you not to do anything foolish. Just sit back down."

Bruce glanced from the frightened face of John Morton to the determined one of Irene Volker. So . . . so this

meant it was all connected? No, that was impossible. Yet
. . . yet . . . He reached back with one hand and slowly sat.

"That's right, Mr. Fitzgerald, nice and calm. I'd hate to
have to kill you now." Dundeen shrugged. "It would be
so wasteful when actually you could be so useful. I'm
sorry you discovered what was going on. It really wasn't
all that terrible. With the exception of Alex Hale, all the
ones we chose would have died anyway. And it really is
better, isn't it, that we used them so that others might
live . . . in sanity?"

"This is absurd," muttered Bruce.

"Oh, no, it's not."

"Dundeen, someone's going to pick up on this. Someone's going to follow the same trail I did and come right
here. When I don't return this afternoon, Nina will go to
the police."

"No, she won't. We're seeing to her right now. And as
far as the trail, it will simply lead to John and Irene, but
they'll have disappeared. In just a few hours they'll be out
of the country." He nodded at Morton and Volker. "Go
ahead."

Bruce watched as the older couple started forward,
slowly descending on him. Shit, thought Bruce, staring at
the syringe in Morton's hand. He couldn't give up. He
couldn't let him take him.

"Just sit still, Mr. Fitzgerald," said Dundeen, approaching him and placing the barrel of the gun on Bruce's
temple. "This isn't going to hurt. It's just a simple
injection. You're not afraid of a needle, are you?"

Bruce's eyes darted toward his right arm. Irene Volker
was unbuttoning his shirt sleeve, now pushing it up.
Then she wrapped her fingers around his upper arm and
squeezed with a tourniquet-like grip. His fingers dug into
the chair. Oh, Christ. Oh, God. He looked up. The
syringe was filled with a dark liquid, and Morton was

tapping it, clearing the chamber of air. Bruce turned his head just a bit, and the cold metal of the gun pushed into his temple.

"Again," Dundeen said, "please don't do anything foolish."

His eyes bulging, Bruce watched as Morton lowered the needle. When it was only inches from his arm, Bruce lunged forward. But it was too late. Dundeen dropped the gun, forced him down, and Volker pinned his arm to the chair while Morton jabbed the stinging needle into him. In that last second, Bruce saw Morton plunge down on the syringe. As the dark solution emptied into Bruce's veins, a hot, piercing sensation immediately buzzed through him.

"Ah!" he screamed.

His body was seized by an enormous jolt and then thrown forward, hurling Dundeen, Morton and Volker aside. Bruce clutched at his arm, then his throat. And then his chest. He shook, stumbled and then fell face first on the floor of Dundeen's den. He tried to get up, but couldn't move his legs. He tried to push with his arms, but couldn't even move a finger. Gasping for breath, he looked up. Dundeen, with a victorious smile spread across his mouth, towered over him.

"Your death," said the doctor, "will be a very, very slow one, but an incredibly helpful one, too, Mr. Fitzgerald. And I thank you. The donation of such a healthy body as yours is invaluable. Medical research will be forever indebted."

"Ah . . . ach . . . ba . . ."

Bruce tried to speak, but his tongue had swelled, filling his throat. He struggled onto his side and glanced up, but saw gray fading to black. And then he was seized again, his body twisting like a muscle, while inside he screamed no, no, no . . .

# 30

By late afternoon Nina was so nervous she couldn't stop moving. She played the tape six, seven, eight times. Jenny's cries, Marcel's giddy voice. It nearly drove her crazy, and she paced the house, from the living room through the den and the dining room, past the curtain that separated the burned kitchen, then circled around through the hall and back to the living room. Each round she made she stopped and peered out the front. The funeral home across the street was lifeless. Not seeing any sign of Mikey or Morton agitated Nina only more, and she made this circle fifty, sixty times, and more. As she walked, her mind surged ahead, imagining every terrible possibility.

She sobbed. She stared at the phone, at the tape recorder. She collapsed on the couch. Dear God, was Jenny alive? Was she all right? What about Alex? And now Bruce? Jesus, he was supposed to bring word back, he was supposed to visit Dr. Dundeen, seek out some sort of help. But he should have been back an hour ago. Could it mean the one thing, that something had happened to Bruce, too?

No, no. Push that away. Bruce was fine, just late. Maybe he couldn't find Dr. Dundeen right away. Maybe he had to wait. And Bruce hadn't called because he was afraid to. He was afraid to call her, to tie up the line, afraid that they might somehow find out and punish Jenny for his indiscretion. Yes, Bruce was right not to call.

Still . . .

As the day wore on Nina grew more frantic. She listened to the tape yet again, heard her hungry baby. A large red rash spread across her chest. She twisted her hair into a knot. She couldn't be still. She paced back and forth. Then, terrified that she would lose her milk, she got out the breast pump again and expressed it away. Soon it would be time for Jenny's feeding. God, was she eating? Were they getting her to take a bottle?

She glanced at the clock. It was nearly five o'clock. Dr. Dundeen's secretary would be leaving within minutes. Without an instant of hesitation, Nina rushed to her purse, pulled out the small leather address book. She flipped through the pages, tore one of the sheets free and ran to the phone. Clutching the receiver in one sweaty hand, with the other she pushed the buttons.

"Doctor's office," came the polite, calm voice of the woman.

Nina's lungs seemed to cave in on themselves. She tried to speak, to force air over her vocal cords. Seated at the little desk in the den, she bent over and focused every bit of energy on the phone.

"Doc . . . Doc . . ."

"Hello? Hello? Is someone there?"

Panic raced through Nina's veins, pulsing through her body with each quick, short beat of her heart. She doubled over fetuslike, so that the receiver was now pressed between her thighs and her chest. She wanted to burst out crying and screaming, spreading her pain away from her body, over the rest of the earth until it bathed her child and brought her back. But how could Nina do that? No, absolutely not. It would only endanger little Jenny's life. Still, Nina wanted to shout out. How, after all, could this woman on the other end of the line not know a thing, not suspect anything and be so calm and normal?

Nina gasped: "Dr. Dundeen . . . p-please."

"Oh, well, I'm sorry, the doctor's not in today. Who's calling please?"

"This is . . . Nina . . . Trenton."

"Oh, Ms. Trenton. Good afternoon." The secretary carefully asked, "Are you all right? Is there something I can do for you?"

"Please. It's very important. I need to . . . to speak to Dr. Dundeen."

"I'm sorry, but he works at home on Mondays. He should be calling in for messages shortly. Can I have him call you?"

"His number. Give me his number."

"I'm terribly sorry, but I'm not allowed to give that out."

Nina screamed: "I need his number!"

The friendly voice was shocked into momentary silence. "As I said, I'm sorry. I'll have him call you as soon as possible. He'll be checking in shortly and I'll tell him you called. May I have your number?"

Tears began to drip from her eyes. They bubbled up and out and began to flow as if from a fountain of pain. With her head over her legs, the drops fell from her face and onto her pants. She began to shake in long, deep spasms.

"No . . . no . . ." she managed to mumble into the phone.

Defeated by fear and exhaustion, Nina dropped the receiver in its cradle, then rolled off the chair and onto the floor. She flicked on the tape player, heard Jenny and then she herself began to cry. She wrapped her arms around her shins and pushed her legs up tight against her chest. Her reddened face twisted and she just lay there, looking at the floor.

In the exact same position several hours later, she blinked. Had she slept? She didn't know, and she gazed around, her eyes following the oak flooring into the living room. She noticed the bottom of a chair, the underside of the coffee table, and gradually she remembered. Jenny was gone. Alex's body was missing. Gradually, she realized it was getting dark, the sun was setting.

She propped herself up on one arm. "Bruce?"

Yes, Bruce had gone out. Much earlier. Hadn't it been early afternoon? He had gone out to see Dr. Dundeen, to ask him a few questions, to request his help. But Bruce hadn't come back, had he?

"Bruce, are you here?"

The empty house sucked up her words. Slowly Nina began to pick herself up, first sitting, then pushing herself up on her knees, and finally standing. She smelled musty smoke and stepped into the dining room. Behind the thick plastic curtain was her charcoal gray kitchen. Yes, a fire, thought her groggy mind.

Without turning on a light, she passed as in a dream into the dark front hall, held onto the banister, turned her head upward and knew there was no one up there, either. So black. So empty. Was Bruce gone now, too? Was he missing? Had something happened to him as well?

"Dad . . ."

He was gone, his body tethered to earth, his mind floating further and further away with each passing day. If only she could tell him about this terrible thing that had happened, if only he could help.

The hysteria had burned away most of her nervousness, leaving Nina not calm but exhausted. Her mind had become relatively clear. Looking out the living room window at the big dark funeral home, she knew what must be done, where she must go. Night was coming and she could wait no longer.

From the den she gathered her purse, swung it over her

shoulder. She passed back through the dining room and her eye was caught by the black telephone. Was this the right thing to do? Or should she call the police? She could contact them, get the officers working on the case. A missing child, a missing body and, could it be, a missing man? They could tap her phone, be ready to trace it in the event the kidnappers called. But Marcel's call . . .

No, Nina couldn't risk it. Not yet anyway. First she'd go to Dr. Dundeen's house to inquire if he'd seen any sign of Bruce. That's where, she figured, Bruce had probably headed after not locating Dundeen at the ECRI. But where had he gone after speaking with the doctor, or had Bruce made it there at all?

Hurrying now, she rushed outside the house and down the steps to her car. Nina brought the engine of her Mazda to roaring life and, as she shifted into gear, looked around. Marcel couldn't be watching, could he? Could someone be in the funeral home? Could Marcel have left someone there specifically to observe her, to make sure she didn't contact the authorities?

Perhaps. But she was going, anyway. She had to. This is the right thing to do, she thought as she turned on the headlights. Her baby. And Bruce. She wouldn't go to the police. Not yet. First she'd speak with Dundeen and see what he knew. Hopefully, she'd find Bruce, too, who might have learned something useful.

Nina headed toward town on Ridgewood, then turned north. As she drove, in the rearview mirror she noticed a dark green car and a pickup truck. Could one of the vehicles be following her?

When she and Alex had been looking for a house, the realtor had shown them a place up this way. Very, very desirable area, the woman had said to Alex and her. See, she had said as they passed the Dundeen estate, this is where the richest man in the county lives. Yes, thought Nina now, she hoped he had the power to help her.

Speed steady, Nina checked behind her one more time. Half a block back was a small car. Behind that car, the pickup truck. But was it the same one that had been there before? Yes, yes, it was.

Ahead, Nina spotted the fluorescent lights of a gas station. Waiting until the last minute, she swerved into it, bounced over the sidewalk and came to an abrupt halt by the tire display. Immediately she focused on the pickup truck and watched as the vehicle, driven by a young girl, drove right on by. Relieved, Nina put the car in gear and rolled on.

Still concerned, Nina checked again at a stoplight a mile later, and again was pleased to see no sign of the truck. Glancing in the side mirror, however, she could make out a green fender some two or three cars back. Hadn't there been a green car behind her not long after she'd left the house?

The light changed and she continued straight, as did two other cars, including the green sedan. One of the vehicles, a small foreign one, turned a block later. Another car pulled out from a side road and behind her. Then as Nina continued out of town and night bore down on the road, she could no longer tell if one of the cars behind her was the green one.

Keeping her speed even, Nina drove steadily on, passing through dark fields and hills, then a forest. Dr. Dundeen's place was, she believed, just another mile or so up the road. But there were still two sets of headlights trailing at a distance behind her. If indeed one of the vehicles was following her, the last thing she wanted was to be seen entering Dundeen's estate.

Nina pressed down on the accelerator, leaving the headlights of the other two cars in the distance. She passed around a curve and out of sight, then spotted a small dirt road just up on her right. One last time Nina eyed the dirt road ahead and then, just before the other vehicles had rounded the curve, Nina killed the head-lights. Instantly she was swallowed up by the darkness and the dirt road disappeared. She thought of hitting the brakes, but was afraid her taillights would give her away. Instead she downshifted into second, and the engine growled and grabbed at the car. Then she saw it in the dark. A faint tan band just up ahead. She downshifted again, and the engine roared, seemed ready to explode. She heaved the wheel to the side and the small car twisted off the pavement, bounced off the road and skidded across the loose surface of the dirt road. She was going too fast. The car started sliding sideways. She raised her foot to tromp on the brakes, but then caught herself as the car fishtailed across the dirt and through the night. Nina struggled to make out the sides of the road, but could not. She saw a clump of trees straight ahead, leaned on the wheel and with all her strength turned it in the other direction.

Finally the little maroon Mazda slid into something soft, and with a dull thud came to a halt. Nina gasped in relief, turned, and saw the road behind and the forest around her growing with murky light. As all grew brighter and brighter, she trained her eyes on the main road. The two cars shot past in a final whoosh. In that moment, captured in the headlights from the second of the two cars, Nina saw the image of a large green sedan.

Desperate to make it to Dundeen's, Nina put the car in first, let up on the clutch, pressed the gas and felt the small vehicle nudge forward a few inches. But no more. She gave it more gas and the front wheel, spitting dirt and rocks, dug deep with power.

"Shit."

Still without the lights on, Nina depressed the clutch, and the car relaxed. Then she tried again, this time more gently. The car budged forward and was about to pop out of the rut when the power wheel burst into a spin, digging deeper still.

Pretend this is winter, she told herself. Pretend you've just driven into a snowbank and you just have to get yourself out. Pressing down on the gearshift, she put it in reverse, rocked back, then popped it into first and rolled forward. She could sense the car's progress, repeated it, felt the car rock more. But then suddenly the car carved deeper yet into the sandy soil.

Nina turned on the headlights and climbed out. The front wheel was embedded in a good eight inches of dirt. She'd have to dig her way out or abandon the car and make her way to Dundeen's on foot.

A glowing light caught her eye. Nina turned. The way up the road, the direction the green car had gone, was filling with light. Was it simply a car headed to town or was the sedan headed back her way?

Fearful of the worst, Nina reached in and turned the headlights off, then shut the passenger door. Standing in the dark, she focused on the lights that slowly grew closer. Whoever was driving was not making great speed, as if they were searching for something or someone and doing so very carefully. It seemed minutes before the vehicle neared the intersection of the dirt road, and as it passed, the car slowed even more.

"No," muttered Nina, recognizing the car.

It was the same sedan. In disbelief she watched as it cruised past the tip of the dirt road, slowed and then stopped. Then the car's headlights circled around as the car turned in the middle of the road. Nearly paralyzed with fear, Nina watched as the lights aimed at the dirt road, then turned in.

Nina bolted for the woods. She jumped a ditch, ran through brush and bush, and made her way to the top of a knoll deep in the forest. Positioning herself behind a thick oak, she stopped and peered down at the road. Her car was caught in the lamps of the sedan, held still in the beam like a deer about to be slaughtered. And the closer the car came to hers, the more it slowed. Finally it came to a stop only some ten feet from the rear bumper of the Mazda.

In the glow of light that spilled into the woods, Nina could see the shape of a man. Was he favoring his left arm? Was that Marcel? She couldn't tell, and she watched as the figure, with pistol in hand, carefully circled her car, then threw open the door. The man reached in and shut off the engine. Alternately bathed in glaring lights and heavy darkness, he moved gracefully alongside the car. His eyes on the ground, he stopped at the edge of the road.

"Ah, so you run from me!" said a thick, rolling voice. "Shame, shame on you. But I can see where you've gone, oh, yes!"

Dear God, thought Nina, recognizing the voice. So it was Marcel, and he'd found her footprints. Had he likewise followed Bruce from the house and caught him? If Bruce had indeed been captured, then she was the only hope. She couldn't let Marcel catch her. She had to make it to Dundeen's.

Quickly, Marcel pulled a flashlight from the sedan and started in her direction, slowly at first, with his eyes on the ground. At once Nina turned. Safety lay in the dark woods, and she started picking her way through spindly black branches and black-green leaves. But it was so dark. She couldn't see more than a few inches and she had to be careful, to make as little noise as possible. She reached out. Rough bark scraped her wrist. Then she moved on. A few feet later she came to a small opening. Glancing up between the trees she saw a half moon hung lazily in the east. She just had to keep that white orb on her right, which would mean she'd be heading due north. She could do it. The Dundeen estate had to be straight ahead.

Arms held out front, she picked her way along, stumbling, but moving on. Behind her she saw the flashlight bobbing over the top of the knoll. Then suddenly Nina's foot pressed down on an unseen branch and there was a dry snap.

"Oh, how nice of you to call out to me like that, my little Nina," shouted Marcel. "Why, yes, you're right over there!"

Nina burst forward, her hands held out front like a blind person's, fending off pointed branches and tough trunks. She stumbled through leaves, over a log. She tripped in a hole and grabbed onto a tree. Pulling herself up, she hesitated, scanned the woods and saw the flashlight off to her right.

The sky was gone, the moon eaten up by the dense trees. She pressed on, picked her way through a strand of young pines.

"Oh, my dear Nina!" came Marcel's taunting voice. "You put such a nasty hole in my arm—why, I had to have stitches! But don't worry, I'm all better now, I'll catch you!"

Fuck you, you bastard, thought Nina pressing on. Go to hell. If I had a gun, too, I'd—

A wave of laughter swept over her. But it wasn't from behind. No, it came from up ahead. Drums and music, singing and happy voices. People. Lots of them at a party or a barbecue or something. God, they'd help her!

Rushing toward the noise, Nina suddenly tumbled out of the forest and found herself in a broad alley-like opening. Before her stood row after row of corn, the stalks reaching above her head. The music and the drums were clearer now. They came from over there. Just from the other side of the field.

The moonlight bathed the clearing. She heard something to her right and saw Marcel burst out of the forest some fifty feet away.

"Ah, there you are, my pretty!" shrieked Marcel, swinging the gun at her.

Nina lunged into a row of corn, her feet stumbling through the furrows, her hands pushing aside the silky tassels and paper-sharp leaves. Smashing aside first one, then a second thick stalk, she ducked over two rows.

Marcel was back there, madly running through the corn after her. She glanced back, saw stalks plowed aside, heard steps and heavy breathing. Nina tripped, caught herself. Just run to the music, she told herself. You'll be safe in numbers.

"Help!" she screamed. "Help!"

His steps short but quick, Marcel burst into view just some twenty feet back. Nina dove between two stalks, darted down another row and tried to keep her course focused on the noise ahead.

"Run, run, run, or I'm going to get you!" chuckled Marcel. "Oh, yes!"

Then she saw a light. Thank God. A house. Her feet dug into the earth, pushing her faster ahead. The music was louder now, the voices singing to the sky. There must be thirty, forty people. She'd be safe. She was going to make it!

Suddenly Nina broke through the last of the corn and flew into an opening. There was music everywhere. A house with a light and open windows. But there were no people. No. No, she thought, twisting from side to side, this couldn't be. She'd heard singing, people calling out.

She glanced back. Marcel shot out of nowhere, then oddly slowed. Nina charged toward the house.

"Help!" she screamed. "Someone help me!"

As if a button had been simply hit, all at once the music stopped. Then, as she ran across the grass, Nina saw a figure cut past several windows. An outside light burst on. A screen door was pushed open.

"Help!" gasped Nina, sweat pouring down her face.

With her last bit of energy, Nina stumbled forward to the house. She reached some steps beneath the door, lunged for a railing.

"This man . . . this man . . ." she began, pointing to Marcel. "He has a gun and you've got to . . . got to . . ."

Nina looked up at a woman whose espresso-black face was sharp and severe. From the top of the steps, the woman stared down at Nina, then looked over at Marcel, who stood motionless in the yard.

"He's been chasing me," began Nina. "And . . ."

From behind, Nina heard a loud laugh. She looked back and saw Marcel drop the gun and double over, hooting almost uncontrollably.

To the woman at the top of the steps, Marcel called, "Dear wife, this is the *blanc* I told you of."

"What?" cried Nina. "No!"

And before Nina could do anything, the woman seized her by the arm.

# Chapter

# 31

"All that's left is to take care of Nina Trenton," said Dr. Dundeen, rubbing the back of his head. "We have no other choice."

Seated on the couch behind him, John Morton asked, "Does that mean we'll have to kill her father, too?"

"Really, John," said Irene Volker, sitting next to him. "You're so nervous. Why would we have to get rid of him?"

Dundeen, a glass of mineral water in hand, turned around. Volker was right. At this stage of the disease, Nina Trenton's father was most certainly not a threat. If, in the off chance, he did pose some sort of problem, Dundeen could always administer a disabling drug.

Dundeen tried to ignore his throbbing head and said, "Even if Bill Trenton somehow brings up the subject of murder, no one's going to take him seriously. But I doubt he'll do even that—his mental deterioration continues at a steady rate. Within a few years he'll be nonverbal, soon after that he'll be dead of natural causes."

John Morton shrugged his big, bony shoulders. "So he's not a problem. But what about her? And, dear Lord, what about the baby?"

Yes, thought Dundeen, the infant. Upstairs his housekeeper, Martha, was attending to the child. Jenny, the woman had reported, had refused all but a very little milk and had been crying a great deal. Her mother's breast, body-temperature milk, the familiar scent—that's what the baby wanted.

"We have both the baby and Bruce Fitzgerald—and, by the way, Fitzgerald wasn't given enough solution to keep him down for very long," said Volker. "We do have a problem there. One that's only going to get worse by the time Marcel finishes." She checked her gold watch. "He should have her by now, so it won't be too much longer."

Dundeen rubbed the back of his skull where the pain was the worst. There was only one way, he knew. Dispose of all three of them—Fitzgerald, Trenton and the baby. The trouble was how. It would have to be done without causing suspicion. In a way that seemed completely natural.

"We have no choice. If we don't keep pushing through, we'll all be caught." Dundeen turned and looked at Morton, the one weak link. "And we can't have that, can we?"

Morton's white face wagged from side to side. "Heavens no."

"Right." Dundeen paced away from the window. "Then we'll load all three of them into Fitzgerald's car. I think an accident should take care of the matter."

It would, he thought, have to be a vicious crash, and there would have to be flames enough to destroy any incriminating details.

Dundeen shook his head. A pity it had gone so wrong at the last moment. If all this were handled efficiently, however, there shouldn't be any real problems. All that mattered was to wrap this up.

"The . . . baby, too?" asked Morton.

"Yes," answered Dundeen.

Volker rubbed her hands together. "He's right."

"Of course I am." It was time, thought Dundeen, to conclude this matter. He had to retreat downstairs. "But

we'll need more of Marcel's solution to carry this off—
more for Fitzgerald and then enough to knock out Nina,
of course. There should be more at the farmhouse,"
concluded Dundeen, referring to the little house on the
edge of his estate that he had let to Marcel.

"No, unfortunately not," said Volker. "He gave the
entire batch to me and it's all back at my house. But John
and I can go and—"

A side door was pulled open, and Dundeen turned
sharply to see Mikey standing there. The young man
looked at them, his usually placid face puffed in a frown.
He walked directly into the den and stood in front of his
father. Martha, Dundeen assumed, must have been so
busy with the baby that she didn't see Mikey slip away.

"Baby cry," he muttered. "Baby cry."

Morton rose and took his son by the hand. "Yes, I
know, Mikey. I know. But she'll soon stop. I promise.
The baby's fine. Don't worry. Now come along, I'll take
you back upstairs."

"Baby cry!"

"It's all right, Mikey, just come along," said Morton,
leading his son out.

The pain in Dundeen's head was growing quickly and
sharply. It was past time. His body was calling out. He
could wait no longer. He had to proceed down to his lab.

He rose, and, to Volker, said, "The solution—you
should leave right away. Can you be back in an hour?"

"Absolutely, we'll go just as soon as John comes
down."

"Good." He started out of the room, then stopped.
"Before you leave be sure and put Mr. Fitzgerald's car in
the back."

"Of course. That would be wise and . . ."

His head suddenly swelling with intense pain, he left
Volker, who mumbled on about something. He blinked
but could barely see in front of him, let alone hear. He

stumbled down the slate hallway, rubbed his head, braced himself against the wall. He took a deep breath, exhaled. That was better. Yes. Glancing behind, he was barely aware of Volker back there, now standing in the hall and asking if he was all right. He waved her away and pushed on, finally reaching the door down to his lab.

When he'd unlocked the door and swung it open, however, the stairs below seemed to fall away like a waterfall. He held the railing. He'd needed an injection hours ago. Then, however, Bruce Fitzgerald had arrived and . . . and . . .

He stumbled into his basement working quarters, which consisted of his office out here, and the lab through the next door. With trembling hands, he reached into a cabinet for a syringe. He popped it free of its sterile plastic case, then stumbled across the room to a small refrigerator. Bending over, he seized the small vial of clear solution. He jabbed the needle through the bottle's rubber top, then sucked the precious fluid into the syringe. He tried to check how many cc's there were but could barely focus his eyes.

"Ah!" he cried when a knife-like spasm rippled through his forehead.

Dr. Dundeen tore away his collar; there was no time to waste. He stepped to a mirror on the wall and felt along his neck for the jugular vein. Sensing the line of pulsing blood, he plunged the needle through the skin. His eyes on his reflection, he pulled back until a trickle of blood filled the syringe's chamber. Satisfied that he had indeed penetrated the vein, he emptied the solution into his body and took a deep breath. It would only take a matter of moments for the spun-down gangliosides to soothe the screaming cells of his mind.

# Chapter

# 32

Her hands bound with rope, Nina sat in a corner of the big old kitchen. Sweat dripped from her forehead, swirled down her face and neck and dampened her clothes. Her heart still racing wildly, she stared at Marcel's wife, who stood leaning against the sink.

"You will go soon, yes, soon," proclaimed Aline, whose high cheekbones pushed her eyes upward at narrow angles. "My husband will be right back with the auto."

"Where's my baby?" demanded Nina.

"Baby? Baby?" She shrugged. "We have no baby here."

"But—"

"No! No babies here. *C'est bon*, because Marcel—he detests little ones!"

As Aline turned and started to drink from the faucet, Nina scanned the room. The back door was to her left, just a few steps across the linoleum. On the counter were some canisters and an espresso pot. Overhead, a single fluorescent fixture. To the right the refrigerator, the living room door and . . .

Nina stopped, looked down. Aline was staring at her with eyes that were deep and dark and unblinking. At once Nina felt a chill. She looked up. On a counter behind the woman stood a knife holder, a block of wood that held the kitchen's finest chopping instruments and perhaps Nina's only hope.

The minutes dragged slowly. Nina sat there, hands in her lap, as Aline glared at her. Finally a distant noise broke their way, the sound of a car making its way around the cornfield and toward the old farmhouse.

"Ah, there's Marcel," said Aline. "So now we go."

The black woman approached her, and Nina knew she had but moments. As Aline took her by the arm, Nina's entire body stiffened and her hands heaved upward. With a single bound fist, she jabbed into Aline's neck, smashing into bone and muscle and cartilage. A split second later, Nina raised her foot and kicked the other woman in the stomach. Gasping for air and wheezing with pain, Aline tumbled back against the counter.

Nina lunged for the knives and grabbed one in her tied hands just as Aline came flying at her. Nina spun, and the two of them locked and fell to the floor. Hitting the linoleum with a hard thump, Nina felt the handle of the knife twist in her hands, sensed the blade cut into her skin. Aline was on top of her, pushing and hitting, yelling and beating Nina's face with her fists. The knife slicing through the air, they rolled across the floor and smashed into the refrigerator.

Within moments, Aline was again on top, now lunging for the knife and grabbing onto the blade itself. There was a spray of blood, she screamed, but did not let go. Nina bucked her waist, throwing Aline off center. Quickly Nina pulled the knife blade from the other woman's bloodied hands, shoved her off and scrambled to her feet. As Nina stood, Aline dove at her knees. In quick response, Nina bashed the handle of the knife against Aline's temple, and the black woman dropped, sinking unconscious to the floor.

Nina heard a car door out front, and charged out the back. Kicking open the door, she leapt down the few steps, then out into the yard. As she ran, she cut the ropes from her hands, looked back at the white farmhouse and heard voices and yelling. She looked to the sky. The moon hung full and bright. Yes, it was rising in the east. All she had to do was keep it to her right. All she had to do was run north, keep running north, and soon she'd be there. Then everything would be fine. Just get me to Dundeen, thought Nina as she ran. He'll help.

She saw a fence up ahead. Yes. The edge of the Dundeen estate. That had to be it. The house had to be up here, up at the top of this ridge. Safety was only a matter of minutes away.

As she clambered over the old wooden fence, she heard a screen door slam. So they were after her now. If only she could maintain her lead. With her pregnancy just a matter of months behind, however, she wasn't as fast as she once was. Taking a deep breath, she peered back and saw two dark figures racing across the field. Oh, God. She bolted onward, plunging into some woods. From behind she heard the rustling of brushes and now muffled voices. Her hand tightened still more on the kitchen knife. No, Marcel and Aline couldn't catch her again. Not when she was so close.

She charged on through the mass of trees, trudged as fast as she could up the hill. Near the top, the forest began to thin. Up ahead, branches and leaves seemed to glow. A light twinkled. And another. It was Dundeen's house. Those were outdoor lights and, yes, a few inside, too. They had to be. Running faster than ever now, she pushed herself through leafy branches and dense, scratchy evergreens.

Up ahead she saw a clearing. Swinging the knife wildly, she cut and batted branches aside, then leapt from the woods and onto immaculately trimmed grass that lined a drive. The sprawling stone house sat there, the front door less than one hundred feet away, the front light a warm beacon of safety. Nina checked the forest. Marcel and Aline were only seconds behind her.

"Help!" she screamed, racing on. "Dr. Dundeen!"

Her plea smashed against the stone walls of the house. Wasting not a moment, Nina ran up the driveway. Now that she was so close to safety, panic overwhelmed her. There had to be someone home.

"Dr. Dundeen, help! Help!"

Up on the second floor a curtain moved, a face appeared. She called out again, circled the fountain out front and hurled herself against the door. Frantic, Nina hit the doorbell, then pounded with the knife handle on the heavy wood. She twisted, glanced back. Marcel was there, one foot in the woods, one on the grass.

"Please, someone!"

Suddenly there was a man's voice from within. Through a leaded glass window Nina saw a hall light burst on. It had to be Dr. Dundeen.

"Please, it's me, Nina Trenton! Please, hurry!"

Almost at once the door was thrown open, and Dundeen stood there, his square body rigid, his face blanched with shock.

"My God . . ." he mumbled. He spotted the knife in her hand and jumped back. "What the—"

Rushing inside, Nina said, "I was attacked. He ran my car off the road, and then . . . then." She swung the knife outward. "Marcel . . . Marcel Dufour. He chased me through the woods and . . ."

But as she looked out the front door, past the fountain and to the woods beyond, there was no one. Marcel and the woman had retreated into the forest.

Gasping, Nina said, "Marcel and his wife chased me . . . they . . . they had me tied up."

Dr. Dundeen stepped halfway out the door and peered around. Satisfied that there was no one, he retreated back into the house.

"Well, they're gone now."

"But . . ."

"Don't worry. Here, let me take that," he said as he carefully lifted the kitchen knife from her hand. "Come inside."

He shut the heavy oak door and bolted it tight. Then he stepped to the side of the door and lifted a small panel. Beneath it was a keypad of numbers and a series of lights. Dundeen punched in a code, a light flashed green, and he closed it back up again.

"There, the security system is armed. Not to worry, it's quite sophisticated. Now let's get you settled in the other room. How badly are you hurt?"

"What?"

"Your hand—it's bleeding. How bad is the wound?"

"I . . . I don't know." Nina exhaled, rubbed her face, then said, "They had me at this house. Down the hill. A wooden house near a cornfield."

"Was anyone else with you?"

"No, I was coming here because . . ." Christ, she thought, where do I begin? Jenny had been kidnapped, Bruce was missing and someone had tied her up in a house. Had they intended to kill her? "I . . . I . . ."

"Does anyone else know?"

His question shocked her. "What?"

"Anyone . . . anyone see you?" he stammered. "Did anyone see you and call the authorities?"

"No. No, I'm sure no one did."

"All right, then come on. We'll take a look at that hand and then call the police."

She was grateful for the gentle hands that steered her across the slate floor of the entry hall. They entered the den and he took her over to a wet bar, where he deposited the bloodied knife in a lower cabinet and then ran water. As the doctor washed her hand in a warm stream, Nina stared out the windows. How desperate was Marcel to silence her? What would he do now? Dear God, would Jenny be all right?

"It's not too bad," said Dundeen, wrapping a white bar towel around her hand. "Clench down on the towel—that should stop the blood. I'll bandage it up later. Now come over here and sit."

As Dundeen steered the way to a couch, Nina continued to stare out the windows. Marcel, gun in hand, could be right back there. And here they were in the den, so obvious.

"But . . ." she began.

He saw what she was looking at and understood. "Oh, yes, of course."

Immediately, Dundeen cross the room and closed the curtains. Then from the bar he pulled a bottle and poured Nina a glass of brandy.

"Here, drink this while . . . while I—"

"No!" she shouted. "We can't call the police!"

"What? But for heaven's sake, why not?"

"We can't because . . ."

"What is it?"

Nina blurted, "Did Bruce Fitzgerald come here this afternoon?"

"Who?"

"He's a reporter and he's a friend of mine."

"No, no one came by. I've been here working all day, and there's been no one." Dundeen was silent, looking at her. "Why?"

Nina couldn't stop herself. "Someone took my daughter!"

"What?"

"They kidnapped her last night. Bruce Fitzgerald—he's a friend. He . . . he went looking for you this afternoon. But they must have got him, too."

Dundeen sat down next to her. "Dear Lord, you'll have to tell this all to the police."

"But they said not to! They said not to tell anyone or I'd never see her again."

"I see."

But obviously she could wait no more. Marcel had chased her through the woods and up to this house. Of course he would know that she'd tell Dundeen. He'd make certain, too, that whoever else was involved would know what she'd done. So what would they do with Jenny? God, it was so hopeless. So incredibly hopeless.

The glass of brandy slid through her fingers and dropped on the cream-colored carpet.

"Jenny . . ." How would she ever get her back again? What were the kidnappers going to do next?

As Nina fell into her grief, her entire body shook. The tears came quickly, but Nina wasn't even aware that her face was dripping wet. She slumped forward, her head in her lap, and she would have stayed that way for a long while had not two hands descended on her shoulders.

"Come with me," said Dundeen's calm, soothing voice. "That's right."

Somehow she was on her feet. Two hands were wrapped around her, and through her tears Nina saw a blur of carpet and chairs as she was moved out of the den, through the hall. She didn't care what happened now, where she was taken. It was useless.

A door opened in front of her.

"Careful, there are some steps down."

She stumbled slightly and fell into Dr. Dundeen's strong arms. Talking to her in a string of soothing words, he led her into the basement.

"Where . . . are we . . . going?" she muttered.

"To my office."

"Oh."

Within moments she was seated in a chrome chair with gray, officelike upholstery. She took a deep breath, looked up and saw Dr. Dundeen on the other side of the room. He was reaching into a cabinet, taking out a small bottle and a syringe.

"What are you doing?" she asked.

"Just relax."

"But what . . ."

"You're under much too much strain," said the doctor.

"I'm all right."

He started toward her, needle raised. "I just want to give you something to calm you down."

A sedative? No. Maybe there was something she could still do. She could always handle herself. And she had to now. Jenny. She had to be alert and awake for Jenny and Bruce's sake. At once her eyes were dry.

"But my daughter. Maybe we should call the police. Maybe I should talk to them."

"Of course," he said, his voice smooth. "This will just help calm you down."

Nina quickly stood. "No, I've got to be alert. I don't want anything!"

A shrill sound pierced her ears. It came from far away, then stopped almost as soon as it began.

"Was that a baby crying?"

They both were still for but a moment. There was, however, no peal of an infant's voice.

Dundeen looked at her with a kind smile. "Nina, please. You've been under a great deal of stress."

"But I heard a baby!"

He shrugged. "Perhaps you heard something from the kitchen. My housekeeper has a two-year-old. Now Nina, please, you're exhausted and—"

Suddenly he was coming toward her, syringe in hand. All she knew was that she mustn't let this happen. Jenny might need her. Bruce might need her. And she had to find Alex's body. No matter how exhausted she was, she must remain fully alert.

"No!" she shouted, rushing behind his desk.

"Nina, control yourself," ordered Dundeen, his face flushed with anger. "I just want to help you."

"No!"

On his desk lay a long, thin letter opener, capped with a brass handle. She grabbed it and raised it up in her fist. Dundeen froze.

"Stay away from me! I don't want any drugs!" She glanced toward the stairs and said, "I want to call the police right now."

"Soon. First I just want to give you something to clear your mind, to help you think more clearly."

"No!"

He started toward her again, his steps short and slow, his body rigid with intensity. What was this? What was going on? Why wouldn't he let her alone?

"Stay where you are!" she demanded.

"Nina, I just want to help," he said, his tone soft and coaxing as if he were dealing with an ECRI patient. "Now put down the letter opener."

"You put down the syringe!"

But he didn't. He was still for just a moment before starting forward again. Nina's hand tightened on the letter opener. I'm going crazy, she thought. I just need to get away. I just need to find my daughter. I want to call the police and talk to them. Maybe they could rescue Jenny and Bruce.

Before her, Dundeen kept coming, stalking her one slow step at a time. Nina turned, caught her foot on a chair and tripped, falling hard against a tall metal cabinet.

"Oh, my God, careful!" shouted Dundeen.

Nina struggled to catch herself, seized the handle of the cabinet and tried to pull herself up. But the cabinet wasn't sturdy enough. It began to rock, tip toward her. She heard something inside slide.

"Look out!" yelled the doctor.

She tried to steady the cabinet, to brace it, but it was

too late. The lever in her hand twisted, the gray metal door swung open. Something slid against the partly open door, dropped off the shelf and tumbled to the floor. Glass shattered, liquid splattered. Nina glanced down and saw a large cauliflower-like mass resting in a smashed jar.

Oh, Christ, thought Nina, recognizing the grayish mass. That's a brain. And she sensed many more slipping off the shelves. One, two, three. A half-dozen jars cascaded out of the tipped cabinet and crashed at her feet.

Cloudy liquid and soft masses spilled around Nina. She screamed. The entire cabinet came tumbling over. Dundeen shouted out, leapt forward as the bank of brains mashed like dud bombs on the floor.

Nina spotted a door. An exit. A way out. She had to flee. Get away. She lunged for the knob.

"No!" shouted Dundeen. "Don't go in there! Don't!"

His anger flared intensely, propelling him forward. All the more frightened, Nina hurried faster, threw herself against the door and pushed it open. She tumbled into the next room, a laboratory that was lit by a faint blue light. Suddenly she forgot about Dundeen and everything else. There, surrounded by an array of equipment and laid out before her, were three bodies, all covered with white sheets. Wires and tubes coiled snakelike around their heads.

"Wh-what . . ."

Dundeen came rushing behind her, then stopped himself in the doorway, and, gasping, said, "Nina . . . Nina, I've discovered something very wonderful. Something quite incredible, really, that will benefit people with Alzheimer's disease."

"What . . . what are these people doing down here?"

"They're helping me, Nina. They're producing something I need—gangliosides."

"But . . ."

"Listen to me, Nina. Gangliosides are the real key to curing Alzheimer's. The body produces only a very small bit each day—just a few milligrams. But it's entirely crucial. Gangliosides—they promote healthy nerve cells and even regeneration."

Nina heard it now, the deep slow hissing of air. She saw it, too. The chests rising and falling. And then she noticed the monitors with the green lines going up and down, up and down, with each heartbeat.

"They're alive," she muttered.

"Their bodies are alive, yes, but in every other aspect they're dead."

Behind her, she heard him say something about patients with do not resuscitate orders and a Haitian drug that could dramatically lower the metabolism. But, no, this can't be, thought Nina. This . . . this . . .

"Nina," begged Dundeen, "please try to understand. Please. The only pure source of gangliosides is the human body. That's why I must keep these bodies functioning—so I can extract the gangliosides from their spinal fluid."

"Dear God . . ."

"I won't need them for much longer. I won't, really," continued Dundeen. "You see, Nina, I'm only weeks away from being able to biogenetically reproduce a true ganglioside that actually works for our needs. Once I've done that, Alzheimer's will be—"

"No!" gasped Nina.

Horrified, Nina looked at the first body, that of a heavy, bald man. On the next table and surrounded by a stack of equipment lay a woman, her skin, like that of the others, white and flaky. A dark-haired man lay at the end.

"Nina, try to understand!" pleaded Dundeen. "I have early-onset Alzheimer's! To keep my mind functioning I need the gangliosides these bodies produce. It works, too.

Don't you recall the day your father was so much better? Well, I injected him with a few milligrams of the spundown solution."

Barely hearing him, she was stumbling forward. The one on the end. That hair. The color was so familiar.

No longer pursuing her, Dundeen stood on the edge of the room, begging her attention. "I'm so close. So very close. Once I've discovered how to reproduce gangliosides that are effective, once I've learned how to synthesize them without any side effects, then Alzheimer's disease will be a thing of the past—I will have saved millions and millions of lives!"

Nina could barely breath. The one on the end, the one with the brown hair. But it couldn't be. His skin was so pale, so wrinkled, so deathly. She hurried up beside the table, saw his chest moving up and down as the air was pumped in and out of him. No, no, it couldn't be . . . She glared at Dundeen.

"I'm sorry," he said. "Truly I am. But he stumbled onto us and he would have ruined everything. All the others would never have recovered. But . . . but him, what should we have done? It was either his life or my research. Just think, Nina, I might be able to save your father's mind. And there's more Nina, much more. Listen carefully. There's something I haven't told you. Something you'll be quite surprised to—"

"No . . ." she groaned low and animallike.

Nina stared down at the mask-covered face. No, it couldn't be. The hair was so thin now, the skin so withered, so old looking. Then she studied the eyes, and knew.

Nina clutched her hands to her chest, opened her mouth and screamed, "Alex!"

And then the bright lights faded to darkness. She clutched outward, found nothing and collapsed on the floor.

## Chapter

# 33

Where was the blanket? On the floor? Why wasn't the heat on? God, it was freezing in here! Was something wrong with the furnace? How were they supposed to live in a house like this? Chicago wasn't like this. Chicago was warm. Not cold like here. Let's go back to Chicago.

Nina rolled on her side, felt her head pound in pain. Then she opened her eyes. She saw a metal wall only ten inches from her face. She touched the platform on which she lay, finding the orange vinyl cold. What was this bed-thing? Where was she? And why did her head hurt so much?

Shivering, she rolled on her back and first saw a lightbulb encased in a wire cage, then a big fan covered by grillwork. The fan whirled and whirled, blowing cold air freely upon her. What was this? What had happened? Without moving her head, she looked about. This was a small room, no more than eight by ten feet, and she lay against one wall. Yes, she'd been at Dundeen's, but what was this, one big refrigerator?

She turned her head a bit further. A body. There was a space and then there was another trolley with a body on its flat hard surface.

"Bruce," she whispered. Thank God.

Struggling, she pulled herself up, then swung her legs over the edge of the table. Sitting there, rubbing her sore head, she understood where she was: a refrigeration room for bodies. There was this hard platform on large wheels and the one that Bruce lay on was across from her.

"Bruce?"

She slipped down, but had to stop a moment. Her head throbbed with deep, hard pain. Had she been drugged or had she hit her head? She'd passed out and fallen. Yes, there was a large bump on the back of her head. Yes, that was it. She'd seen . . . seen Alex and fainted.

Alex. She trembled. Dear God. She'd seen his chest rise and fall. She'd seen his heartbeat bleep on a monitor. Was that possible? Had she really seen that? He was alive, but wasn't alive. He was dead, but wasn't dead. All these months he'd simply been suspended between two worlds. It couldn't be. No. Alex.

Chilled with shock, she looked up. "Bruce."

She braced herself, then took a lunge across the narrow space and caught herself on the other trolley. Why wasn't he stirring? Why was he lying there so still, his arms laid so peacefully at his side? No, she prayed, not like Alex. Not another one.

Taking his hand in hers, she squeezed it but received nothing in return. She brought his hand to her lips. Dear Lord, she thought, why is his skin so cold? Why is he not responding? Please, no.

"Bruce!" she called.

She bent over him, stared into his lifeless face, then patted his cheeks. The skin was as cold as if he'd been out for a blustery walk. Why wasn't he shivering? Why hadn't the cold woken him, too? She rubbed his whiskery face, tried to stir blood and movement and hope.

"I'm here. It's me, Nina. Bruce, Bruce, wake up!"

Flushed with panic, Nina was suddenly very awake. She pushed two fingers into his cold, clammy neck, and found nothing but squishy flesh and muscle. Her fingers worked quickly, pressing all up and down the side. There had to be a pulse. Bruce had to be alive!

"Bruce!"

Sensing no pulsing blood in the side of his neck, she grabbed one lifeless arm, lifted it and searched his wrist. Again nothing. Lord, she thought. Had Dundeen killed him? Had Bruce walked right into the middle of all this and been killed, all because of her?

She pushed back her hair, bent over and placed her ear just a fraction of an inch above his lips. She couldn't, however, sense a trace of air emerging from his still body. Frantic, she ripped open the top buttons of his plaid shirt and then placed her ear on his chest. But there was nothing. She dragged the side of her head over his rib cage, then froze. All she wanted was a subtle beat of life, something that proved he lived.

But nothing. Bruce was dead. His body offered no response, not even any warmth.

"I'm sorry . . ." she gasped.

Nina stared at Bruce, then touched his cheek one last time. There was still Jenny, her baby. She might be in this house and she might be alive.

Next to the door were two switches, and she rose and crossed to them. Nina flicked one of them, and the bulb in the wire cage went off. Just as quickly, she turned it back and the light came on again. When she pushed down on the other switch, the ceiling fan shut off.

The door before her was big and obviously thick, covered like the rest of the room with mottled galvanized steel. There was no door handle, no lock or switch. To the side was a plunger, which she pushed. Nothing happened. The emergency-door release had been disconnected.

Immediately, Nina leaned on the door. She put her weight into it and pushed, but the door didn't budge. She pressed her ear to the cold metal wall, but could hear nothing from outside.

Frantic, Nina started pounding with her fists. Beating and kicking at the door, she knew only one thing. She had to get out. She had to find Jenny. They'd killed Bruce. And they'd taken Alex. They'd taken him and kept him hidden from her all these months. But they weren't going to have her baby! No, she was going to find Jenny and then somehow take care of Alex. Maybe he could be revived. Maybe he still lived. Alex!

"Let me out!" she shouted, the rage returning.

No sooner had the words passed from her lips, than she heard two thumps on the other side of the door. Nina stopped and stood still. A moment later she heard a handle being turned and saw the door begin to move. Then the seal was broken. At once she hurled herself forward.

"Ah!" came a small cry from behind the door.

The door flew open, the person tumbled on the floor and Nina bounded into a dark hall. She raised her fists, lunged forward, but the young man merely raised one open palm in a wave.

"Hi."

Stunned, Nina stared down at the soft, frightened face, and said, "Mikey."

At the sound of his name, he smiled, his cheeks big and round, his eyes narrow and slanted. He got up, brushed off his hands and came over. He started to take her by the arm, then looked past her and saw Bruce lying on the trolley. Silently, Mikey let go of her and stepped directly into the refrigeration room. Extending his hand, he laid his palm over Bruce's forehead, waited a moment, then reached down and felt his prickly moustache. The young man giggled.

Mikey turned to Nina, and, as if this were just one more, said, "Like dead."

Dear God, thought Nina, had this poor person spent his life poking and chortling at bodies as they passed so briefly through the funeral home? What kind of demented entertainment had Morton provided him with?

Nina asked, "Mikey, are you alone?"

He looked around a bit sheepishly, then nodded as if he'd done something quite wrong.

Quickly, he tugged on her, and said, "Baby cry."

Nina gasped. "Jenny? Jenny? Is she all right?"

"Baby cry."

"Yes, I understand. Jenny's crying because she needs me. Can you take me to her?"

His head bobbed up and down in an eager nod. Dear God, thought Nina. Jenny was crying. She was here, crying. That meant she was alive.

For a second Nina was filled with confusion. She looked back in the refrigerated room, saw Bruce lying there so deathly. And Alex. He was down here, alive yet no longer human as machines pushed and prodded and maintained his body in some suspended state.

To Bruce, as he closed the heavy door, Mikey said, "Bye."

His simple word clarified it all for Nina. Jenny was alive and crying. Nina had to take care of her first, get her to a place of safety, then do what she could—if anything— for Alex and Bruce.

Nina said, "Okay, Mikey, take me to the baby. But we must be very quiet, right? Very, very quiet."

He nodded and smiled and raised a finger to his lips. "Shh."

Mikey glanced in both directions, then started off, leading the way toward the rear of the basement. At the end of the corridor they came to a bifold door. Mikey stepped through, looked back at Nina and again pressed a single finger to his lips.

"Shh."

They entered a dark room, and as Nina's eyes adjusted she could make out a series of shelves on one wall, a pile of materials and a stack of boxes. This was, she guessed, some sort of work room. Mikey moved quite quickly, and Nina struggled to keep up. It was, thought Nina, as if he'd spent his entire life treading on the very edge of normal life. He knew not how to enter its heart, only to sneak around it without being detected.

Eventually, they reached an old wooden staircase, which they mounted. At the top, Mikey froze and nearly ceased breathing as he cracked the door and peered out. When Mikey was certain there was no one ahead, he inched open the door and led Nina into a huge kitchen, where a single bulb burned over the sink.

Looking about, Nina could detect no one as they passed through the butler's pantry and servants' dining room. It was darker here at the rear of the house and most of the light now came through the windows; outside a security light burned boldly.

Without hesitation, Mikey scooted around a chair, went past a coat rack and to a small door. He checked on Nina, then held up a single finger and beckoned her forward.

It was just then that she heard it—Jenny's cry. Lunging past Mikey and through a door, Nina found herself at the base of a dark, narrow staircase that led up to what must have been the servants' quarters. Her baby was up there, alive and crying, and she rushed forward, stepping on the first stair.

Smiling, Mikey caught her arm. "Shh!"

He twisted to the side and squirmed past her, moving carefully and quietly up the stairs. The door at the top was open a bit and light seeped down. Nina was right behind him, and the higher they climbed, the louder grew Jenny's wails. Now Nina could hear another voice, a woman's, talking and hushing and trying to comfort the baby. There's nothing wrong with her, Nina wanted to call out. She's fine. She just wants my milk, she just wants me to hold her and nurse her and love her!

The baby cried louder, and Nina lunged forward. Her baby. She just had to reach her. But in her excitement, Nina missed the next step and she tumbled forward, her shoes and hands slapping loudly on the oak. Above her, Mikey stopped and looked back in fear.

Suddenly a voice upstairs called, "Mikey? Mikey, where are you? Come here right this minute!"

Nina heard steps coming, and quickly whispered, "Go on, Mikey! Go on, I'll be right there!"

At first Mikey seemed not to understand and he stared down the dark staircase in puzzlement. Then somewhere deep inside he caught the idea that Nina mustn't be seen. All at once he scrambled quite noisily up the stairs, pausing at the top. He looked back at Nina, waved and then started into the upstairs hall.

"Mikey, where are you?"

"Here!" he shouted, as if this were all a game.

"What?" came a stern voice. "I told you not to leave the TV room. Now get back in there right now! I have enough trouble on my hands without your running around the house."

Nina was moving at once, crawling up the stairs. At the top she froze, then slipped through the door. Finding herself in the middle of a narrow, dimly lit hallway, she ducked into the first room, a bathroom. Immediately she started searching the medicine cabinet, finally finding a pack of razors. She took a double-edged blade and wrapped a washcloth over one end of it. Throwing a towel over her shoulder, she started out, beckoned by Jenny's cries.

Nina edged her way down the hall and saw the woman's shadow spill from a room. The dark outline grew smaller as the stranger neared the doorway, then swelled as she turned and headed back toward the middle of the room.

Turning the corner, Nina reached the woman in two large strides. She thew one hand over the woman's mouth, and with the other pressed the razor to her neck. The woman stiffened and began to twist.

"I have a razor in my hand," said Nina. "Don't move and don't make any noise or I'm going to slit your throat. Do you understand?"

The woman, now rigid with fear, barely nodded. Jenny, hearing her mother's voice, was quiet for just a moment, then began crying louder than ever.

"Good. I don't want to hurt you. I just want my baby. If you try anything, though, I'll kill you. I'll kill you real fast. Now just hold the baby nice and steady." Nina turned her head and called, "Mikey!"

He was there within seconds. His eyes big and curious, he walked around Nina and the woman, just staring at what was going on.

"Mikey, take the baby in your arms. That's right. This woman is going to hand you the baby and I want you to take her. But you must be very careful. Can you do that for me?"

"Okay."

"Good." Into the woman's ear, Nina said, "Just hand the baby to Mikey."

Surprised by her lightness, scared by her crying, Mikey gasped as he took Jenny in his arms.

"Very good, Mikey. Don't let her crying frighten you, she's just hungry." She nudged the woman in the right side. "What's your name?"

"Martha," she said in a small voice.

"Okay, Martha, I'm going to take you to that chair and I want you to sit down."

"Yes, of course. I'll do whatever you say. Just don't hurt me . . . please."

"Just get in that chair."

"Yes . . . yes . . ."

"Is the baby all right?" asked Nina as she seated Martha. "Has anything been done to her?"

"No . . . nothing. She's fine . . . just hungry. She . . . she wants your milk."

"Believe me, I intend to feed her."

Nina used the razor to cut the towel into long thin strips, the first of which she tied over the woman's mouth. Minutes later and without any struggle, Nina had Martha tied securely to a wooden chair. Torn strips of material pinned the woman's arms around the back and to the frame of the chair, while her feet were bound to the wooden legs.

"Good boy, Mikey. I'll take her now."

Hands shaking, Nina lifted the little body from Mikey's arms and clutched her to her body. The sweet smell of Jenny, her soft folds, her squirming arms—all this Nina drank in.

"Oh, baby!" she cried, and kissed the thin, soft hairs on Jenny's head.

Nina unbuttoned her blouse and unfastened her bra and lifted the baby to her. The eager infant sucked in Nina's breast and the first of the milk so quickly that she choked a bit.

"Shh. I'm right here, Jenny," said Nina, patting her on the back. "I'm right here, sweetheart. Everything's all right. Everything's all right."

Jenny ate as quickly as she could drink and was soon calmed. When she was sated and quieted, Nina changed her, then checked to make sure Martha was still securely tied to the chair.

"Can you breathe all right?"

The woman nodded.

"Just don't do anything, and you'll be fine. I'll be checking on you," lied Nina.

Nina, with the baby now sleeping in her arms, headed down the back staircase, Mikey just a half step behind her. As she moved to make their escape through the rear door, however, she stopped. Alex and Bruce were both through the kitchen, down another staircase and in the basement. How could it be that Alex, who'd been so dead, now had air hissing in and out of his body? When they'd found him crumpled in the snow he had appeared so dead.

"Mikey, my friend downstairs. Is he . . ." She saw the confusion on his face, and so she held one hand to her upper lip and rubbed it. "You know, the man with the moustache."

He nodded quite rapidly.

"Is he dead?"

Mikey hesitated. "Like dead."

"But not dead?"

Mikey frowned and thought a minute. "Like dead."

"Does that mean he'll wake up?"

His eyes flitted around the room and he shrugged.

Shit, thought Nina. Had Bruce been given the same drug that slowed one's metabolism, had he already been pushed over the edge, had he already fallen into the same state as Alex? No. Not yet, she realized. Alex needed a host of sophisticated machinery to keep him artificially alive. Not Bruce. If indeed he was somehow still alive, his body was functioning on its own.

"Mikey, can you take me to the basement again, back to my friend with the moustache?"

"Yeah."

"But we have to be very, very careful, just like before. We have to be very, very quiet, because if Dr. Dundeen or anyone else hears us we'll be in big trouble. Okay?"

"Yeah, yeah."

He eagerly reassumed the lead, and soon they were passing through the kitchen, then down the steep staircase that led into the back of the basement. As they started through the work room, Nina stopped.

"Mikey, wait a second."

Clutching Jenny, Nina carefully made her way to a darkened wall. She felt along a rough table top, felt paint cans, then moved a little bit farther. On the wall was a pegboard, and she could just make out the silver blades of screwdrivers and two saws. Finally she found a large, thick wrench.

The tool in hand, Nina started after Mikey, moving quietly down the hall. When they reached the refrigeration room, Nina grasped the heavy metal handle and opened the door. The naked light burned painfully bright, and Bruce lay there exactly as Nina had left him. She took half a step in and froze. She was mistaken. Surely this long, motionless form of cold flesh could not be alive.

Full of doubt, Nina went to Bruce and gently pushed two fingers against his throat. Where there should have been a rhythmic throb, there was nothing. She bounced Jenny a little higher up in her left arm, then bent over and put an ear again to his chest. The cage of flesh and bone was quiet and peaceful.

Mikey came up beside Nina and pushed her aside. He bent over and pressed his right ear against Bruce's ear. Then Mikey stood absolutely still. Finally a smile on his face, he stood up.

"Like dead!"

Nina whispered, "Mikey, what do you mean?"

"Like dead!"

Without asking, he reached for Nina's watch and tugged it from her arm. Then as careful as a glass blower, Mikey held the watch, crystal down, less than a quarter of an inch from Bruce's lips. He pulled it away once, was not satisfied, and put it back. Seconds later, Mikey lifted it away, studied it and smiled.

"Like dead."

He held the watch to the naked bulb. Covering the thin crystal was a fine film. Moisture.

"Oh, my God." Was it just the last of the heat emanating from his body or could he really be alive? "Mikey, do you know how to wake him up?"

Before he could answer, a door down the hall creaked. Nina froze. Heavy steps started moving their way. Dundeen, she thought. It had to be him.

Shit, she thought. She was stuck in here. There was no escape. Immediately she thrust Jenny into Mikey's arms. Next she lay down on the empty trolley, tucking the bulk of the wrench beneath her right thigh. Beside her, Mikey started crying. He heard the steps, pushed at Nina and squeezed Jenny too tightly. The baby woke with a huge wail.

Against every instinct, Nina pressed her eyes shut and forced herself to lie perfectly still. She concentrated on the steps rushing down the hall. Finally the heavy door was swung back.

"Mikey!" exclaimed Dr. Dundeen. "What in the hell are you doing here?"

"Ahh!" he cried.

"Out, get out of there right now!"

Nina heard Dundeen come in, grab Mikey and pull him out of the room.

"How in the hell did you get that baby down here? Just wait there in the hall. Don't move." He shouted, "Martha? Martha, are you down here?"

Nina heard him move, sensed him approaching. Barely able to contain herself, she stiffened as she felt his hot, moist breath spilling over her face. But she couldn't restrain herself as he reached down and tried to push back her eyelids.

All at once, Nina's eyes exploded and she shrieked, "You fucking bastard!"

Dundeen screamed and fell back. Nina leapt up, her left hand grabbing him by the collar. Her right hand came back, and then in a powerful stroke she smashed him with the heavy metal wrench. He yelped and stumbled.

"Damn you to hell!" cursed Nina.

The vision of Alex filled her mind, and she struck Dundeen a second and third time. He brought his hands up, but she kept beating him with the wrench until he passed out and collapsed. Jenny. He'd taken Jenny from her. And look what he'd done to Bruce! Out of control, Nina reached down and grabbed Dundeen by the shirt. That face—she wanted it to be nothing but a bloody pulp. She raised the wrench again. She was going to whack him over and over again until his teeth and his brains were spilled and splattered all over the room.

Behind her Mikey screamed, "Baby cry, baby cry!" and tears ran down his face.

Nina hesitated for an instant, and then hurled the wrench down. It missed Dundeen's face by an inch and smashed against a leg of the trolley. She wanted nothing more than to kill Dundeen, to mutilate his life as much as he had hers. Instead, she fell on the edge of the table, her breath whooshing out of her.

In the doorway, Mikey and Jenny cried on.

"I'm okay . . . it's okay . . ." she gasped.

Gathering her strength, she stumbled to Mikey and fell against him in a big hug. She lifted Jenny from his arms, rocked her, opened her blouse and began to nurse the baby again. Within moments Jenny fell quiet.

"I'm sorry you had to see that, Mikey," sighed Nina. "This man—he did something very bad."

With Jenny still sucking at her breast, Nina entered the room again and stared down at Dundeen. A curling ribbon of blood slipped down the side of his head. Was he dead? She hoped so.

Sniffling, Mikey came in, nudged Nina aside and

stepped over Dundeen. He looked down at the unconscious doctor, then bent over Bruce, placing his ear once
again to Bruce's. Next, as Nina watched, Mikey made a
fist and started dragging his knuckles up and down
Bruce's breast bone. He stopped, hammered on the hard
bone, then placed his ear on Bruce's chest. Not satisfied,
he again started dragging the knuckles over Bruce's chest.
A frown spreading on his face, Mikey continued this for
over a minute.

Nina didn't know what to think. Clutching Jenny in
one arm, she reached around Mikey and took Bruce's
wrist. Her fingers pressed the cold flesh and . . .

"Oh, my God." She could feel it. A glimmer of movement, a dull swelling of blood in veins. "There's a pulse,
Mikey!"

Biting his lower lip, he quickly pushed Nina back,
moved down and reached Bruce's legs. With his forefinger
and thumb, he grabbed one of Bruce's inner thighs and
started to pinch. Putting his weight into it, he bent over
Bruce and squeezed and twisted.

A faint moan squeaked through Bruce's lips. Nina
started patting his cheeks. He was alive. Oh, God, she
thought, he was alive! Alive!

"Bruce! Bruce, wake up!"

Nina and Mikey continued pushing and prodding
Bruce. His chest began to rise and fall, his head twitched.
A small cry of pain fluttered over his lips. His eyes began
to move.

"Bruce, Bruce!" called Nina.

She was silent, hoping for a response. Instead, though,
she heard muffled voices and distant steps. She froze.
Someone was upstairs. Oh, Christ, she thought. Who was
it? Marcel?

"Mikey, how long is this going to take?"

He smiled and shrugged. Among other things, the
concept of time was something he'd never learned.

# Chapter
# 34

"Hello?" called Morton as Irene Volker and he passed down the main hall. "Hello?"

They checked the den and found it empty, as were the living room and dining room also. Morton called into the sunroom, received no response, and then Irene checked the kitchen. When she emerged with a puzzled look on her face, Morton knew there was only one place Gregory Dundeen could be.

"He must be down in his office."

"Really? You don't think he went anywhere, do you?" asked Irene Volker, the bottle of Haitian solution carefully in hand.

"No, of course not. Especially not in view of the time situation."

Morton returned to the slate hall and headed to the basement door. Finding it open, he ushered Irene Volker through and then started after her.

"Greg, are you down here?" called Morton, descending into the office. "Hello, anyone—" He spotted the broken jars, the spewed lab samples. "Lord!"

Volker rushed over chunks of glass. "Oh, no!"

Fearing all was ruined, Morton began shouting, "Greg? Greg, where are you? Are you all right?"

His eyes ran from the mess, over the gray metal cabinet

and to the open lab door. Hurrying into the next room, Volker and he found nothing amiss. The three bodies, their breathing and heartbeat regulated by machinery, lay in the soft blue light. Morton only glanced briefly at them before hurrying through the lab and to another door, this one also swung wide. With Irene Volker just behind him, he pressed into a dark basement hall.

"Greg?" called a panicked Morton. "Greg, are you back here?"

With no response, they turned back into the lab. Suddenly Volker stopped, grabbing Morton by the arm.

"What was that?" asked the short woman.

He spun, looked back into the dark hall. "I didn't hear anything."

"No, there was something." Volker pushed around him. "I heard something."

Morton followed her, and then he heard it, too. From somewhere down here he heard pounding, and then a muffled voice. Drawn by the noise, they rushed down the corridor until they stood just outside the cooler.

Morton touched the door with one hand, and said, "Good God, Greg, are you in there?"

"Yes!" came his muted response.

His hands shaking, Morton pulled on the handle and swung open the door. Gregory Dundeen, blood dribbling down the side of his head, stumbled out.

"What happened?" demanded Volker.

"Nina Trenton . . . I had her locked up. I should have drugged her, but I . . . I was waiting to give her Marcel's solution. She . . . she caught me off guard."

"Oh, my God," moaned Morton. "Where's Fitzgerald?"

"He must be with Trenton and her baby."

Morton raised a hand to his chin. Her baby? If she'd found her child, didn't that mean she'd been upstairs? He tensed, ready to hurry off.

"What . . . what about Mikey? Is he all right?"

Dundeen stumbled along. "Come on. We don't have any time to waste!"

"But . . ."

"We've got to stop them!"

Morton didn't move until Dundeen grabbed onto his arm and started pulling. Morton still hesitated.

"But . . . but Mikey."

Her voice full of fright, Volker said, "I'll check on him, John. I'll take care of him. You two go. If Trenton and Fitzgerald get away, it'll be the end. Hurry!"

"Yes, yes. All right." Morton added, "We didn't see anyone upstairs . . . or outside for that matter."

Irene and he struggled to keep up with Dundeen, who charged through the lab, his office, up the stairs and disappeared into the rear of the house. In the front hall, Morton put his hand to his chest and tried to catch his breath. He just wasn't so young any more. All of this was too much.

Irene asked, "Are you all right?"

"Just go check on Mikey."

"Of course," she said, rushing toward the main staircase.

Dundeen came running through the dining room, shouting, "The kitchen door's open—they must have gone out the back. Damn it!"

Morton watched as the doctor hurried down the hall and into the den. He reappeared with a double-barreled shotgun in each hand, one of which he thrust at Morton. The older man took the thing and stared at it. He'd never fired a gun before.

"Come on!" shouted Dundeen.

"Yes . . . yes, of course," responded Morton.

He took one last look up the main stairs, but there was no sign. Hoping that Mikey was all right, John Morton followed Dundeen out of the house and into the darkness which enveloped the estate.

# 35

Though he was reviving with each shaky step, Nina had to support Bruce's tall body. With her arm around his waist and one of his over her shoulder, they made it out the back door, around the garage and, hugging the woods, toward the front of the house. Mikey, clutching Jenny, stayed a half step behind.

The drive, Nina figured, was their best chance, and they furtively made their way up it. The main road couldn't be too far away, and if there wasn't a house nearby, then perhaps they'd be able to stop a motorist. A phone, thought Nina, cursing herself. Her instinct had just been to get as far away as fast as possible. But she should have hunted out a phone in the house and called the police. She glanced back at the stone dwelling. Morton's big Oldsmobile was parked out front. How long would it be before they found Dundeen? How long would it be before they came charging after them?

"That's it, Bruce," coaxed Nina as they made their way along the blacktop. "Just keep going."

"My . . . head. Oh, Jesus."

"You'll be fine. We have to hurry."

He was like a drunk. A big drunk who stumbled on, one lazy foot in front of the other. And, thought Nina, he was so heavy. He was easily 30 or 40 percent bigger than she was, and she could barely support him. If only she could keep him steady. He stepped on a rock, teetered and nearly pulled them both to the ground.

They made it around a bend, leaving the house some fifty yards behind. Suddenly, though, there were no footsteps behind her, and Nina turned. Clutching the baby, Mikey was stopped in the middle of the road as if he knew he shouldn't go this far. He glanced at Nina, then back down the road, ready, it seemed, to bolt away.

"Come on!" urged Nina, her voice hushed.

Mikey took a hesitant step, and Nina called after him again. He moved only slightly. She couldn't let Mikey run back to the house. She needed him to carry Jenny.

"Mikey!"

He trotted after her, Jenny bouncing in his arms. Nina checked behind them again, and was relieved to see how much progress they'd made. But how much time did they have? And how long was the driveway? Before them, the pavement curved ahead and disappeared into the blackness. Was it a half mile or mile long? Nina hoped it wouldn't take more than another ten or fifteen minutes to reach the main road. If only they had that much time.

"What happened?" mumbled Bruce.

"They gave you a shot of some drug."

"Oh, man."

He rubbed his head, and Nina could see that he was reviving with each second. His steps were more solid, too, and Nina felt the burden of his weight lift from her.

Suddenly through the dark came the distant sound of voices. She looked back, but couldn't see anything through the trees. Then she heard footsteps running over blacktop.

"Over here, Mikey!"

Leading the way, Nina pushed Bruce off the drive and across a narrow band of grass. They rushed along the edge of the woods, but Nina knew it was useless. She saw a thick pine and steered Bruce off the grass and behind the tree. Once she had helped him to the forest floor, she quickly dashed back and pulled Mikey in. She lifted Jenny from his arms, then took Mikey by the hand and led him to Bruce, where they all crouched down.

Hidden with them in the branches, Nina whispered, "There's a bad man out there, Mikey. We must be very quiet."

He nodded and put a finger to his lips. "Shh."

"Right. Be very, very quiet or we'll all be in big trouble."

The steps were clear, running up the drive and drawing closer and closer. Nina glanced at Bruce, who sat, his head in his hands. Then she cradled Jenny in her left arm, nestling her close to her breast. Just be quiet, baby. Just be quiet.

As the steps neared, Nina again whispered to Mikey, "Shh."

She took his soft hand in hers and squeezed. In response, his fingers also tightened. Then Nina saw something beyond the branches. A figure. Someone desperately charging up the drive. Dundeen. Yes, in the moonlight she caught sight of his bald head and, in hand, a long gun. He drew nearer and nearer, and finally passed just some twenty feet away. Moments later he was gone, having charged up the drive. What would he do when he didn't find them? Start searching the woods? Head off toward the river?

Nina tried to plot a course. She could let Mikey wander back to the house and she could leave Bruce, hidden here in the woods. She, carrying Jenny, could try to make it through the woods to find help. Yes, perhaps that was best. She looked over at Bruce. Would he be safe here? Or perhaps he could make it on his own now. Maybe . . .

More steps came running from the house. Who was this? Morton? Marcel? Nina put her fingers to her lips and again hushed Mikey. But the baby. Jenny started to squirm. Quickly, Nina lifted her blouse and pressed the baby to her breast. There, feed, thought Nina. Feed and be quiet. You can't make any noise now. You must be quiet. Whoever was coming was much slower than Dundeen. Nina strained to see through the branches, at first catching only a brief glimpse of a tall dark figure. Then she saw the silver hair. Morton, gun clasped in two hands. Nina gently pulled Mikey back, hoping the boy wouldn't recognize his father. But as she reached for Mikey, her shoulder slightly moved and suddenly Jenny fell away from her breast. The baby gasped, and then a short cry bust from her lungs, a shrill noise that rose out of the woods.

Morton, just some thirty feet away, stopped still. "Who's that?"

Panicking, Nina folded the child into her breast, and Jenny was quiet again. Nina looked through the branches. Morton was raising a gun in their general direction. She turned and looked at Bruce, who, although more awake, was still.

When no response came, Morton grew agitated. "I hear you in there. Come out! I have a gun!"

Mikey recognized the voice and looked through the dark in puzzlement. He started to rise, but Nina caught him by the arm. Dear God, she thought. What were they going to do? How would they get away?

"Come out right now!" Morton shouted nervously.

A happy grin zipped across Mikey's face and he broke away from Nina. She lunged for him but missed as he scrambled to his feet and started pushing through the branches. Nina's eyes darted past Mikey. In the distance she could now see Morton taking aim.

"Come out slowly!" shouted the terrified Morton. "Slowly!"

But Mikey was so excited to see his father that he rushed as fast as he could. Bull-like, he threw himself through the evergreen branches, charging toward Morton.

"Stop . . . stop right there or . . . or I'll—"

Nina saw what was about to happen. She screamed, "Wait!"

"I said stop!"

As if it were all a game, Mikey rushed on, bursting all at once from the dark woods.

Nina shouted, "Don't!"

Mikey said, "Hi—"

Yet before Mikey could say anything else, the terrified Morton fired. The gun cracked the deep night with flame and explosion, the shot blasting into Mikey, hitting him squarely in the chest. He cried out, his voice high and confused, and stumbled onto the grass. A strange word bubbled from his lips. Clutching his shattered body, he staggered toward his father, reached out toward him, then toppled over.

"Mikey!" screamed Nina in horror.

For a terrible moment everything was oddly quiet, a moment of shock, disbelief. Slowly and cruelly, though, Morton began to understand. He lowered the gun and lunged forward.

"No! No, dear God, no!"

In horror, Nina pushed her way out from behind the pine tree. She held aside a few branches, picked her way through . . . and there lay Mikey, his chest ruptured and gushing with black-red blood.

"No!" roared Morton, dropping to his knees and seizing Mikey's hand.

With the last of his life, Mikey gazed up in confusion, his moonlit face as gentle and calm as ever. His lips lifted in a small smile, and his narrow eyes closed once, twice and then forever.

"Oh, God, no!" sobbed Morton. "Mikey, Mikey!"

Nina stood nearly paralyzed. Only when it was too late

did she notice the dark figure standing some twenty feet away.

"It's all your fault," said Dundeen's shaking voice.

Nina stared at his gun.

"None of this was supposed to happen. We could have kept on. I would have had the solution I needed to continue my work and . . ." His words rose over Morton's sobs. "In another three or four months I would have perfected a synthetic ganglioside that was both effective and safe. Alzheimer's would have . . . would have been a thing of the past."

Nina said: "My husband, you . . . you . . ."

"Killed him? In a way, yes, but all because he went poking around. Don't you see? We had to stop him." A pitiful laugh dribbled from his mouth, and he dropped his head and shook it. "It's not just that I could have saved your father, Nina. No. Oh, God, no." He stared at her and, half mocking, said: "I could have saved you."

Nina wrapped her arms tighter around Jenny. "Wh-what?"

"I also developed a genetic test for early-onset Alzheimer's. And remember those cell samples I took from you and your baby? Remember?"

Nina felt her stomach give way. No. No, she didn't want to hear this.

"Well, I ran them, Nina. I sent them to a research lab and had them fully analyzed. And you know what? Your baby's fine. Just fine. But as for you . . ." he said, smiling, "you have the classic defect on the twenty-first chromosome."

"No!"

"Oh, yes. Early-onset Alzheimer's disease. That is your inheritance, your gift from the Trenton family. Just imagine, you'll probably begin showing the first signs of deterioration before your daughter's even a teenager. You'll start losing your mind and she'll think you crazier and crazier. The courts will probably have to find a foster home for her and lock you up. She'll be effectively orphaned. Who would have thought that such an attractive person as you would lose her mind—and all within the next decade, no less."

"You're wrong!"

"You know I'm not."

"But—"

Dundeen raised the gun. "Now where's Mr. Fitzgerald? He couldn't have gone far."

Nina stared at him, kissed Jenny. Alzheimer's? Her? No, no she had to be there for Jenny.

"Tell me or you're a dead woman."

Nina couldn't stand it, couldn't bear it. The thought of her mind disintegrating, of being locked away before this baby was even a youth—impossible!

"Nina," ordered Dundeen, "tell—"

A voice from the dark woods said, "I'm right here."

Dundeen said, "Come out . . . slowly."

Above Morton's desperate crying, Nina heard Bruce falter, steady himself and continue on. Clutching a branch for support, he emerged from the woods some fifteen feet away. Almost immediately Dundeen took aim.

"Bruce!" screamed Nina.

An instant before the gun fired, Nina saw Bruce dive to the side. The shot missed and, now on the ground, Bruce struggled to rise.

Dundeen laughed as he took aim again, saying, "This, my friend, I guarantee is going to hurt. Just—"

Suddenly, there was a second blast, a noise so loud and close that Nina thought at first she'd been shot. Jenny screamed, her shrieks reaching the skies. Nina madly groped for blood—on the baby's back, her arms, her legs. But there was nothing. Incredibly, Jenny was unharmed. Nina spun to the side, expecting the very worst. However, Bruce was slowly pushing himself up.

Turning to Dr. Dundeen, she saw that he still stood, but that half of his face and part of his throat had been blown away. A thick liquid covered the top of his torso, and like a butchered chicken, the upright body stumbled, turned and took a few steps. The shotgun slid from his hands, then Dundeen dropped to the ground.

Behind her, gun in hand, John Morton said, "I believed him. I . . . I believed it might all work."

Awash with shock, Nina kissed her baby, held her tightly, tried to quiet her. I love you, I love you, I love you, she thought. It's all right. It's going to be all right. Oh, Lord. They were surrounded by bodies, but they were all right. She rushed to Bruce.

"Are you—?"

"I'm okay . . ."

She extended her hand, helped him up and gave him a hug that embraced Jenny between them both. Taking a long, deep breath of the summer night air and feeling Bruce's arms around her, she thought how at last it was over, finally over . . .

But when she heard the cocking of a gun behind her and felt Bruce stiffen, Nina knew she was mistaken. Turning, she saw John Morton standing above Dundeen's body. In Morton's hands was the doctor's shotgun. All together there had been two double-barreled guns. That meant four shots, two of which Morton had fired, one of which Dundeen had. There was one left, one in the gun that Morton was now raising in their direction.

"Irene and I did it because we wanted to help Mikey. His memory—we wanted Dundeen's drug so we could save Mikey's mind," he said, his tired face all wet. "That was the only reason. My boy—he was already slipping, and he'd had such a hard life. I had to do something to help him, didn't I? Wouldn't you? Would you want your child to die before you?" The lanky gray-haired man wiped his eyes. "Dr. Dundeen was brilliant. Absolutely brilliant. Just try to save . . . to save his work, as much as you can."

Saying nothing more, John Morton continued to raise the shotgun until it rose straight into the sky. Rotating it still further, he lowered the weapon to his mouth, then carefully wrapped his lips around the barrel. His face streaming with tears, he stared down at his son and pulled the trigger.

# Chapter
# 36

There was just one more thing. Nina had to do it. And it had to be taken care of before the police arrived.

Still groggy from the drug, Bruce could stand only with difficulty. Nina escorted him a little further up the drive, eased him down onto a grassy knoll and then handed him Jenny.

"I'll be back in a few minutes," she said.

"Where are you going?"

"To the house."

"But Volker—"

"I know."

As she suspected, Nina found more shells in the pocket of Dundeen's bloodied coat. She withdrew them, picked up one of the guns and loaded it. Then she started off, weapon in hand.

Bruce called, "Nina, be careful."

"I will."

She'd come back. For Jenny, she would. She'd be there . . . always. Dundeen had to be wrong.

The past months and years swirled in her head. Alex. Her father. Jenny. All of them linked, their fates so inextricably tied to this terrible disease. Forever. Life and death and genetics. The real family ties. They. The doctors. The scientists. If Dundeen was right, if Nina did in fact carry the gene for early-onset Alzheimer's, perhaps there was still a way. Perhaps another scientist could interpret Dundeen's work or otherwise discover a means for saving her, a way of preventing her mind's disintegration. But time—was there enough of it?

As Nina walked through the summer night and down the long black drive, she was transported away. That night, that cold late-winter night. Alex in the snow. Jenny in her womb. The end of one life. The beginning of another. None of what happened had made any sense. She hadn't been able to comprehend it, hence was unable to accept it. But now she saw it all. Dundeen's desperation. Morton's complicity. Alex's unfortunate timing.

When she arrived at the large oak door of Dundeen's mansion, Nina lifted the gun in front of her, ready to blast whoever greeted her. She kicked open the door, made her way down the hall. It was so quiet, so still, however, that she knew almost at once that Irene Volker was dead. Entering the den, Nina found the older woman there, slumped on the couch, an air-filled syringe in her arm. When, she wondered, had Volker shot a bubble of air into her arteries? After she had heard Morton scream in anguish? Or after the fourth shot? Perhaps Volker had even snuck up the drive, witnessed the disaster, then returned and ended her own life.

Now, at least, there would be no interference. Now Nina could accomplish what she knew she must. Yes, before the police, before the detectives, before it all became tangled in the courts. In a trance, Nina passed through the front hall and to the door that led to the basement. Quite sure of herself, she followed the stairs down and entered the large office with the blue carpet. Beckoned by Alex, she barely noticed the mess strewn about. She lay the gun on a table and proceeded on.

The mechanical wheezing of the life-support machines called out, and Nina headed into the soft light of the lab. She crossed directly to the last of the three bodies, a plugged-in mound of flesh surrounded by a mass of electronic monitors. Finding a stool, she wheeled it by Alex's bedside. For a long, long while she simply sat there, staring at her husband. Then she pressed the back of her hand to his cheek and, feeling the skin barely warm, knew at once that Dundeen had spoken the truth: Alex could never return to the world of the living. His body functioned mechanically, but his spirit had long since departed.

Alex . . . you're so thin now. So gray . . .

"We have a baby girl," she whispered in his ear. "Her name is Jennifer, just like you wanted. I call her Jenny, and she's very healthy and very beautiful. She has your eyes but she's blond like me. I'm going to finish putting your pictures in the red photo album. I'll give it to her and I'll tell her all sorts of stories about you. She'll know you as well as if you were here . . . but we'll miss you."

She stroked his withered cheek. So dry. So pale. My poor Alex. Trapped here so long. Tied to earth by all these tubes and plugs. If only . . . if only . . .

The tears were coming quickly. "We'll miss you so very much. Alex, Alex, can you hear me? I miss you so much and I'll always love you. Always."

Her face entirely wet, Nina rolled the stool to the wall and started tugging at the mass of wires. Within moments, three plugs plopped out of the wall. The hissing and pumping of machinery came to a slow but definite halt. The monitors suddenly were quiet, empty, void of pulsing lines. And at last the body of Alex Hale lay at peace.

She stood over him, studied him. For minutes.

"Good-bye," she finally said, and kissed him.

Her eyes wet, she pulled the sheet over her husband's face and started out. Now she understood, felt in her heart that Alex would not and could not return. Not ever. Now she held an image of Alex completely still and without life. Yes, dead. She glanced back. Alex was dead. She could see his unmoving body beneath the sheet, the last of life finally allowed to slip away.

The pain shook her, but did not overwhelm. She had to move on. She had to go upstairs and call the police. Yes, she told herself, moving quickly. Go upstairs, call the police, tell them to come at once, tell them to go after Marcel and his wife. Hurry.

Aware of just what she had to do, Nina emerged from Dundeen's office. She'd make the call and then seek out Jenny and Bruce, who'd been waiting so long.